BODIES AND BATTLEMENTS

BODIES AND BATTLEMENTS

A Ravensea Castle Mystery

ELIZABETH PENNEY

St. Martin's Paperbacks

This is a work of fiction. All of the characters, organizations, and events portrayed in this novel are either products of the author's imagination or are used fictitiously.

First published in the United States by St. Martin's Paperbacks, an imprint of St. Martin's Publishing Group.

EU Representative: Macmillan Publishers Ireland Ltd., 1st Floor, The Liffey Trust Centre, 117-126 Sheriff Street Upper, Dublin 1, DO1 YC43, Ireland.

BODIES AND BATTLEMENTS

For information, address St. Martin's Publishing Group, 120 Broadway, New York, NY 10271.

www.stmartins.com

ISBN: 978-1-250-37005-1

Our books may be purchased in bulk for specialty retail/wholesale, literacy, corporate/premium, educational, and subscription box use. Please contact MacmillanSpecialMarkets@macmillan.com.

Printed in the United States of America

St. Martin's Paperbacks edition / June 2025

10 9 8 7 6 5 4 3 2 1

To my readers: thank you.

CHAPTER 1

We have always lived in this castle, this jumbled, tumbled heap perched above Robin Hood's Bay. We were the Asquiths of Ravensea Castle, scrappy defenders of the Yorkshire coast since 1138. But for the past century or so, we've been hanging on by our fingernails, the threat of losing everything hovering over us like the broadaxes we once wielded against our enemies.

Now, in the oddest twist of fate, modern technology might save this old pile. At any moment, the first guests would arrive at the castle, having found us through a shiny new website. Although we had only three suites fit for human habitation right now, it was a start. Income from my herbal apothecary business and estate rents were barely keeping us alive.

Standing in the front courtyard, I tipped my head and studied the castle's towers and battlements, trying to see the place the way our visitors would when they drove across the causeway. On the website, I'd glossed over the fact that guests might be stranded here—or in the nearby village—during storms and full-moon tides. Unless they traveled by boat, of course. Maybe I could put a positive spin on this enforced isolation . . .

The arched front door creaked open to reveal Janet Fagan's round, pleasant face. Our chief cook and housekeeper wore a gray shirtdress and starched white bib apron, a kerchief covering her brassy curls. "There you are, milady. I wanted to tell you that the cheese and fruit plates and the drinks are set up in the drawing room, as you asked."

"You're a gem," I said. "I don't know what I'd do without you."

I didn't bother to correct how she addressed me, because I'd tried a million times. She'd been calling me "milady" since I'd turned eighteen, replacing "Miss Nora," which had been bad enough. Janet had come to work for us when I was ten, right before the loss of my mother, who had been the true lady of the castle. Even at age thirty, that role didn't quite fit me.

I sat on a stone bench next to a potted topiary tree and patted the space beside me. "Come. Sit."

Through the open front gate, the bench had an excellent view of the causeway and the village, which was set around a cove hugged by emerald-green hills. My plan was to watch for the vintage Land Rover piloted by Janet's husband, Guy. He'd gone to the train station to pick up our guests, one couple and a singleton. Another couple was arriving later by car.

Janet emerged from the castle, followed by Rolf, our English mastiff, who hated to be left out of the action. As Janet settled beside me, two hundred pounds of dog collapsed onto my feet.

He smelled like rotten fish.

"Oh, Janet, did he . . . ?" I jerked my new leather flats from underneath his sprawling body.

"He did, I'm afraid. He got out while I was hanging up the laundry."

Rolf had a bad habit of foraging along the beach, digging through heaps of seaweed in search of tasty *dead* snacks. Over our heads, a seagull wheeled and cried, no doubt scenting the dog and confusing him with a carcass. Rolf lifted his head and woofed thunderously, sending it flapping away.

"Not much going on in the village this afternoon," I said.

Monkwell's cluster of white stucco and sandstone buildings sat quietly in the June sun, only a few people walking in and out of the shops. Out in the bay, fishing boats chugged, and once the tide turned, they would deliver turbot, scallops, and sole to the fish market on the quay.

"All that will change when the summer visitors start arriving." Janet turned her face to the sun with a sigh. "Ooh, this feels good. The heat is warming me right to my bones."

And they were weary bones, thanks to me. I felt a stab of guilt at how hard Janet had been working. The past couple of months had been a frantic whirlwind of cleaning, repairs, paperwork, marketing, creating menus, and more paperwork. Permits, licenses, floor plans . . . mind-boggling.

"I'll clean the guest rooms, Janet," I said. This extra duty was my job until we could afford to hire help. "I'm not adding that to your plate."

She patted me on the knee. "Don't worry yourself, milady. I've enjoyed helping you with this new venture." Excitement lit her blue eyes. "I'm really looking forward to cooking for a crowd like in the old days." The "old days" meant when Mum was alive and my parents used to entertain everyone in the county.

Dishes made from local meat and fresh-caught seafood

featured heavily in Janet's recipes, along with delectable baked goods and desserts. The accommodations might be marginal but the food would be spectacular, thanks to my talented chef.

On impulse, I kissed her soft cheek. "Bless you, Janet. Your food is going to win us five stars." The lodging site allowed guests to rate their stays, a double-edged sword in itself. Our aim, naturally, was five-star all the way.

She gave a pleased chuckle. "I don't know about that. But I'll do my best." She smiled up at the sun for a moment then said, "Do you suppose Sir Percival will bother the guests in the red room?"

Like any self-respecting castle, we had several resident ghosts. Sir Percival, our woebegone knight, moaned and rattled chains, mostly during the full moon. The corridor near the red room was his favorite, um, haunt.

"The moon is waning, so I hope he doesn't decide to stray from his usual routine." I shuddered at the idea, then recalled a more pressing issue. "Cross our fingers that the water closet doesn't act up again."

Each room had its own en suite bath, a definite plus, although the age of the fixtures was an entry in the minus column. We'd soon learn if "quaint" was acceptable when it came to bathrooms. We didn't have the funds for upgrades yet.

Tension knotted in my belly at the thought, an all too familiar feeling as of late. So much was riding on the success of our new venture—the rest of our lives, in fact. Trying to force myself to relax, I inhaled deeply—and got a nasty whiff of rot. *Rolf.* We'd better keep him away from the guests until I had time to give him a bath.

So many chores, so little time. But maybe once the guests were settled, I could slip out to the herb garden.

Over the next few weeks, the busy harvest time for Castle Apothecary would begin, and I would be in the thick of preparing tinctures, creams, teas, and balms. Yes, I'd definitely get out there soon, even if I had to work by moonlight, with Sir Percival looking over my shoulder.

"Here they come," Janet said, tipping her chin toward town.

I squinted at the hillside and spotted our light green Land Rover buzzing along the road. They'd be here in about ten minutes, judging by past experience. I thought of another pressing issue. "Is Dad ready?"

My father, Arthur Asquith, was the official host of Ravensea Castle, and as such, he needed to be washed, dressed in his best tweeds, and ready to greet our visitors. Simple as that sounded, we basically needed to excavate him from his study, where he was holed up writing a family history. Right now he was lost in a labyrinth of dusty fifteenth-century documents, hot on the trail of Sir Percival's story.

Janet rose to her feet. "He said he would be, but I'd better go give him the ten-minute warning."

"Thanks, I appreciate it." He seemed to listen to her much better than me.

Rolf lumbered to his feet and followed, leaving me alone to watch the Land Rover approach. Guy had now reached the village, and for a few moments the vehicle was lost to view. I counted down the seconds, knowing exactly when it would reappear, even if he had to stop at a crosswalk or slow for traffic.

Right on time, the Land Rover popped up on the street leading directly to the causeway. Another vehicle was behind it, something low-slung and black. And then to my surprise, a third appeared, a gray sedan. Strange. We were supposed to have one more party coming, not two.

And what was this? A black van raced over the rise before slowing to tail the sedan, followed by a tiny red car I recognized. A full-blown caravan was on its way to the castle, including Father Patrick, our parish priest.

The five vehicles rolled over the paved causeway, moving almost as slowly as a mob on foot—or horseback. I stood, my nerves crawling with anticipation and anxiety. Instead of an army at my back to greet the horde, I had my father, Janet, and one large dog who might look forbidding but was actually a big baby. A smelly one, too.

The Land Rover swept through the gate and slowed, then pulled up and around the circle to park in front of the door. One by one the other vehicles followed. Doors opened and people spilled out, voices clamoring.

In addition to our inaugural guests, I spotted my siblings, Tamsyn and Will (*what were they doing here?*), local workmen (*hurray, the garden path*) and Hilda Dibble, our favorite pain in the arse, as Janet called her. Hilda had opposed our plan every step of the way, and now here she was on opening day, along with her sidekick, Sandra Snelling. Typical.

Dad and Janet appeared in the doorway, Dad thankfully wearing his best tweeds. But he still had his slippers on, and a battered felt Robin Hood hat was perched on his curly red head, complete with moth-eaten feather. A crumb of something nestled in his thick beard.

"Welcome, welcome to Ravensea Castle," Dad roared with a wave of his arm, his voice easily cutting through the ruckus. Guy began to herd his passengers toward the door. The guests, a sleek middle-aged couple and an attractive man in his thirties, huddled together with necks craning as they took everything in—the massive walls, the flags flying on the tower, the oddly dressed lord of the castle.

Father Patrick was the first to reach me, the sea breeze tossing his gray hair, which was on the long side, as was his beard. As usual, he wore clerical clothing and collar. "Good afternoon, Nora," he said, his voice holding an Irish lilt. "I've come to give your endeavor a wee blessing."

I glanced around at the chaos, at the throng about to descend on me, seeing to my horror that Rolf had escaped from the house to join the fray. I cringed when he jumped up and swiped Hilda's face with his huge tongue. That certainly wouldn't improve our relationship.

"Thank you, Father Patrick," I said fervently. "We're going to need it."

CHAPTER 2

Moving fast, I ushered Father Patrick into the castle, tempted to bar the door behind us against Hilda and her friend. The Great Hall was empty, but I could hear Dad's voice booming in the drawing room, which overlooked the knot garden, one of the castle's best features.

"Want a glass of mead?" I asked Father Patrick. "And we've got nibbles."

"I won't say no," he said, looking pleased at the prospect.

We were halfway across the hall when the front door opened and my sister, Tamsyn, slipped inside. "Hold up," she cried, running to join us, long legs flashing.

I braced myself, since she did not approve of me renting "her" castle. "I thought you were on location." Tamsyn had a lead role in *Highland Lass*, a period costume drama filmed in Edinburgh.

"We were," she said, bestowing her famous smile on Father Patrick. We both had our late mother's strawberry blonde waves, green eyes, and pale skin that freckled. But my sister was incredibly photogenic and I was not. "But we're on break, so I'm here to help."

Great. "Wonderful," I said, thinking of a way to kill

two birds with one stone. "You can be our room attendant." That would take her down a notch plus give me more time in my garden.

My suggestion earned me a dirty glare until Tamsyn realized Father Patrick had noticed. She dimpled. "Whatever you need, *my dear.*"

My smile was equally insincere. "And I'll hold you to it, *my darling.*"

The front door opened again and my brother walked in. To my relief, he was by himself. No Hilda yet. "You two go ahead," I said to Tamsyn and Father Patrick. "I need to talk to Will a sec." They scooted off to the drawing room.

"Oh, good," Will said in a low voice as he approached. "I was hoping to get you alone." Lean and lanky like us, and sharing our reddish hair and green eyes, my brother wore a close-cropped beard and an air of distraction. Will's company, Monkwell Mead, produced the finest honey wine in England and we planned to feature it heavily.

"Did you get rid of Hilda?" I asked. "The nerve—after all she's done—"

Will nodded, but then the door creaked open to reveal my nemesis and her friend. "I tried. Honestly." He placed a hand on my arm, speaking rapidly as the two women hurried our way. "Make sure you give the Cargills the royal treatment."

"The Cargills?" Oh, he meant the middle-aged couple now drinking mead in the drawing room. "We'll treat them well, of course. Why the concern?"

He winced, screwing up his face in an expression I recognized. A confession was coming. "I invited them to stay. They own a chain of high-end wine shops all over the UK, you see. They're considering taking on Monkwell Mead. It's a big order, with national promotion."

"Oh, I get it. You want to make sure I don't blow your deal." Suspicion dawned. "You didn't comp them, did you?" I hadn't taken the reservation. That must've been Janet, I thought.

He rubbed a hand over his face. "I might have mentioned that they would be our guests."

"*Will*." My whisper rose to a muffled shriek. "Don't do that again without asking me. I'm paying the bills here."

"Sorry," he muttered. "I won't." Then his eyes widened. "Which room did you give them?"

I knew where this was going. "The red room," I admitted. "Which we now call the King's Chamber, by the way. But don't worry, it's not his time." I was referring to Sir Percival's haunting schedule, which was more or less reliable. Will opened his mouth to object, but before he could speak, I said, "They have to stay there. Another couple has the white room, aka the Queen's Chamber, and our single guest is in the Knight's Chamber."

My brother winced. "Let's hope the good sir keeps a low profile." He jerked his thumb toward the front door. "I'll go help Guy bring in the bags. See you in a few."

He strode across the hall, nodding as he passed Hilda and Sandra. Feeling I must out of politeness, I waited for the two women to join me before going into the drawing room.

As she strutted along, pigeon chest out and tiny feet tapping, Hilda's heavily made-up blue eyes darted around, landing everywhere except my face. I could practically see the drool forming behind her pursed, red-painted lips as she took in the hall's tattered splendors. As the self-appointed doyenne of Monkwell—even though she'd moved here only last year—Hilda was relentless in her efforts to control what we did at Ravensea Castle. Unfortunately for her, Dad and I were skilled at digging in our heels. We had centuries' worth of inspiring examples behind us.

The other woman stayed one step behind Hilda, faithful sycophant and friend. I didn't know Sandra well, but she was the type to poke her finger into every village pie.

"Nora," Hilda said when she reached me, penciled brows rising. "I had no idea that your sister would be gracing us with her presence."

"I'm such a fan." Sandra's voice was a coo. "She's so beautiful. And talented, too."

"Isn't she?" I said, deciding not to reveal my own surprise at Tamsyn's arrival. Maybe her presence would prevent Hilda from voicing her views about our bed-and-breakfast. "Will you join us for a glass of mead? Or wine?"

Hilda glanced at Sandra. "Shall we? I don't usually drink this *early* in the day but—"

"But we don't usually get to rub elbows with a television star either." Sandra wiggled in place as if eager to keep moving. "Let's go."

"We shall accept your kind invitation," Hilda said loftily, as if channeling Lady Violet from *Downton Abbey*. She charged through the archway into the drawing room, only to stop short. Sandra bumped right into her with an "oof."

I peered over their heads but saw only Dad ranting eloquently about Monkwell's delights while our guests and Father Patrick listened. Tamsyn was curled up on a nearby sofa, bare feet tucked up under her legs and her slim fingers cradling a glass of golden mead. The single man in the party kept glancing her way, naturally, but she pretended not to notice. Already smitten, poor sot. As for Janet, she was fussing over the food trays while Ruffian, the battered tabby who ruled Ravensea, watched hopefully for a stray tidbit.

"Er, Sandra." Hilda whirled around so fast she smacked right into her friend, who grabbed Hilda by the shoulders to steady herself. "We must leave. Right. Now."

"But why?" The two women danced back and forth for a moment, each trying to get around the other. "I want to meet Tamsyn. Get her autograph."

Hilda shouldered past her friend, which made Sandra step back, her heel almost landing on my toe. "Let's go," Hilda said between gritted teeth. "I'll explain later."

Sandra sniffed. "All right. All right. No need to make a fuss." Adjusting her skirt, she trotted after her friend.

"Thanks for stopping by," I called. "Have a nice evening." I might have allowed a note of glee to seep into my tone. Good riddance to bad rubbish, as Janet would say.

Inside the drawing room, I joined the group near the fireplace. Dad stopped pontificating to boom, "This is my other daughter, Nora. She's the brains behind this outfit."

Looking pained, Tamsyn turned her pretty profile toward us and gazed pensively into the fireplace, where a small fire was smoldering.

I smiled, extending my hand to the guests in turn, introducing myself to Lorna and Gavin Cargill and Brian Taylor. "Welcome," I said, smiling warmly. "I do hope you're settling in all right. Your bags have been delivered upstairs to your rooms, and dinner will be at six. A buffet. Until then, wander around, relax, enjoy."

"I love this place already," Lorna gushed. Much younger than her husband, she had a pleasant, broad-cheeked face and an expensively tinted blonde bob. Her country outfit of tan plaid slacks and jacket was Burberry, her sleek leather boots enviable. "It's like something out of a fairy tale."

A Gothic novel more like, with the room's dark walnut wainscoting and heavy Victorian furniture, but I murmured thanks, grateful for good early feedback. Maybe I could encourage her to repeat her thoughts in a review.

"Your father mentioned the bearded vulture that was spotted on the moors last summer," Brian said, his face aglow with interest. With horn-rimmed glasses and a brush-up hairstyle, he looked bookish but trendy. "I'd love to add that to my list."

This comment pegged him as a birdwatcher, a favorite visitor pastime. "A rosy starling was also seen recently," I said. "Pink beak and all." Rosy starlings were also rare here in Yorkshire and it was believed that the wind had blown this one from Eastern Europe.

"A pink beak? Ooh, how darling," Lorna said. "I want to see one of those."

Gavin Cargill, trim and polished in his tweed suit, said, "We won't have much time for tramping on the moors, my dear." He rocked on his heels. "Golfing, sailing, and fine dining, that's my idea of a vacation."

Lorna's smile drooped but she merely said, "Don't forget trying out new brands for the stores." She raised her empty glass with a tinkling laugh. "And it's time for a refill."

As she drifted toward the drinks table, where Janet waited to serve, her husband began to go on about his friend's yacht, presently moored out in Robin Hood's Bay.

I tagged along behind Lorna, wanting a glass of mead myself. It had been a long day.

"Another splash, Mrs. Cargill?" Janet asked, holding the bottle of golden juniper mead aloft.

"Please," our guest said. "And call me Lorna." She set her glass on the table and watched while Janet filled it. "Perfect."

"How about you, milady?" Janet's brows rose in inquiry.

"The same," I said, although I liked the elderberry, which had a rich red hue. While Janet poured, I topped a water cracker with Brie and a grape, accidentally dropping a small chunk of cheese onto the floor. Ruffian pounced and it disappeared.

Janet gave me a complicit smile as she handed me the glass. "Enjoy."

Lorna had wandered to the tall windows overlooking the terrace and the garden. After hastily piling cheese and crackers on a small plate, I followed.

"Want to step outside?" I asked, nodding toward the closest French door.

She threw me a glance and then turned the crystal knob and stood back to let me, juggling my glass and the plate, go out first. Up to his usual tricks, Ruffian wound between my ankles, hoping I'd spill more cheese. But I made it across the pavers to the terrace wall without incident and set down the plate. The glass stayed in my hand, at the ready. I took my first heady swallow, savoring the sweet yet dry flavor.

Lorna perched on the wide balustrade and gazed down into the knot garden, where a long rectangle was broken into curving beds edged with box and filled with flowering plants. In the center was a fountain featuring a lady in Grecian garb pouring water. Head-high walls edged the entire space, with gates leading into the kitchen garden and maze.

The stonemasons were working on a section of path, resetting the pavers. Previously, they'd been jutting up and uneven, a real trip hazard for our guests.

"What a beautiful garden," Lorna said. "Such a variety of plants."

"They're mostly herbs, many of them medicinal," I explained. "It's modeled after the physic garden my ancestors designed." Ruffian leaped up to sit beside me on the wall, grace in motion despite his battered ear and bulk. I gave him a tiny piece of cheese. "I make bath and beauty products plus select herbal remedies." Ruffian's big eyes begged for more cheese, so of course I gave in. "You'll find a basket of Castle Apothecary bath luxuries in your room. Gratis." I sold my products in stores around the area, and being able to offer them here was a nice touch, I thought.

"That sounds wonderful." Lorna sighed. "I can't wait to fill a hot bath, lie back, and relax."

I said a silent prayer that the hot water supply would cooperate. "Busy schedule?" I murmured, for something to say.

Lorna swigged mead like a fisherman at the pub swilling beer. "Oh, you don't know the half of it. Gavin believes in being hands-on in our business. We visit all our twenty-five stores on a regular basis plus meet with our British vendors at least once a year. Then travel to French wineries every other year. We live in York but I hardly ever see the place."

"It's nice to help him with the business, though, right?"

I heard the question in my voice. Something told me she was more reluctant than not when it came to traveling so much.

Her answer was a head shake and another sigh. "It's one of those things . . . sounds good on paper but he's so busy and driven . . . I feel more like an employee than a partner sometimes."

I racked my brain for something positive and tactful to say. Finally I settled on, "Well, I hope you both enjoy your stay here and take some time to unwind. If you need suggestions for date nights, let us know."

Janet opened the French door. "Guests incoming," she trilled.

Our last couple had arrived. "That's my cue," I said. "Please excuse me."

Lorna waved a hand as if say no problem. "I'm going to sit and enjoy the garden a little longer." Ruffian, who had more emotional intelligence than most people, jumped up beside her. By the time I reached the door, she was crooning softly to him and rubbing his chin. Good boy.

When I arrived out front, a good-looking man with dark hair and a goatee was getting out of a white luxury sedan. Seeing me, he paused and waved, giving me a blinding smile before going around to the passenger side.

But I didn't see anyone sitting in that seat, which was odd. He opened the door and bent inside, the angle such that I couldn't tell what he was doing. Then he turned and gently set a white French bulldog on the ground. She wore a pink collar and matching leash.

"Come on, Lady," he said, tugging on the leash. "Let's say hello to our hostess."

Our guests were a man and his *dog*? A giggle erupted

behind my hand. Not over the fact of someone traveling with a pet. That was totally ordinary and yes, Ravensea Castle was pet-friendly.

But talk about crossed signals—Janet had booked this pair in the *bridal suite*.

CHAPTER 3

Finlay Cole's expression as he took in the frilly Queen's Chamber was priceless. "It's, er, lovely," he said. Released from her leash, Lady trundled across the floor to the four-poster bed, where she stopped and woofed. With her short legs, she'd never be able to jump up there.

"You can put her on the bed," I said. "The coverlet is machine washable." As he picked up the sweet little dog, I added, "Sorry for the mix-up. Janet thought you were bringing a female companion. Human, I mean, not canine."

He glanced over his shoulder at me, one brow raised. "I did say I was bringing Lady. She must have thought I said, 'my lady.'"

"Probably," I said. Looking totally content, Lady was snuggling up on the lace-trimmed pillows. "I think she's given her sign of approval." I backed toward the door. "Make yourself comfortable. We have drinks and appetizers downstairs when you're ready. Dinner is at six," I added in case he didn't come down to mingle. "Buffet-style, so casual."

Instead of responding, he gazed fondly at his dog. "She's a rescue, you know."

"Really? How kind of you to adopt her." I leaned against the doorjamb, knowing I should stay and listen. Even if I were impatient to move on to my next task, this was what being an innkeeper was all about. Build relationships, the manual had said. Engage your guests in conversation about their passions and interests. And hopefully not about possibly troubled marriages, like Lorna's.

Besides, now that his companion—and naked ring finger—signaled his single status, I took a closer look and was pleased. His features were chiseled, gray eyes keen under dark brows. A couple of inches taller than my five nine, his build was both lean and strong. Oh yes. He was definitely my brand of tea.

Finlay ran a hand through his hair, rumpling it. "It's quite a harrowing story, really. She was left in a dark, cold house when her owners scarpered." He studied Lady, now making the cutest little snorts as she slept. "The poor thing was so glad to see us."

"How awful. I'm so glad you saved her." Mindful of Janet working alone downstairs, I said, "I'll get out of your hair now. Give you a chance to get settled. See you later."

"Thanks, Nora," Finlay called. As I shut the door, I saw him stretch out on the bed beside the dog and kick his shoes off. Finlay and his Lady made a lovely couple.

I found Janet in the kitchen, seasoning a large and lovely beef roast for the oven. "There you are," she said. "Guests all settled?"

"Yes. And Finlay Cole loved the Queen's Chamber." I stole a cracked pepper cracker from an open packet, watching Janet for a reaction. "And so did Lady, his bull-dog."

Janet's mouth dropped open. "His *bulldog*? You mean he isn't here with a female companion?"

"Not a human one, no." I tied on an apron, ready to tackle the vegetables. We were having roast potatoes, brussels sprouts, and Yorkshire pudding with the beef, all locally sourced. A classic English dinner.

"I certainly got my signals crossed." Janet shook her head. "Sorry about that."

"It's fine. He's happy so we're happy, right?" I picked up a peeler and got to work on a large brown potato.

With flagstone floors, arched windows, and a beamed ceiling, the castle kitchen was both vast and cozy, kept warm by a huge old AGA. The AGA range was temperamental to be sure, but easier to cook with than the oxen-sized fireplace and ovens used in centuries past. Janet's favorite classical harpsichord music accompanied us, playing from the speaker next to a red geranium on the windowsill.

How many meals had I helped make in this room? Hundreds, if not thousands. But this dinner was special, our first as official hosts. The first meal that anyone rated. My stomach gave a lurch. A lot was riding on that roast beef.

Glasses clinked as Tamsyn strolled in, carrying a tray. She went over to the dishwasher and began to load it.

"Who are you and what have you done with my sister?" I scooped peels into the compost bucket.

"Oh, stop." Tamsyn continued to slot the glasses. "Just because I'm a television star, it doesn't mean I've forgotten how to work."

Janet and I exchanged glances, but we didn't say anything. "I was wondering, milady . . ." Janet said.

She called Tamsyn that too, and Will was "young sir." Even more quaint, her husband was, in public at least, "Mr. Fagan" instead of Guy. I wasn't sure if it was the Victorian novels she devoured or living at Ravensea, but our dear cook could put most historical reenactors to shame.

"Yes, Janet?" Tamsyn asked. She shut the dishwasher door, then came over and perched on a stool.

"Would you mind setting the table for me, please?" Janet asked. After much debate, we'd kept the banquet table in the dining hall. Our guests would be served from a meal station and then sit together. Or not, since the table held twenty people easily.

"I can do that. In a few." Tamsyn grabbed a piece of the carrot Janet was chopping. "Who would have thunk it? Two dishy men out of four guests," she said between bites. "I sure picked the right time to visit." Another crunch.

I gave her a sharp look. *Hands off,* I wanted to say. *Finlay is mine.* "When did you meet Finlay?"

She shrugged. "He came down while I was clearing the glasses. Asked me about the local walking paths."

"So he can take a romantic stroll with his Lady," I said, unable to hold back a grin. "How sweet."

At Tamsyn's frown, Janet jumped in, trying to run interference. Even after all these years, the poor thing didn't realize that sparring was our love language. "Lady is his dog," she said. "So he's probably single."

"Oh," Tamsyn said, brows rising. "Sweet." Then those perfect brows drew together. "But why is he single, do you suppose? Maybe there's something the matter with him." After having several Mr. Rights go terribly wrong, she had good reason to be skeptical.

"Probably. Wouldn't doubt it." Pretending to focus on

dicing potatoes, I hid a smile. "How about I investigate
and let you know?"

Three hours later, I was trudging up the winding stair to
my room on the third floor, every body part either aching
or numb with fatigue. But my heart was warm with the
satisfaction of a challenge well met.

Tail twitching and a smug look on his face, Ruffian
was waiting for me when I finally hauled myself up the
last steps. "I know, I know. You're much more fit than I
am." He darted ahead toward my room. "Rub it in, why
don't you?"

While taking a shower—using my own lavender-and-
lemon goat's-milk soap—I reviewed the evening, thankful it was behind me. With Tamsyn and Will's help,
dinner had gone amazingly well. Tamsyn helped me set
up the buffet and monitor guest needs while Will carved
roast beef and poured wine from grapes grown in Yorkshire, which often surprised people. Dad had joined us
in the role of head bon vivant and chief raconteur. The
guests loved him, and in the excitement of his new status, he didn't eat enough. After several glasses of wine,
Janet's husband, Guy, and Will had to steer him upstairs
to his room and pour him into bed.

Dad couldn't keep up that pace, so we'd have to make
adjustments going forward. As I toweled off and slipped
on pajama bottoms and a T-shirt, I thought about options.
Maybe he could do a welcome speech at the beginning of
dinner, lead a toast, and then retire.

"Knock, knock." Tamsyn. "I've got Ovaltine and
cookies."

How thoughtful. A hot sweet drink before bed was a
favorite childhood ritual of ours. We'd enjoy it in my room

or hers, which was adjacent to mine and separated by a walk-through closet. "Come in," I called, picking up a comb and tugging it through my hair.

As she carried in a tray, I went to the window and opened the casement, still combing my hair. The sill was wide enough to sit upon, so we both perched there, bookending Ruffian, who always chose the middle. He gazed out into the warm night, nose twitching in response to the aromas drifting in. Salt from the sea. Fragrant herbs and roses. Ancient stones warmed by the sun.

"Did you put in lighting?" Mug cradled in both hands, Tamsyn leaned forward, peering down into the garden, where little lights outlined the paths and hung in the trees. Finlay and Brian strolled past with Lady, footsteps crunching on gravel. How nice. Our two singles had become friends.

"Solar lights," I explained. "Expensive but worth it, I thought. Doesn't the garden look beautiful?"

"It really does." She inhaled deeply, a signal I knew well. She wanted to talk about something and was gathering her thoughts. Or her courage.

Finally she said, "I have to admit I didn't think much of your idea at first." So she was sidestepping. What she was saying wasn't news to me. "But it's lovely, Nora. The castle seems . . . oh, I don't know, *happier* tonight. It's meant to be filled with people and good food and laughter. I suppose that sounds idiotic . . ."

"No, it doesn't. I totally agree." I couldn't hold back a huge grin. "Janet said something similar." Despite my doubts about my hostess skills, I had as my vision, my goal, exactly what she was talking about. Providing warmth and comfort and camaraderie within these thick old walls.

A woman's scream rang out downstairs.

Tamsyn and I stared at each other. Ruffian stiffened, ears swiveling. When he arched his back and hissed, we knew.

At the same time, we said, "Sir Percival."

After setting our mugs down, we bolted out of the room. "He's not supposed to appear during this moon phase," I said as we ran down the tower stairs.

"Maybe he was excited about having guests?" Tamsyn suggested, breathless.

At the bottom of the stairs, we charged along the corridor to the King's Chamber, located in the northeast corner of the castle. We found Lorna Cargill huddled at the end of the hall, outside the door.

"I saw something over there," she whispered in a trembling voice, pointing. "First there was a blast of cold air . . . and a weird sound like chains rattling . . . and then I saw *him*. Looking at me." Her hands shook as she gestured. "A face but no *body*. It was *horrible*."

Tamsyn put an arm around Lorna's shoulders, easing her away from the wall. "This is a very, very old castle," she said in a soothing voice. "And sometimes one of our ancestors, Sir Percival, pays us a visit." She reached for the room door, which was unlocked. "I promise you, he never hurts anyone. Come with me while Nora . . . takes care of him."

I pulled out the drawer in an end table standing under a bad portrait of the first Baron Asquith, thankful I'd stocked up on emergency supplies. After fumbling around for a sage smudge and a box of matches, I struck a flame and lit the bundle of herbs. Not for the first time, I considered asking Father Patrick to perform an exorcism. But when it came down to it, I'd never had the heart. Ravensea had ghosts, yes, but they were *our* ghosts. Remnants of our history, so to speak.

"You're a bad, bad boy, Sir Percival." I waved the bundle around and wisps of fragrant smoke drifted through the corridor. "Don't you be scaring our guests, you hear me?" I marched along the carpet, stopping every few feet to wave the sage, watching to make sure no sparks escaped.

Near the gallery overlooking the Great Hall, the air stirred, more a gathering of molecules than anything solid. Ah, there he was. I went in that direction, aiming the smudge like a weapon. "Go on, scoot."

Dust motes began to swirl, someone sneezed, and then, with a dismal clank of metal, the air cleared. Good. He was gone. And hopefully he would stay that way.

Ruffian nudged the staircase door open and padded out, mewing. "Giving the all-clear signal?" I said to him. At times I thought about renting Ruffian out as a ghost hunter; he was that skilled at detecting paranormal activity.

I was stubbing out the smudge in a crystal ashtray when Tamsyn emerged from the King's Chamber. "How's she doing?"

"More or less recovered from the shock," Tamsyn said. "I got her calmed down enough to focus on running a hot bath. Those rose petal and jasmine bath salts smell fantastic, by the way."

I smiled at the compliment. "Glad you think so. There's a jar next to our bath." I tucked away the smudge for another haunting. "Where is her husband? Did she say?"

Tamsyn shrugged. "She didn't. He wasn't in the room, that's all I know."

Odd. I wondered where Gavin was. Maybe out getting some air or sneaking a cigarette. We fell into step, heading back to the staircase. "What did you want to tell me? Earlier?"

In response, she ducked her chin, warning me off with a head shake. Another gesture I knew well. She had reconsidered confiding in me, at least for now. "First one upstairs gets the most cookies," I said, putting on a burst of speed. We jostled for the lead all the way up the spiraling stairs, giggling and pushing and having fun, like two sisters without a care in the world. Certainly no worries about bankruptcy or bad reviews or whatever was troubling Tamsyn.

Dawn arrived far too early, pink and lovely over a pearly sea. I groaned, thinking I should sleep another half hour or so. But then I thought of my garden. If I went down now, I could get in a good hour or so of weeding before breakfast preparations started. I'd never made it out there last night, as I had hoped.

Ruffian blinked at me from the nest of bedclothes as I pulled on soft old jeans. "Stay here if you want, sleepyhead. I don't blame you." We'd both had a restless night, me because I'd been worried about my guests and their comfort—and Sir Percival's return—him because I'd rolled around far too much, clutching at my pillows and trying to find cool spots on the sheets.

During the wee hours, I'd heard a dog bark. Lady, perhaps, taking a potty break outside. That high-pitched yip certainly wasn't Rolf. But the episode was brief and hopefully hadn't disturbed anyone else.

I slipped my feet into clogs and slung the loop of a gardening apron over my neck and tied it around my waist.

Combed my hair and washed my face. I was halfway through the door when I heard a thump behind me. Ruffian, who suffered greatly from fear of missing out.

In the kitchen, I put on water for coffee and fed the cat, then buttered a crusty roll to carry out with my travel mug. Footsteps creaked overhead. Guy and Janet, in their apartment. We slipped out through the side door and strolled through the kitchen garden. Pea vines climbed up trellises and sprouting greens and young transplants filled the beds. Soon we'd serve homegrown vegetables to guests.

I opened the red-painted gate to the knot garden, noticing that it wasn't fully latched. Not that it mattered, really, except I didn't like Rolf to get in there and rampage around. Drinking coffee as I went, I stumbled and almost fell when I kicked something hard. Ouch.

An ornamental stone ball about the size of my fist lay in the path. Picking it up, I glanced around, trying to figure out where it had come from. Now and then crumbling mortar let go and we had to patch the stonework back together. Too bad the workmen hadn't noticed it was loose and mortared it. Now I'd have to get them back, sometime in this century.

I couldn't see a gap on the wall at the moment, so I continued on, thinking I'd ask Guy about it later.

Halfway to the fountain in the middle, Ruffian let out a cry and darted right between my legs, which made me wobble on my feet again. "Hey," I called. "Don't do that." I dropped the ball, letting it fall onto the grass. I swiped my jeans leg with damp fingers, wishing I had been wearing the gloves tucked in my apron pocket.

Ruffian ran to the foot of the fountain and began sniffing around at a heap of cloth on the ground. What was that? Had one of our guests dropped their coat or a lap blanket? I suppressed a sigh, figuring this kind of thing went with the territory.

But as I got closer, terror squeezed my midsection, threatening to send the coffee in my stomach erupting upward.

That wasn't a bundle of cloth. It was a *person*. Hilda Dibble, to be exact.

CHAPTER 4

I stood frozen, my gaze skipping over the dreadful sight. Hilda lay on her front, legs slightly splayed and her arms flung outward. She was wearing the same clothes as last evening: a flowered skirt with a blouse, boiled wool jacket, and low-heeled leather shoes. A small handbag sat open near her feet.

Something dark matted the hair on the back of her head.

Blood.

Ruffian looked at me and mewed.

I sank to my knees, letting go of the travel mug. *Her pulse. I should check her pulse.* Giving little grunts of distress, I crawled the short distance. When I touched her neck, it was cold. Nothing beat under the skin.

Hilda was dead. In my garden. Why? How? When?

"No. No. Someone help . . ." I scooted backward, crablike. I needed to call 999. Rouse the castle. Where was my phone? Oh yes, in my apron pocket.

Gravel crunched, followed by a light whistle. "Lady, come." Finlay, out on an early morning stroll.

I scrambled to my feet and waved my hands. "Finlay. Help. Please. There's an . . . emergency."

After another whistle for the dog, Finlay began to run

toward me. "What's the matter, Nora? Are you hurt?" Lady dawdled along behind, tongue out.

I shook my head, pointing. My mouth was trembling now and I didn't dare to speak, in case I burst into tears. My hands fumbled with the phone as if I'd forgotten how to make a call.

He came to an abrupt halt when he saw Hilda lying on the grass. "Lady. Stay." She sat. A cool, wary alertness replaced the worry and concern on his face, as if a hand had wiped his expression clean. "Who is that?"

"H-H-Hilda Dibble," I stammered. "She lives—lived in the village."

Noticing my phone, Finlay put his hand up in a *stop* gesture. "I'll make the call." With measured steps, he approached the body, bent to touch her neck. "Don't move," he barked. "Don't touch anything."

"What? Who are you to talk to me that way?" I huffed. "Telling me not to call. It's *my* castle." *My dead body?* Ugh.

He whipped around, wallet in his hand, and flipped it open. "I'm a police officer. Detective Inspector Finlay Cole."

The absurdity of this struck me and I let out a very inappropriate laugh. "Seriously? You just *happen* to be staying here? Huh." I wasn't sure where I was going with this, what I was thinking. It was strange, that's all.

His brow furrowed. "An unfortunate coincidence," he growled. He shoved his wallet into his pocket and took out his phone. "Hold tight, 'kay?"

I sank to the ground again and wrapped my arms around my knees. Hilda. Dead. Although I despised the woman, I was horrified. She was only, what, fifty or so? She must have been stumbling around in the dark and fallen. Or—?

The ball I'd found. My eyes searched the grass. Had

someone *hit* her with it? A sick feeling in my gut told me the answer was yes.

"A team will be right out." Finlay stepped away from the fountain. "When did you come out to the garden?" He was still holding his phone.

"A few minutes ago. I was hoping to do some weeding. You came along right after I found her."

"You weren't out here last night?"

I latched on to what his question implied. Had Hilda been lying out here all night? Maybe so, judging by the coldness of her skin. "No. I went to bed around, um, ten or so. I saw you out here, with Brian, before that." I winced at the accusation in my tone.

He tapped away on the phone and I realized he was taking notes. "She wasn't here, then," he mused. "Which means . . ."

She was killed sometime between nine at night and six in the morning, when I came out. Way before six, I guessed, for her to cool off so much.

Shuddering, I pressed my face to my knees. After a struggle to control my churning stomach, I looked up. Finlay was crisscrossing the grass, searching.

For evidence. For the weapon.

"On my way into the garden," I said, "I stumbled on a stone ball that fell from the wall."

His head jerked around. "A stone ball?"

"About so big." I showed him the size with my hands. "It's over there. On the grass."

He stared at me for a long moment, as if probing my brain, as if wondering if this was a subtle attempt at confession.

It wasn't. I did have something to tell him, though. "I'm sorry, but I touched it. I had no idea . . . I stubbed my toe on it."

"Where was it exactly?"

I showed him and he hunkered down to examine the spot. "You may go, Ms. Asquith," he said. "Don't leave the property. I'll come find you later."

My knees flexed, ready to run. Then I hesitated. "What do I tell people?" My family, the guests . . . they'd be wondering why the police were in the garden.

He lithely rose to his feet, his gray eyes boring into mine. "Tell them there has been an accident and that's all you know. No one is to leave until I give the say-so, got it?"

"Got it," I mumbled. I picked up my mug and hurried away, doing my best to hold back the cascade of emotions looming like a cresting wave. Horror. Dread. Fear. If I gave in, let it crash over me, I'd be swept away. And I couldn't afford that, not now, not with the future of the castle at stake.

While alive, Hilda Dibble had done her best to derail our new venture. Ironically, her death might be what finally succeeded.

The scent of baking cinnamon buns greeted me when I burst into the kitchen. Janet, who was mixing eggs in a bowl, swung around in surprise. "Milady. You startled me."

"Sorry." Wondering how to frame the news, I crossed the kitchen to make a fresh cup of coffee. "Um, Janet—"

"Make me one, Nora?" Tamsyn slunk across the kitchen, yawning, her hair tumbling about her shoulders. She pulled out a chair and sat. "I'm so, so tired."

What I was about to say would definitely wake her up. "We have a problem." I found a new filter and placed it in the pour-over cone.

Tamsyn blinked. "Don't tell me you're out of coffee?"

"No, no, that's not it. Plus we have the pods." We'd bought a machine for the guests and set it up in the dining room.

Now Guy tromped through the back door, stamping his feet. "What's the to-do in the garden? I see the bobbies arrived."

That was fast. How long before the guests noticed?

Now Dad appeared, fresh in a starched white shirt, his hair and beard neat. This was an improvement. Usually he immediately holed up in his study, fed by deliveries of pots of tea and toast as he dug into the records.

"Something smells good," he said, his eyes twinkling. "I'm in the mood for a big fry-up."

"And you shall have one, milord," Janet said. "Soon as Nora shares whatever is on her mind." She gave me an encouraging nod.

All eyes fastened on me, expectant. "Something awful has happened." I swallowed. Finlay had said to call it an accident, but surely my family had the right to know the truth. "When I went out to weed, I found Hilda Dibble dead by the fountain."

A brief silence like a held breath—and then the exclamations and shouts of shock and disbelief began.

"Hold on, hold on," I cried. I got up on a stepstool and waved my hands so they would notice me. When they calmed down, I put my fingers to my lips. "Shh. We don't want the guests to know. Yet. Finlay said—"

"Finlay?" Tamsyn asked, her brow furrowing before she remembered not to do that. "What's he got to do with it?"

"Turns out he's a detective inspector. So this . . . situation . . . is right up his alley, it seems." I shrugged. "Anyway, I suppose he wants to manage the truth, be the one to deliver it. I mean, I would if I was investigating a murder—"

"Murder?" Janet's eyes were huge. "The poor woman was *murdered*?"

"In our *garden*?" Tamsyn put in. "That's horrible." She shivered, rubbing her arms.

Finlay was going to kill me. Bad choice of words. "In short, yes, it appears that way. So we need to let the police handle it."

Guy pushed back his cap, scratching his head. "That woman would do anything to put a spanner in it, wouldn't she?" When his cheeky remark surprised a rueful laugh from us, he blushed. "Just saying."

"You're right, Guy," Dad said. "She certainly worked hard to make life difficult for us." He crossed himself. "God rest her soul." We murmured the same.

"Who could have done such a terrible thing?" Tamsyn asked. "One of our guests?"

Her suggestion landed with the thud of a catapulted boulder, stunning us.

"I sure hope not," I blurted. The idea of renting a room to a killer was unthinkable. "Finlay, for one, is definitely innocent. Besides, Hilda didn't meet any of the guests." Then I reconsidered. Maybe she'd run away from the social because she'd seen someone she didn't want to encounter. "That we know of, I mean."

"One of her many enemies must have followed her here," Dad said. "Though I'd love to know why she was skulking about."

So would I, and Dad was right. Hilda wasn't exactly liked in the village.

Guy was frowning, something obviously on his mind. "What is it, Guy?" I asked.

He shuffled his feet. "Just some rumors I heard . . .

there's talk of smugglers in the area. She might have run afoul of them, like."

For centuries, this section of rocky, remote Yorkshire coast had been a smuggler's haven, with coves and caves providing perfect cover. His theory seemed far-fetched, but Hilda had no problem interfering in other people's business.

This time, it appeared, she'd gone too far.

Janet glanced at the wall clock. "We'd better get a move on. The guests will want to be fed." She donned a pair of mitts and opened the oven door to retrieve the buns.

Guy withdrew, headed back to the vegetable garden. No doubt he would also keep an eye on the police.

"Dad, why don't you wait in the dining room to greet our guests?" I suggested. The water was boiling so I put together a tray with a teapot, a cup, and milk. He meekly carried it out.

"Coffee," Tamsyn whined, still slumped at the table.

"Coming right up," I said, sarcasm lacing my voice as I poured boiling water into the coffee filter cone. "We could use a hand here, by the way." Chafing dishes needed to be lit and platters ferried. Thankfully we'd set up the dishes and silverware the night before.

Tamsyn came over and leaned against the counter, arms folded. "So what exactly happened?" she whispered. Her tone became wheedling. "You can tell me."

Janet was just as interested, flashing us glances as she stirred eggs and flipped bacon.

"What I said." I motioned her back until I had safely put the hot kettle down. "I went out to weed and found her lying beside the fountain. She'd been hit on the head." Horror once again rushed up my chest at the memory. "I touched the weapon. I think."

Tamsyn put a hand on my arm. "What was it?"

"A stone ball from the wall. I moved it after I stubbed my toe."

"You touched it?" She shook her head. "Oh, no. Nora. If that is what killed her, they're going to blame you."

"Me? But she'd been there for hours . . ." My voice trailed off. That didn't matter. I could have beaned her with that ball last night and staged the "discovery" of her body.

Dad appeared in the doorway, clearing his throat. "Hate to interrupt, but we've got some early risers."

"We're on top of it, milord." Janet began spooning eggs into the chafing dish. "The hot water urn should be ready for tea. Or they can use the pods for coffee."

He saluted before disappearing again.

Since Tamsyn was in her nightgown, it was up to me to ferry the food. I ran back and forth between the dining room and kitchen, pausing only to light the chafing dishes. Then I carried a fresh cup of pour-over coffee to the dining room to check in.

The three guests and Father were seated at the table, high-piled plates in front of them and mugs of steaming drinks close to hand.

"Everything okay?" I asked.

Brian Taylor barely broke chewing stride to nod. "Delicious," he said. "Fueling up for a good long day in the field." He took a swallow from his mug.

"Sounds wonderful." I considered breaking it to him that he wasn't going anywhere. Not until Finlay had spoken to him.

I'll wait until after breakfast. Pretending to be casual, I wandered over to the window overlooking the knot garden and peeked out. Dad had cleverly pulled the curtains partway closed, the excuse being the sunlight beaming in from the east. Heads clad in police caps bobbed along the paths and I recoiled, hoping no one else had seen them.

Brian continued. "I've chartered a boat today. I'm going to see how many seabirds I can bag—for my book, I mean—along the coast from Whitby to Scarborough."

I pictured him on the water, binoculars trained on the cliffs, spotting storm petrels and shearwaters, shags and great skuas.

"We're going to be out on the water today as well," Gavin Cargill said. Freshly shaven, cheeks ruddy and teeth gleaming, he exuded contentment and good cheer. "My friend, Patrick Horn, is anchored offshore in his eighty-foot Oyster."

"Nice," Brian said, brows rising. "Sweet boat."

Gavin's smile was condescending. "Very." He patted his wife's knee. "Lorna is going to put on her bikini and sunbathe, aren't you, darling?"

I cringed. Another outing sure to be canceled. Our bed-and-breakfast would fail before it even got started. One night with guests and we were over. So pathetic it was laughable. In and out of business in record time.

"Maybe," Lorna said. "If it's warm enough." In contrast to her husband, Lorna looked wan and tired. One side of her collar was up and the back of her hair wasn't quite combed. Had Sir Percival kept her awake all night? I hoped not. Maybe I could discreetly ask her later. Not that it really mattered, I reminded myself. They'd be checking out and posting bad reviews before the day was out.

Gavin pushed back in his chair. "Would you like something else from the buffet, darling?" He picked up his empty plate.

Lorna shook her head and I noticed she'd barely touched her food. Then she peered into her mug. "Another cup of tea would be nice."

I sprang into action. "I'll get it." Rather than refill her used mug, I pulled another off the stack.

Her husband came over to the table, picking and poking his way along.

On this side of the room, a window overlooked the side drive to the former stable block, an entrance used by the family and service vehicles. Now, as tires crunched on gravel, Gavin looked out. "An ambulance? What's that doing here?"

Over at the table, Dad said matter-of-factly, "They must be here for the body."

CHAPTER 5

Gavin recoiled. "Body? What body?"

Lorna gasped. "Is it the other guest? The young man with the adorable dog?"

Brian's complexion paled. "I hope not. He's a very nice chap."

"Finlay Cole is fine," I said, having finally gathered my wits. Dad was sitting mute, his eyes apologetic. I gave him a little shrug to let him know I forgave him. "It's someone else. A local woman. There was a . . . um, an accident. And unfortunately . . ." *She was hit on the head and died.* Rather than lie about the cause of death, I stopped there.

"Who was it?" Brian asked. He sat frozen, fork poised in the air. Noticing, he set it down.

Hilda hadn't even made it into the wine social so I doubted any of the guests had met her. "Her name was Hilda Dibble."

Lorna frowned, testing the name under her breath, and then shook her head.

Brian pushed his chair back with a squawk of wood on stone. "Sorry. I just remembered something. Please excuse me."

He strode out of the dining room and I hoped he wasn't heading for the hills. Finlay wouldn't be happy with me if all the guests left before he could talk to them.

Well, except for barring the door—literally—or locking them in the dungeon, there was nothing I could do to keep Brian or the Cargills at the castle.

Even if—a sudden thought stole my breath.

Even if one of them killed her.

It wasn't any of us who lived in the castle, I knew that much. After a horrified moment imagining Brian and the Cargills as killers, I reined in my imagination. A more likely scenario was that the culprit had accompanied Hilda. Or followed her here. That begged the question: What on earth had she been doing at the castle in the middle of the night? The answer would probably lead straight to the killer.

Despair swamped me. If it had to happen—which it shouldn't have, not by any stretch—why hadn't the dastardly deed been committed elsewhere? We'd been well and truly dumped on.

Lorna turned in her chair. "Honey, maybe we should . . ."

Gavin was still standing by the window, watching the activity in the garden. "Ready when you are."

His wife stood. "Nora, we'll be checking out this morning." Her lips twisted in an apologetic yet determined grimace. "We weren't charged, correct, so there's no refund to process—"

"Hold on," I said, a trifle desperately. "You can't leave."

They stared at me. "Why on earth not?" Gavin blustered. He gestured toward the garden. "This isn't anything to do with us." His eyes narrowed. "It's not as if you'll lose money."

"Finlay Cole has requested that we all sit tight. *Detective Inspector* Finlay Cole, to be exact."

Their mouths flapped open and shut. "He's a police officer?" Lorna squeaked, her shoulders raised. "I had no idea."

Me either. "I guess we got lucky." I motioned toward the buffet. "You might as well get comfortable. It will probably be a while." *Brian.* I had to track Brian down before he took off. I pivoted on my heel. "Now, if you'll excuse me."

Dad had continued to eat quietly and when I glanced back over my shoulder, he lifted his cup with a wink. His way of reassuring me that he had this.

I ran a finger across my lips, signaling that he'd better keep mum. Who knew what other beans he would spill given the chance? Not on purpose. Duplicity just wasn't in his nature. *Too good for this side of heaven*, Janet often said.

Tamsyn was coming down the staircase as I headed up. We met on the landing. "Hey, can you cover for me in the dining room?" I asked before giving her a quick overview.

"Sure. I was headed there anyway." Tamsyn's brows drew together. "Where are you going? Taking a break?"

"Hardly. I'm trying to stop Brian from leaving. He left the dining room rather suddenly, right after Dad blew it."

Tamsyn snorted. "Not a surprise. Dad, I mean. Don't worry, I'll charm the Cargills. They'll be begging to stay on once I'm finished with them."

She sauntered down the steps, hips swaying, and I could tell she was already immersed in her role as host with the most. Tamsyn Asquith: actor, fairy princess, and queen. When didn't she get her way?

* * *

I knocked on the door of the Knight's Chamber, aka the blue room. "Brian? Are you in there? It's Nora."

Faint footsteps sounded and the door opened a crack, revealing a sliver of Brian's face. "What's up?" His morose tone and the sad expression in the one eye I could see told me he was upset. Quite a contrast to his earlier excitement about his birdwatching boat trip.

"Are you okay?" Bringing the hammer down with an order to stay on the property and then leaving felt wrong somehow.

The eye blinked then glanced down. "I'm fine," he said, injecting heartiness into his tone. "Why?"

Because you don't seem fine? "Uh, no reason." I shrugged. "I mean, I'm not that happy this morning. About the . . . accident. It's so sad." I paused. "Anyway, the police have asked us all to stick around. They want to talk to everyone."

With a sudden jerk of his hand, he opened the door wider. "Police. You mean Finlay?"

"So you knew?" I remembered the two of them taking a walk yesterday evening. It made sense that they would discuss each other's occupations, as you do with any new friend.

I thought back to the conversation at dinner. Finlay hadn't mentioned his career then, I was pretty sure, because I'd been hanging on his every word. He'd merely said that he was relocating to Monkwell and his flat wasn't ready yet.

Brian's complexion had gone sickly again. "About Hilda Dibble? No, I had no idea."

I could sympathize with his reaction to a mention of the dead woman. Every time I thought about discovering her body, I wanted to hurl. "I meant Finlay, but no worries. I just wanted to let you know that he has asked us all to stay put. Until he's had a chance to talk to everyone. You'll be able to leave after, I should think." I injected a sprightly tone into my voice, trying to hide my dismay at losing a paying guest. Brian was supposed to stay for a week.

His brow furrowed. "Leave? Do you want me to? I booked for—"

"No, no. You can stay." My laugh was a sick little trill. "I thought you might not want to, after all this." I began to back away. "But I'm glad you're staying. You probably should reschedule your boat trip, though." I grimaced. "I'm sorry."

Brian's expression eased. "I'll do that." He started to close the door.

"We'll be serving lunch around noon," I called, hoping he heard me. Although we didn't normally offer a midday meal, if guests were forced to stay in, we'd feed them.

Now that I was upstairs, I figured I might as well tidy the rooms. Our eco-friendly rules required changing linens every three days unless otherwise requested. I still planned to make the beds, dust, vacuum, and empty the trash cans daily. Or rather, make Tamsyn do it. Janet and I had plenty on our plates.

Because Brian was in his room, I pushed the carpet sweeper and cleaning cart to the Queen's Chamber, where Finlay was staying. Far as I knew, he was outside directing the investigation, but I knocked twice and called out, "Housekeeping," anyway, before inserting my key in the lock.

To my shock, the door opened, revealing Finlay, Lady at his feet. She gave a gruff little woof, either greeting me or warning me away, I wasn't quite sure.

"I'm sorry, I thought you were in the garden, busy with . . . stuff." I gestured at the cart. "I was going to tidy your room."

Finlay poked his head out, looking up and down the hall. "I was taking a quick break to check on Lady. Have you done the other rooms yet?"

"No, yours is the first."

He gnawed at his bottom lip. "You can go ahead in." His gaze fell on the vacuum. "Stay out of the other rooms for now, okay?"

A jolt of adrenaline made my heart jump. "You think one of the guests had something to do with Hilda's death?" Was he worried I might accidentally hoover up evidence? It was possible. Couldn't they match sand or soil or tiny fibers?

His expression closed, exactly like shutters being pulled across a window. "Right after you're finished here, I'd like to talk to you. Meet me downstairs."

Talk to me? My heart began to pound, even though it made sense for him to interview me. I was the one who had found Hilda. Who had touched the possible murder weapon.

Trying to divert his thoughts in another direction, I said, "We told the guests they need to stick around to talk to you. Both parties—Brian Taylor and the Cargills— were headed out on excursions so I had to say something."

He regarded me steadily with those cool gray eyes. "What exactly did you tell them?"

"Only that there had been an accident." I bit back a mention of Dad's faux pas. "The Cargills want to check out now. Brian is good with staying put."

After another staring session, he snapped his fingers at

his dog. "Lady, Come. I'll see you downstairs, in what? Fifteen minutes?"

"Give me twenty." I needed to maintain control somehow. I'd take any extra time and try to compose myself.

"Good enough." The pair began to stroll down the corridor and I pushed my way into the room, pulling the cart behind me.

I surveyed the room, assessing the tasks ahead. Finlay Cole was an orderly guest. The covers were pulled up and his clothing was hanging neatly in the wardrobe. A water glass sat on the nightstand, along with reading glasses and a book.

Lady's bowls were in the bathroom, clean, one filled with water. A few toiletries sat on the pedestal sink and a travel bag on the toilet tank. Towels were hung on the rack.

He'd used my signature soap for men, I noted with pleasure. It had an earthy yet fresh citrus vetiver scent, both relaxing and invigorating. I'd leave another bar.

Ten minutes later, I was finished. If all guests were like Finlay, this part of the inn-keeping business would be a breeze.

I was putting the cart away in the linen closet when I saw Lorna Cargill leaving her room. She came trucking along the hallway, arms swinging, head down and shoulders hunched.

"Lorna," I called softly. "Mrs. Cargill."

She stopped, head going up. "Nora. Hello." She shifted her stance, clearly uncomfortable. Because they were leaving so quickly? Was she afraid I'd berate her or try to get them to stay?

She didn't need to worry about that. My concern was a little more, um, otherworldly. I waited until I was closer to

ask, "How was your night? Any more *unusual* events?"
Behind my back, I crossed my fingers that Sir Percival had
retreated for good after the sage burning.

Her eyes flared, mascaraed lashes making a doll-like
fringe. "What do you mean?"

She was going to make me say it. "Remember the
chains clanking? The cold spot? I was hoping that you
weren't disturbed again." I refrained from mentioning the
disembodied head, his most frightening display.

Lorna waved a hand. "Oh, that. No. After my bath—
which was heavenly, by the way—everything was fine. No
sign of anything spooky."

But everything wasn't fine. As she rushed past me with
a muttered *Excuse me*, her averted gaze and slumped posture revealed the lie.

Something was bothering Lorna Cargill. And if not
Sir Percival, was her struggling marriage to blame? Or
Hilda Dibble's death?

We assigned the solar, a sunny, graciously furnished space
adjacent to the drawing room, to Finlay for his interviews.
Dad had the library, so the solar was my combination
office and sitting room, the spot where I curled up with
Ruffian and read or dreamed up new herbal recipes.

"I'll get these out of your way." I gathered the folders,
loose papers, journals, and books littering the Hepple-
white desk into an untidy stack.

Meanwhile, Tamsyn moved two sturdy upholstered
armchairs so they faced the desk. I gave her a nod of appre-
ciation. The last thing we wanted was a well-built man like
Brian or Gavin breaking one of my delicate antique chairs.

Finlay set his tablet, phone, a notepad, and pen on the
cleared surface. "Thank you. This will do nicely."

"Tea?" Tamsyn asked, clasping her hands at her chest. She was playing the role of winsome housemaid now. All those period dramas were coming in handy. "Biscuits?"

"That'd be nice, thanks." Finlay rested his hand on the back of the chair. "I'd like to talk to you first, Nora." He cleared his throat. "Ms. Asquith."

"Certainly, Detective Inspector," I said crisply, trying to show I wasn't daunted by his switch to formality. I took it as a warning to remain on guard and be very careful about what I said.

I chose a chair. "Tamsyn, can you bring me a cup, too?"

A frown flitted over her face. While she could be kind—witness the Ovaltine last night—she resisted any request she viewed as ordering her around.

"Please," I added.

"Right away, I'm certain," she replied, using yet another of her accents as she flounced around and made for the door.

"Close the door, please," he called.

She shut it none too gently. Finlay's eyes met mine, the flash of humor on his face matching my reaction. Then his expression grew formal, chilly even.

Disappointment sank my spirits. When we'd met yesterday, I'd thought there were possibilities. I liked him and he was definitely attractive.

Now we sat on opposite sides of a desk, and despite the slightly small and feminine scale of it, it was a perfect metaphor for the barrier between us.

Finlay was on one side, representing the law, and I was on the other, insides shivering in presumptive guilt, like when blue lights flashed in the rearview.

Then I sat up straight, tensing my jaw. Finlay Cole was not going to bowl me over. I was innocent, my family—including Janet and Guy—was innocent, and I would stand my ground, sword in hand, so to speak.

My chin lifted and I allowed a hint of cold challenge to enter my gaze. We stared at each other a long moment and I could practically hear the steel clashing, the shouts of battle.

He tore his gaze away and tapped at his tablet. "I have a few questions, Ms. Asquith. Your cooperation will be much appreciated." Ms. Asquith. Not Nora.

My mouth opened, a protest on my lips. Of course I was going to cooperate. I wanted to find out who had killed Hilda Dibble as much as he did. More, even.

Then I shut my mouth, a smile curving my lips. His incendiary remark was a tactic, a way to put me on the defensive.

"Of course." I folded my hands in my lap. "Fire away."

He took a moment to fiddle around with his phone. "I'm going to record this, if that's all right with you."

I shrugged, watching as he tapped away, then gave his name, rank, the location, and the date. He had me give my name as well.

Now I wished I had an official title, so as to pull rank. "Eleanor Sibilla Asquith." *Sibilla*, he mouthed. "It's a family name, from the fifteenth century." Sir Percival's wife was called Sibilla.

Was it my imagination or did I see a drift of tiny sparkling lights in the corner? "Sibilla," I said again, experimentally. The particles danced and I smiled to myself. Sir Percival was monitoring the situation, it seemed. Somehow I found that comforting.

"All right, Ms. Asquith. Take me through your movements this morning."

I detailed the time I'd gotten up, and my journey out to the garden to weed. My discovery of Hilda Dibble's body lying by the fountain. As I spoke, I tried to focus on each word, doing my best to keep shock and horror at bay. Of course, this reserve might work against me. Maybe dissolving into a heap of shattered nerves would testify to my innocence.

"You're doing fine," he murmured, letting me know that he saw right through my efforts at control.

Then I glanced at my lap, at the absolutely shredded tissue in my hands. I didn't even remember taking it from the box.

"One more question. Did you see a cell phone anywhere? Either on your way to the garden or near the deceased?"

I thought back. "No, I didn't. Her handbag was there, with things spilled onto the ground. I didn't look inside it, though." Was Hilda's cell phone missing? That was a shame, especially if she'd planned to meet someone in the garden.

"Moving on," Finlay said. "Tell me about Hilda. Any idea why she was at the castle last night?"

"None. In fact, after the way she acted at the wine— oh, you weren't here yet." I told him how she'd shown up at the castle unexpectedly and invited herself to the social, only to change her mind at the last minute.

"Any idea why she decided to leave?" he asked. "Who was in the drawing room?"

I gave the list, then added, "It was really strange, especially because she was very interested in fawning over—I mean, talking to Tamsyn."

A glint of humor flashed in his eyes and my tension eased a notch.

"Those two workmen," he said, surprising me. "What were they doing here?"

"You're observant," I said, surprised that Finlay had

noticed them, what with the novelty of arriving at the castle.

An odd expression flitted across his face. "Hazard of the job. If you don't pay attention, well, things can go sideways pretty fast."

"I imagine so," I said. "Anyway, Shawn Boswell and his helper, Joe, were fixing one of the flagstone paths in the garden. Do you think they had something to do with it?" What reason would two stonemasons have to kill Hilda?

He gave a head shake, indicating that he wasn't going to answer. "Do you have their number?"

"Certainly. Shawn's, anyway. I can get it for you." However, if I set the police onto them, I'd never get them to finish the rest of their projects. "Don't tell them it was me."

Busy looking at his tablet, he didn't respond. "Back to Hilda. How well did you know her?"

A pulse beat in my ears. This is where I had to be careful. Hilda and I had what you might call a history.

"I didn't know her well at all." I tried to sound unconcerned, airy, even. "She was pretty new to the village."

"Long enough to be a thorn in your side, I understand." He drilled me with his gaze. "She didn't approve of your bed-and-breakfast?"

My eyes went to a thick folder I'd moved off the desk. Inside was all the correspondence with the council, applications for permits and licenses, answers to their endless inquiries. Plus clippings from the local newspaper, including letters to the editor from Hilda and articles about our plans for the castle.

To say that the approval process had been like a spell on the rack wouldn't be an overstatement. Thanks to Hilda, every step of the process had been fraught with needless complications, public dragging, and nitpicking criticism.

There was no point in lying or even glossing over the topic. Finlay could find out the dirty details in a heartbeat, either through gossip or by perusing the newspaper and council archives. Someone—a bobby?—had already given him a heads-up.

"She, ah, made it her business to put obstacles in our way," I finally said. "Which was strange. I never could figure out why she cared so much."

He sat straighter, alert like a game dog scenting prey. "How did you feel about that, Ms. Asquith?"

"How do you expect?" I replied in astonishment. "It was hell. I didn't kill her, though. I didn't need to. We succeeded and she failed. She was old news, far as I was concerned." The time to bean her on the noggin was months ago. I didn't say that, of course.

I still hadn't wanted her anywhere near the castle. Her next trick might have been to file complaints about sanitation or the food. She was a devious and nasty piece of work.

Thankfully he left the subject there and moved on.

"Last night. Can you tell me when you went to bed?"

I did my best to estimate the time, explaining that Tamsyn and I had sat on the windowsill to drink Ovaltine first. At the thought of Tamsyn, I remembered the tea. She was taking an awfully long time to bring it.

"Where were you the rest of the night?" Finlay asked.

"In bed." Here came the crux of the matter. I matted the tattered tissue into a ball.

"The whole night?"

"Well, except for a loo visit. No idea when that was. The loo is adjacent to my room," I added quickly, meaning I hadn't wandered the castle or gone outside.

"Can anyone vouch that you were in your room the entire night?"

My underarms dampened. Did he really believe I'd crept out of my room to kill Hilda? "No . . . only the cat. Ruffian."

Tamsyn chose that moment to barge through the door. She lugged the tray to the desk and set it down. "Sorry to take so long. Janet was pulling lemon curd tarts out of the oven so I waited to snag a few."

Despite the stress of being under interrogation, my mouth immediately watered. I adored lemon curd. Judging by the eager expression on Finlay's face, so did he.

He splashed milk into a mug and I got up to do the same. Then I grabbed a tart and sat down again.

Tamsyn hovered. Finally, at Finlay's questioning look, she said, "I can vouch for Nora." The minx must have been listening outside the door.

"How's that?" Finlay asked, munching on a tart. He'd tapped the recorder off before fixing his tea.

My sister's face flamed with color, meaning that what she was about to reveal was highly embarrassing to her. Not much rattled her, so this had to be good.

"I was awake during the middle of the night." She reached into her apron and pulled out her phone. "I can prove it."

"Hold on." Finlay used his ring finger to turn the recorder on. A bare ring finger. "I want to get this." He put her through the same routine as he had me.

"Tamsyn Lucia Asquith," she said clearly, perching on the chair adjacent to me. She held up the phone. "I was texting in the wee hours. Nora didn't stir all night. Except a visit to the loo at two. She went right back to bed, after."

My face was burning. I'd already covered the loo business and we didn't need to discuss it again.

"You can look at my texts," she said, her bottom lip quivering. "They're time-stamped, obviously."

"Who were you texting?" I asked. "Ben?" She'd been dating Ben Morrison, another actor on her show, for just under a year.

The quiver became outright trembling, and to my dismay, I saw tears in her eyes. "Yes, I was texting Ben. Our show has been canceled. And he . . . he's gone back to his wife."

CHAPTER 6

My heart went out to my sister. No wonder she'd been more difficult than usual. "I'm so sorry, Tamsyn. I had no idea."

She curled her lip and sniffed, which meant *back off.* Tamsyn only allowed me to get so close before she would get all prickly and defensive. "Whatever. The point is, Detective, my sister didn't creep out to the garden and hit Hilda on the head. Besides, if we were going to kill someone, we'd cart the body offshore and dump it."

Was that an amused glimmer in Finlay's eyes? "Noted, Ms. Asquith. I appreciate you coming forward." He held out his hand. "May I take a look? I won't, er, read the texts. I only want to see the time stamps."

"Don't worry," she said, placing the phone in his palm. "There's no phone sex or anything. Ben and I are well past that point. Like I said, he's going back to *her.*"

"I thought they were divorced," I said. Tamsyn had been adamant that she wouldn't date him while he was married.

"They are." Hurt and anger flashed in her eyes. "He went off to a family gathering in Scotland and she ambushed him. With the help of his brother and his wife. The ex is her best friend, you see."

"Ah." I made a mental note to check out the tabloids later. I was pretty sure this salacious episode would be thoroughly dissected. Poor Tamsyn. I couldn't imagine having every detail of my personal relationships presented in full color.

A jolt of realization made me gasp. What if the tabloids found out about Hilda's murder? I could see the headline now: YORKSHIRE CASTLE SHOCKER. STAR TAMSYN ASQUITH QUESTIONED IN BLUDGEONING DEATH.

"Does anyone know you're here?" I asked. "Besides Ben?"

"Why?" Her eyes went wide. "Oh, I get it." She put a hand over her face. "I'll never get another part."

"What's that they say?" Acid laced my voice. "All publicity is good publicity?" I was worried about the bed-and-breakfast tanking—not to mention possibly being arrested—and she was concerned only about herself.

"I'll do what I can to keep things low-key," Finlay said, handing the phone back to Tamsyn. "Police press conferences aren't my thing, although I can't vouch for the higher-ups. If the case drags on, they'll get involved, I'm afraid."

Despair tempted and taunted. Everything we'd worked for was about to go up in flames, and we'd probably lose the castle as a result.

Then I rallied, a deep sense of resolve hardening in my gut. I would solve Hilda's murder myself and save us from ruin.

After lunch with the guests, a sullen meal of roast beef and cheddar sandwiches dressed with Janet's biting horseradish, Tamsyn and I went over to Monkwell. Finlay Cole was still doing interviews at the castle, but at least the crime scene team had left, a length of tape around the dire spot the only evidence of their presence.

"I'm so glad to get out of there," Tamsyn said with a sigh as we crossed the causeway in Mum's 1991 red Saab 900. It was my car now, good on petrol and roomy enough to deliver my products to stores. Which is what we were doing today, our destination Tatiana's Bower on the High Street.

"Me too." I'd been totally wrung out after my interview with Finlay. It took a lot of energy to be that guarded, especially after the visceral shock of discovering Hilda Dibble's body. A restorative cup of peppermint-and-ginger tea soon put me right. Returning to my normal activities, however briefly, was a relief.

The causeway became Castle Lane and then intersected with the High Street, which ran through the village, bordering the bay. Tatiana's Bower, a charming shop with a mullioned bow window, was located between the Lazy Mermaid ice cream shop and the Headless Viking pub.

I slid into a spot in front, a little miracle to brighten our day. "Can you help me carry stuff in?" I had two large boxes of soap, herb bath tea, creams and lotions, and aromatherapy roll-ons to deliver.

"If we can grab an ice cream after," Tamsyn said.

"Deal. I'd love that." Walking over to the village for ice cream had been one of our favorite childhood treats.

Between the two of us, we managed to grab the inventory. By the time we reached the door, Darby Walsh, the owner, was holding the door open for us. "Hello, ladies. I didn't think I'd see you today, Nora." Darby, tiny, dark, and fey, had huge brown eyes that revealed her every mood. Right now they were brimming with concern and a smidge of alarm. "Is it true? Hilda Dibble is dead?"

"Yes, she is," I said. "And I found her." I set a box down on the glass counter, inhaling the delicious aroma of spices, candle wax, incense, and chocolate that characterized the shop. Tamsyn put her box next to mine.

Darby put a hand on my arm. "So I heard." Her expression was rueful. "It's all over the village, details more gruesome by the minute."

An image of Hilda lying on the grass flashed before my eyes. "It was pretty bad. She was hit on the head."

"You poor thing." Darby gave me a hug. She turned to Tamsyn. "You need one, too."

Tamsyn usually resisted overt displays of affection but she allowed Darby to embrace her. "It's a nightmare," she said once Darby let go. "The DI was trying to pin it on Nora." She patted her chest. "Until I intervened."

My eyes met Darby's and we shared a secret smile. She'd moved to the village about a year ago and we'd quickly become fast friends. The absolute opposite of the situation with Hilda. I'd confided in her often about my dramatic, difficult, maddeningly adorable sister.

"We're going to find her killer," Tamsyn declared. "Follow the clues ourselves." I half expected her to pull a magnifying glass out of her dress pocket. She loved her props. "I think someone tried to pin it on us. Why else do it at the castle? A dirty trick for sure."

"I was thinking the same thing," I admitted. "Great minds think alike. I mean, Finlay Cole is a fine detective, I'm sure, but—"

"I don't know about that," Tamsyn said. "Why was he sent down to Yorkshire? He told me he was moving here from London. Who would leave London on purpose?"

Darby laughed. "Living here isn't a punishment." Then she saw Tamsyn's lifted eyebrow and crossed arms. "Well, I suppose it might be for some people."

I thought back to Finlay's remark, how missing something could cause things to go sideways. Had he been demoted? It was possible.

"Anyway," Darby said. "You mentioned clues." She leaned on the counter, an eager look on her face. "Do you have any?"

Tamsyn and I looked at each other. "Not really," I admitted. "There wasn't much physical evidence that I noticed. Only the stone ball that was probably the murder weapon. Oh, and her phone is missing."

"That is pretty thin," Darby said after a moment. "Where do you go from here?"

Tamsyn shifted her stance. "Well, in the detective show I was in—a mini season—we always did a deep dive on the victim and the suspects. That's where we're going to start."

"And talk to people, too," I put in. If I wasn't careful, Tamsyn was going to take over the investigation. She could be a bit of a loose cannon and I didn't want to get stuck doing damage control. Better to make a plan and stick to it.

I turned to Darby. "What did you know about Hilda? Did you like her? Did you know if she had any enemies?"

Darby put up her hand. "Whoa. Give me a minute."

"Nora," Tamsyn said, "you can't just barrage people with questions. It will put them off, not to mention give the game away."

I put my hands on my hips. "I know that. Darby is a friend. She doesn't care if our questioning isn't . . . isn't discreet."

"I honestly don't," Darby commented. She went over to a display and returned with three fair-trade chocolate bars. "This situation needs chocolate."

We unwrapped the bars and ate a couple of pieces while Darby organized her thoughts.

"Hilda was one of my best customers," she finally said, chocolate still tucked in her cheek.

"What? Really?" I glanced around the shop, at inventory that was romantic, feminine, sexy, and frivolous. None of those words described Hilda.

Darby nodded as she made her way across the shop, soon returning with a lacy peach silk nightgown and robe set. "She bought one of these last time she was in." She held up the hanger so we could get a better look. "Hilda had a lot of secrets," she mused. "How she behaved toward you, Nora, and other people in the village, was only one facet of her personality."

"A nasty one," Tamsyn said. "She was a royal b—"

A woman walked into the shop. Sandra Snelling, Hilda's friend. Like Hilda, Sandra favored classic styles, as if guided by the Royal Family's dress code. Today she was wearing a pink boiled wool jacket with a plaid skirt and slingbacks. However, in stark contrast to her impeccable appearance below the neck, her hair was a rat's nest and her makeup smudged.

"Darby!" she cried. "He finally did it. He killed her."

After this remarkable statement, Sandra burst into tears. Darby rushed to comfort her and Tamsyn and I stared at each other. Could it really be this easy solving Hilda's murder? We only needed to learn who *he* was. I wasn't leaving the shop until we found out.

"There, there," Darby soothed. "Nora, want to switch on the kettle? I've got some of your Calming Chamomile."

"Right away." I dashed around behind the counter, to the niche where Darby kept tea things, a small fridge, and biscuits. The kettle was full so I snapped it on and then rummaged through the bags of tea looking for the right one.

Sandra was pushing her hands through her hair, revealing how it had gotten into such a state. "Did I tell you he threatened her? Right to her face, it was."

Darby put a hand on her arm. "Come, sit. Tea will be ready in a minute."

Tamsyn leaped into action, arranging several chairs in a circle near the tea niche. Sandra blinked at her, recognition finally dawning. "You're Tamsyn. From *Highland Lass*." The show that had just gotten canceled.

My sister winced, then hid her reaction behind a broad smile. "Yes, I am. Nice to meet you. And you are?"

"Sandra. Sandra Snelling." Sandra fumbled for a chairback and sat, her gaze still fixed on Tamsyn.

"Pretty name, Sandra," Tamsyn said. "I was named that once, in a film."

"Oh, that's right," Sandra crowed. "I remember. You were gorgeous in that role." She leaned forward to study Tamsyn, as if examining her pores. "You're even more so in person, though."

Tamsyn simpered. "How nice of you to say. It must be the sea air. It's positively invigorating."

How could she stand being scrutinized and commented upon like that? If I were famous, I'd never go out in public. Or I'd wear a disguise when I did. One good thing about the sick-making fangirling, though: Sandra was calming down and she also wasn't questioning our presence. I was relieved she hadn't come in accusing us of murdering Hilda.

The kettle whistled. "Who else wants tea?" I asked, filling a mug for Sandra.

We all could use some Calming Chamomile, it was decided, so I made three more mugs and we sat in a circle to drink. A packet of McVitie's chocolate-covered biscuits went around, too.

"I can't believe she's gone," Sandra said. "Hilda was my best friend. Before she moved in next door, I was rather lonely, being new to the village and all."

"So sorry for your loss," Darby murmured. "Nothing like a best chum to brighten your day."

I gritted my teeth, impatient to get to the point. Sandra was a babbler, I recalled from previous encounters. If we went directly at her, she'd divert left or right, deftly avoiding capture like a greased pig. The image made me laugh at the same time I was taking a sip, making me sort of slurp-snort.

"You okay?" Tamsyn whispered.

"Fine," I whispered back, discreetly wiping my nose.

Sandra was now giving a lengthy and descriptive litany of the activities she had enjoyed with Hilda: shopping, excursions to stately homes, sailing, theatre, so on and so forth. Darby looked as though she was about to nod off, the chamomile and Sandra's droning proving to be a potent combination.

Time to rein this in.

When she paused to take a breath, I jumped in. "Um, Sandra. I'm so, so sorry for your loss. Truly." She regarded me with skepticism, no doubt remembering the fraught public meetings and Hilda's scathing letters to the editor. "She sounds like a wonderful friend and I hope whoever did . . . this . . . will pay. Dearly. From what you said earlier, you might know who it is?"

Shaken out of her stupor, Darby sat up straight, and we all looked at Sandra expectantly.

"Ah, um, yes," she stammered. "I'm pretty sure I do."

Don't waffle now, lady. "You said he threatened her?" I prodded. "That's just awful."

Tamsyn widened her eyes, somehow making them shine with fear. "What if he does it again?"

"Oh." A hand went to her mouth. "I hadn't thought of that." The hand went to the back of her head, as if she was imagining herself being struck down like Hilda.

"Who was it, love?" Darby asked. "Hilda would want you to tell us. To help bring him to justice."

"Joe Lumley." Sandra slumped as she spoke, as if she'd released all the air in her body. "The stonemason. He said he'd see her in hell before she got his parole revoked."

CHAPTER 7

I thought about Joe, a big, quiet lug who moved stones and pavers with ease. He rarely spoke and it was hard to imagine him losing his temper and making such a violent threat. However, we were talking about Hilda.

"What provoked him?" I asked.

Sandra's mouth open and shut. "I don't know," she sputtered. "It came out of the blue." Then she frowned. "Does it really matter?"

"Maybe not," I admitted. "When was this?"

She tapped her mouth, thinking. "Day before yesterday? Yes, that's right. We were having a cup of tea in the garden, and he came around the house unannounced, long hair flying, muscles bulging everywhere." She shivered in horrified glee. "He shouted at her and then left. Banged the gate so hard it fell off a hinge."

Joe and I were soulmates, united in our loathing for Hilda.

"Have you told the police?" *Sorry, Joe. When push comes to shove, I'm gonna throw you under the bus.* Finlay had seemed to accept the alibi Tamsyn gave me but that could change. Especially if they didn't turn up any other leads.

"Not yet," Sandra admitted, her shoulders hunched and laced hands fretting. "You think I should?"

The three of us nodded. "Definitely." That was Tamsyn. "I would, love." Darby. "If he's dangerous, they need to get him off the streets." My assertion.

"What if he comes after me?" she asked.

She had a point. "I'm sure they'll be discreet," I said firmly. "Tell them your concerns. Besides, maybe they'll find more evidence when they search her house and arrest him." I assumed they'd search it. Then I remembered Finlay's question. "What does Hilda's phone look like, do you remember? The police couldn't find it."

"Her phone?" A line appeared between Sandra's brows. "It's in a pink case with gold stars. I don't understand why it wasn't with her. She never went anywhere without it."

The killer must have taken it. There might be incriminating messages or calls on the device, maybe even an invitation to meet in the castle garden.

I couldn't imagine Joe setting up a get-together with Hilda, or that she would agree after he threatened her so bluntly. He could have followed her there, though, and impulsively killed her. Then the person she was there to see showed up and what? Took her phone and left, without calling for help? How horrible.

Another question was, why meet at the castle? Why not her home or another place in Monkwell?

The guests. The Cargills and Brian Taylor. They weren't familiar with the area so it would make sense for her to come to them.

Did I dare to ask the obvious question? I took a breath and went for it. "Sandra, do you know why Hilda was at the castle last night?"

She froze like a rabbit in the headlights. "No, I don't. Really, I have no idea."

"She knows something," Tamsyn said. We were on our way into the Lazy Mermaid for an ice-cream cone.

"I think so, too." I held the door open to let her enter first. A thought niggled. Was Sandra trying to divert attention to Joe, away from someone else? Without connections or wealth, he made the perfect fall guy. This realization made me squirm, I so greatly despise people targeting the underdog. I was ashamed I'd considered it.

Liv Becket, another good friend, was behind the counter. Gorgeously blond and ample, she and her husband, Tom, ran the ice cream shop as well as a dairy farm that supplied the milk and cream for the frosty confections.

"I was hoping you'd come in," Liv said. "I saw the Saab parked out front." To the teen slouched behind the counter, staring at her phone, she said, "Astrid. To your station." Astrid was her fifteen-year-old daughter. She also had Ava, ten, and Tom, Jr., five.

"We were making a delivery to Darby," I said, moving to the ice cream case. I studied the flavors before saying, "Small vanilla, please. Regular cone."

Liv and Tamsyn wore identical smirks. "Nora always gets vanilla," Liv said. "I'm trying to get her to branch out."

"Good luck," Tamsyn said. She bellied closer. "I'm going for the mint chocolate swirl today."

"That's my favorite," Astrid said, digging at the vanilla with a scoop. She formed a perfect ball and placed it firmly on the cone.

With a glance at her daughter, Liv said, "How are you two doing?" She widened her brown eyes meaningfully.

Astrid rolled her eyes. "Mum. I know all about the murder. I hear about worse things online."

"That's what I'm afraid of," her mother muttered. She glanced around the empty shop. "I'll take a break and sit with you."

We carried our cones to a small table in the corner, near the window. Liv sat patiently while we enjoyed the first few bites of the creamy treats. People made fun of me for liking vanilla but nothing can top the sweet perfection of such a simple yet complex flavor.

Never able to remain idle, Liv rearranged the few items on the table. "How's the ice cream?"

Tamsyn moaned. "Incredible. If I'm going to be hanging around Monkwell, I'll have to ration myself." She wagged a finger at Liv. "Don't let me buy ice cream more than three times a week."

"Cut it out," Liv said with a groan. "You're so slim." She patted one of her curved hips. "Unlike me." Then what Tamsyn had said sunk in. "What's up with the show?"

Tamsyn leaned forward. "Canceled," she whispered. "So I'm between gigs." She threw me a smirk. "Lucky for Nora I'm around to help."

"Yes, lucky me." I popped the end of the cone into my mouth and crunched. "So. The bad news." I filled Liv in, with occasional interjections from Tamsyn.

Liv was appalled. "I mean, Hilda was a royal pain but she didn't deserve that."

Behind the counter, keen young ears had obviously been listening. "One time, when I gave her chocolate sprinkles, she told me to take them off. That I'd made a mistake. I never make mistakes with orders." Astrid was seething.

"Of course Astrid couldn't take them off," Liv said. "We had to toss that serving and start over."

"She made friends everywhere she went," I said deadpan, making them laugh.

The door opened and a family group came in, several adults and half a dozen children. "Mum!" Astrid squawked.

Liv rose to her feet. "Duty calls. You going to hang out a while? I'll bring you cold drinks after I help with that gang."

I looked at Tamsyn. "Sure. Want to do some research on our phones?" I was itching to do something, anything, to figure out who had killed Hilda. And why.

Tamsyn scooted her chair closer to mine. "Where should we start?"

"Hmm. Let's look at the local community group. If Hilda had a problem with Joe, maybe it started with the stonemason company."

The group was generally friendly, with people posting about events, lost dogs, and the weather. Sometimes the most mundane topics aroused the most controversy and discussion, which could be amusing.

However, we had a few cranks, like Hilda, who liked to complain. They usually got shut down eventually but not quickly enough, in my view. We business owners, having been advised that rebutting would only fan the flames, had to suffer in silence.

I typed Hilda's name into the search function to find her posts.

"Good grief." Tamsyn slapped a hand to her forehead. "'Important Notice,'" she read aloud. "'Whoever so rudely left the dog waste on the steps down to the beach this afternoon: Kindly return and pick it up! This beach belongs to us all, let's not let it go to the dogs.'" She grimaced. "Complete with Exhibit A. Gross."

"That's only one of her helpful missives," I said wryly. "Read this one." I brought up another post.

"'Downtown display,'" she read. "'Hanging flowers are lovely BUT they are crooked. Council, please fix them soonest before we embarrass ourselves.'"

Again, the post was accompanied by photos. I had to admit that the baskets were off-kilter. Thinking back, I remembered workers up on ladders fiddling with them. Although Hilda was a newcomer, people jumped when she barked.

"Bit of a bully, hmm?" Tamsyn commented. "I know the type."

"You have no idea," I said with a sigh. "I battled her for months about the bed-and-breakfast."

She eyed me, puzzled. "You never said anything about it." Then understanding dawned. "Oh. Yeah. I was a jerk, wasn't I?"

I tried to restrain a satisfied smile. To be honest, she had been. Her outraged reaction when I'd shared my plan had discouraged me from confiding in her. "Well, I could tell you weren't in favor so I didn't bring it up." I shrugged. "It almost didn't go through anyway." So why create a rift over something that might not happen, had been my logic.

Her expression was contrite. "I'm sorry, Nora. Forgive me for letting you battle the ogre alone?"

"It's okay. We got our approvals despite her best efforts." A wave of despair hit me and I covered my face. "Now it looks like we're going to fail before we even get started." Not that our problems were anywhere close to an untimely loss of life, but still . . .

I felt her arm sneak around me. "Not on my watch, sis."

After composing myself, I said, "All right. Back to work." Thinking of Joe, who had threatened Hilda in front of Sandra, I added "stonemason" to the search. "Aha. Found it."

The post started out fine, with Hilda seeking a recommendation for a stonemason to repoint her chimney. People soon chimed in with recommendations, with several for Shawn Boswell. Hilda replied to one that she'd reached out to him.

Then, a few weeks later, Hilda posted an update on the post. "'I cannot recommend Boswell Builders at all. So many problems.'" When someone asked for clarification, she said, "'Rather not go into details online, sorry.'"

Tamsyn groaned. "But it's okay to slam the company?"

"I know, right? Before social media, people gossiped, sure. Went by word of mouth, good or bad. Now anyone can say anything and it's everywhere."

Tamsyn rolled her eyes. "Tell me about it." She leaned closer to study the post. "I don't see Joe mentioned. I wonder why she targeted him with the threat about his parole."

"There must be more to the story. Maybe Joe saw her comments and told her off. Then Hilda retaliated."

Liv brought us a couple of ginger ales. "How's it going?" The shop door opened again and more customers came in. "Send me a text later, okay? Drinks are on the house."

I picked up the can and popped the top. "Thanks. Will do." I lifted the can in a salute.

"We need to track Joe down." Tamsyn opened her can. "Unless he's coming back to the castle to do more work?"

"Not right now. They finished the path, finally. So yes, we need to go to him." I sipped soda, thinking. "I can call Shawn's wife and find out where they're working. I have no idea where Joe lives." I'd rather not confront him at his home anyway. If he was dangerous, I wanted witnesses.

"Won't she tell him we're coming?" Tamsyn asked. "We need the element of surprise."

"You might be right," I admitted. "Though I've called her before. It beat waiting for Shawn to get back to me." Like many tradespeople, Shawn was hard to reach and even harder to pin down. It felt like a special dispensation when he finally showed up.

A pair of women waiting in line for ice cream were staring at us, whispering behind their hands. Had they recognized Tamsyn? Or were they talking about my discovery of Hilda's body?

My stomach knotted. I wasn't in the mood for questions or comments. "We should go."

Tamsyn glanced over, tossed her head, and stood, pushing the chair in. Wearing both a wide smile and an invisible don't-talk-to-me cloak, she sauntered, hips swinging, toward the ice cream shop door. The gossipers watched her, starstruck, while I scurried along in her wake, invisible myself in her radiated glow.

And that suited me just fine.

Janet hurried to meet us when we walked into the Great Hall. "There you are, miladies. I wanted to check in with you about dinner."

"How many will be eating, you mean?" I asked. "Just two extra. Finlay and Brian, who said he's staying the full week. Lorna Cargill told me she and her husband were checking out." My spirits sank even lower at this reminder of our struggling bed-and-breakfast venture. Once the news of Hilda's death broke, would we ever get another booking?

She shook her head. "They've decided to stay for a week as well. And even better, they're paying for the extra days." Glee danced in her eyes. "I may have quoted them the top rate. They didn't quibble at all."

This sudden reversal gave me pause. Briefly. Then I decided not to question something going our way for a change. "Great work, Janet. If we give them the royal treatment, maybe they'll leave a good review. Even with . . . Hilda."

Janet drew herself up proudly. "They won't find fault with my cooking, I promise you. Tonight I'm serving roasted chicken with mash and veggies and lots of gravy."

"Yum. One of my favorites." I had another thought. "How are we set for the wine social?" Finlay was probably busy with his new case so we wouldn't have done much for one guest, Brian. Now we needed to rethink that.

"I've got the nibbles handled." Janet smoothed her apron. "And your father is going to share something special: Sir Percival's life story."

"I can't wait to hear it. Maybe we'll understand him better." Maybe we could even figure out how to prevent him from scaring guests.

Several daylily blossoms on the console table arrangement had wilted so I paused to pluck them off. Reminded of the garden chores awaiting me, I asked, "Are the police still gone?" I was worried they might have come back.

"Far as I know." Janet winced. "They left big old boot prints everywhere, I noticed."

"I bet they did." Thankfully the plants in the crucial area near the fountain were ornamental, not edible. An image of poor Hilda made me shiver. If they had been herbs, I would have to pull them up and start over.

"Nora and I have launched our own investigation," Tamsyn said. She glanced around. "Let's go somewhere more private and we'll tell you about it." Voices in the Great Hall tended to carry. If anyone happened to be lurking in the minstrel's gallery, for example, they could hear every word, even a whisper.

Dad's study door was open so we ducked in there, closing the door behind us. He reared up out of his chair, tossing a piece of paper aside after he noticed us. Which had taken a moment, he was so lost in thought. "To what do I owe this pleasure?"

"Do we need a reason?" Tamsyn asked sweetly as she went around the wide walnut desk to give him a kiss on the cheek. "Nora and I had a very interesting visit to the village and we want to tell you about it."

"Sit," I told Janet, who tended to hover, conscious of her so-called position in the household. She perched on one chair while I took the other.

Tamsyn leaned against the desk, arms folded. Her gaze fell on the page Dad had been reading when we came in. "What's this?" She snatched it up. "Someone wants to *buy* the castle?"

CHAPTER 8

I jumped up from the chair. "What? Who?" I joined Tamsyn and read over her shoulder.

It was indeed an offer to buy, in cash and with quick settlement promised, like a cattle prod to the rear, *Get out*. Price to be negotiated, and an offer to chat. Someone named Patrick Horn had signed it, and the embossed gold letterhead read HORN HOTEL GROUP. Thinking the name sounded familiar, I pulled out my phone to search.

"Ooh, splashy website." The main page displayed various hotels, all former stately homes, in a carousel display. "'Luxury at your fingertips' is the slogan."

"And he wants this place?" Tamsyn joked. She took the phone and scrolled. "These hotels are amazing. Four- and five-star."

I took my phone back. "No castles, though." Yet. "Castles have tons of cachet."

Dad cleared his throat. "He also enclosed a personal note." He used his thumb and forefinger to pick up a small square of paper as if it were a disgusting object.

Tamsyn took the note and read aloud, "'Dear Arthur, I'm moored just off your lovely property and would be happy to either come to the castle or have you motored

out to my yacht for drinks and discussion. I look forward
to working with you.' Signed 'P.'"

I put two and two together. "He's Gavin Cargill's
friend. Gavin mentioned him and his big boat at breakfast." Was Gavin involved in the deal? "Maybe he's spying on us to give Patrick inside intel."

This theory gave everyone pause. Then Dad let loose
a barrage of imprecations sprinkled with medieval insults like popinjay, coxcomb, hedge-born, and skamelar.
"What is it with these fopdoodles?" he roared, pounding
his fist on the desk. "This castle was built by Asquiths and
in Asquith hands it shall remain."

In the ringing silence following his declaration, my
sister and I looked at each other and burst out laughing.
Even Dad chuckled, fingering his beard. Janet remained
perturbed. She was very protective of us all.

"I know a few actors who should take lessons from
you," Tamsyn said. "They're pretty milquetoast, shall we
say?"

"No doubt, no doubt," Dad mused. "Toss that letter,
will you, Tamsyn? We're not interested in selling, not to
Patrick Horn or anyone else."

I dropped the letter in the wastebasket and Tamsyn
did the same with the note. If Patrick Horn was like the
others, though, he'd be back. Especially now, after a murder, which put real estate into the stigmatized category.
Unfortunately for prospective buyers seeking a bargain,
the castle's history was rife with murder, mayhem, and
death. Sadly, Hilda's death was only a blip on a thousand-
year scale.

As if reading my mind, Dad said, "Sir Percival was
betrayed and then murdered, right outside the gates."
He patted a stack of papers. "You'll hear all about it this

evening during the wine social. I'm also thinking of writing a pamphlet on our ghosts that we can offer to guests."

"With a guide to expected sightings?" Tamsyn asked. "That might be handy."

I groaned. "I don't want Ravensea to be thought of as a haunted castle." To me, the ghosts were atmosphere, not the main event. "We'll get tons of curiosity seekers and maybe even paranormal investigation teams."

Tamsyn put up a finger. "I know a producer—"

"No, Tamsyn." Even as I protested, I felt myself weakening. We really weren't in a position to turn away any revenue. "Put a pin in it, okay?" If we got over the present hump, we might not need the fees—or the notoriety.

To Dad, who was looking downcast, I said, "Please do write your booklet. I for one can't wait to learn more about our ancestors." I waved a hand at the shelves of books, the papers and ledgers and journals and portraits. "Talk about a trove. You might have enough material for a whole book."

"I'm hoping so," he grumped. "I'm only up to the fifteenth century and it's amazing what I've uncovered so far." He sat down at his desk and placed a pair of readers on his nose, our signal to leave him be. Now was not the time to bring up Hilda and what Tamsyn and I had learned. Dad's brain was like a fully loaded freight train—once in motion, switching tracks wasn't always easy. Or advised.

I put my arm through Janet's. "Why don't we talk in the kitchen?"

The Cargills were the first to arrive at the wine social, dressed casually in expensive slacks and shirts, sweaters tied around their shoulders. The perfect evening outfit for a well-heeled couple on vacation. Their noses were slightly sunburned, I noticed, and they exuded a general air of contentment. Despite everything, they'd had a good day, it appeared.

"I'm so glad you're staying on." *Except if you're spying for Patrick Horn or killers.* I pointed to the bottles on the table. "Red or white? Or fine handcrafted mead, fermented right here in Monkwell? We have several varieties." This wasn't their first introduction to my brother's products but I thought a little promotion wouldn't hurt.

"I'll have the lavender mead, please." Lorna glanced up at her husband. "It's perfect for this setting, don't you think?"

Gavin put an arm around her shoulders. "Definitely. I'm ready to joust for your hand, love." He glanced at me. "The plain honey mead, please."

Lorna snuggled closer. "No jousting necessary. I'm all yours."

I filled two glasses, glad that the castle's romantic setting was working its magic on the couple. Yesterday they'd been miserable, especially Lorna. "What did you do today?" *After being questioned by the police, which we won't mention.*

"We went sailing," Gavin said. "On my friend's yacht. Up past Whitby and then down again. Sun. Sea. Salt air. It was marvelous."

"That's right," I murmured. "You mentioned a friend."

Gavin picked up his glass and took a healthy swallow. "Patrick. Patrick Horn. He's quite the mover and shaker."

"Really?" I asked brightly. "What does he do?" I wanted to hear Gavin say it out loud.

Before Gavin could answer, Dad bustled into the room, hat askew and a folder tucked under his arm.

"Greetings," he bellowed. "Welcome to our social." He officiously settled in an armchair near the fireplace and rested his feet on a footstool. "Glass of mead, Nora, please?"

While Gavin and Lorna moved on to the appetizers, I ferried a glass to Dad and set it on a coaster close to hand. Already leafing through notes, he gave me an absent nod of thanks.

Brian and Tamsyn now came in, Tamsyn chattering away about something or other. The effect of her attention on Brian was notable. He had color in his cheeks and his laugh was infectious.

I hurried back to my station to serve them. "Good evening," I said. "Any luck chasing down a rosy starling?"

"Not yet," Brian said, pointing to the red wine. "I'm hopeful, though. The boat excursion was incredible." He spooned a handful of nuts into his palm. "I checked off quite a few seabirds on my list."

"So you did go. That's great." I had my fingers crossed that his overall experience here would prove to be positive. Also that Finlay would quickly find the killer and obtain justice for Hilda, of course.

Speaking of Finlay. He now strode into the room, Lady at his heels. When everyone stared at him, action suspended, he smiled and made a slicing motion with his hand. "At ease. I'm here as a guest." After a few uneasy glances, conversation resumed.

Brian and Tamsyn moved along to the food and Finlay took their place at the drinks table. "I really know how to command a room, don't I?" His head shake was rueful. "It's a shame I had to break cover and ruin my vacation. And everyone else's."

"A huge shame. Red, white, or mead?" Questions crowded to my lips. Had he made any progress? Had he heard about Joe threatening Hilda? Was an arrest imminent?

Not the time or place. Maybe I could catch up with him later, alone. A waft of his spiced aftershave drifted to my nose and suddenly being alone with him held a whole new set of possibilities.

Stop it. Nothing could be more inappropriate than daydreaming about the man who might possibly put me in jail. Plus a guest. That was tricky, for sure.

"Red, please." Finlay watched as I filled a glass. "In other news, I picked up the key to my flat this afternoon."

I corked the bottle. "Here in Monkwell?" His position was regional so he might live in any of a dozen towns and villages in the area.

He picked up the glass and tasted the wine, nodding in approval. "A very dangerous location. Over an ice cream shop." His eyes twinkled with mirth.

"The Lazy Mermaid?"

"That's it. Right in town, which is convenient, and with a nice view of the bay."

Liv hadn't said a peep about Finlay renting the flat. Of course, we'd barely had time to talk this afternoon. "Your landlady is one of my best friends."

"She seems a good sort. So does her husband."

"Yes, Tom is great. An excellent cook, too. We have really fun dinner parties at the farm." Conscious that I was starting to babble, I shut my mouth.

An awkward pause fell and we smiled uneasily at each other. I didn't know much about him, but my mind was scrambling to find something witty or interesting to say.

Dad saved the moment. "Good evening, all," he said, his deep voice immediately commanding attention. "Welcome to my fireside chat. Since I have a captive audience"—a pause for our gentle laughter—"I've decided to occasionally share a tale from the castle's lengthy history. Tonight's topic is Sir Percival Asquith, who served on the side of truth during the Wars of the Roses. I'm speaking of the Yorkists, of course."

Lorna threw me a wide-eyed look over her shoulder and I nodded. Yes, that Sir Percival. The one who had frightened her.

He gave us a brief overview of Sir Percival's life, his birth, marriage to Sibilla, and birth of several sons. Sir Percival was thirty-two when he fought at Towton in March 1461, one of the bloodiest battles of the decades-long war.

"It took Sir Percival almost a month to straggle home. He'd been wounded and was finally well enough to travel the sixty odd miles between Towton and Monkwell. So it was under the light of a full moon that he finally glimpsed the castle. Alone, on a horse that was also on its last legs, he made his way onto the causeway.

"Can't you see him? Shoulders slumped in relief, his heart glad with the knowledge that he would soon see his beloved wife and children again? He'd hole up here and recover, regain his strength so he could fight another day. Sir Percival was very loyal to his king."

Dad paused for a long moment, heightening the suspense. Those of us in the know braced ourselves, sensing that a tragedy was about to unfold.

One side of an open French door shut with a bang.

Everyone jumped and Ruffian, who was lurking, looking for treats, yowled and bolted across the room like his tail was on fire.

Tamsyn and I exchanged glances. *Sir Percival.* The cat's reaction confirmed it.

"Must've been the wind," Dad said, although the other

side of the doors had stayed open. Rising to his feet, he took up the tale. "Sir Percival had almost reached the gates, mere feet from home, when several men set upon him. Although he put up a good fight, they soon had him down." With vigorous gestures, Dad acted out the scene. It was obvious where Tamsyn got the acting gene.

"Sir Percival was on the ground, a sword pointed at his neck, when the scope of betrayal came clear. These weren't vagabonds looking to rob someone.

"These men were in the pay of Cedric Asquith, Sir Percival's older—and jealous—cousin. While Sir Percival had been away fighting for king and country, Cedric had plotted to steal everything, including Sir Percival's lovely wife."

"Blimey," Gavin blurted. "That is a rum do."

"It certainly was a betrayal of the worst kind. Cedric made sure that Sir Percival knew it was him who had ordered the attack, and after gloating, he told the swordsman to cut off Sir Percival's head."

That was why we sometimes saw only a head floating in midair. Other times we'd get a flash of his whole body but there had always been something odd about the throat area. Namely, a space between neck and shoulders.

Everyone groaned, commenting about the injustice of Sir Percival's fate. "What happened next?" Finlay asked.

"I bet Cedric married the merry widow," Gavin commented with a snicker.

"He did, indeed," Dad said, returning to his seat. "Though rumor has it she was a reluctant bride. She and Cedric never had an heir, only girls, so Sir Percival's oldest son eventually inherited. Poor Cedric died a terrible death after suffering from gout and a nasty ague." A wicked smile flashed. "Sibilla was a noted herbalist so you might think he wouldn't have suffered quite so much."

"No wonder Sir Percival hangs around," Lorna said sympathetically. When her husband, Finlay, and Brian gave her surprised looks, she added, "You didn't know? He's one of the castle ghosts. I actually had an encounter with him." She sounded proud of the experience now, which was an improvement over her original fear and horror. "I bet that slamming door was him, listening in on Arthur's story."

"Really?" Finlay asked. "Do tell."

Sensing that attention was slipping away, Dad said, "And that concludes my talk tonight. I hope you all enjoyed it."

Tamsyn began to clap and everyone joined in. After the applause died, the conversation became general, with plenty of compliments thrown Dad's way, I was glad to see. I refilled drink glasses then nipped over to the food table for cheese straws and cold prawns with cocktail sauce.

Finlay was talking to Dad, who was in seventh heaven, and the rest of the group was laughing about something. It was a good time to slip away to the kitchen and see how I could help with dinner.

My brother, Will, was watching Janet peel potatoes while gobbling a buttered dinner roll. "Hello, stranger," I said. "Janet, I'll do that. You take a break."

"Don't mind if I do." Janet sat at the table, resting her feet on the rungs of another chair.

"Nora." Will crammed the rest of the roll into his mouth and reached for me. "How are you? I would have been here sooner but I was halfway across the county."

I returned his hug. "I get it. I'm okay. Let me get these

potatoes done." When he reached for another roll, I swiped at his hand. "Cut it out. Janet, we maybe should rethink offering dinner. How about only on the weekend? Or maybe Thursday and Friday." On the other nights, guests could eat at one of the local pubs, fish and chip places, or upscale eateries in the area.

"I wouldn't say no," Janet replied. "Although I enjoy cooking for a crowd."

"And we love everything you make." A brace of roasted chickens was already resting, skin crispy and luscious, and broccoli waiting to be steamed. "Will, are you staying?" If so, I'd better add a couple of potatoes to the pot.

He nodded eagerly. "Thanks. Better than a frozen burrito, which is all I have at home."

Janet was leafing through a local paper. "You need decent meals, young man. Eat with us whenever you want."

Will gave me a triumphant smile. Then his face sobered. "I hear that my freebie guests are paying now. I'm glad it worked out, Nora. I won't do that again."

I plopped a naked potato in the pot and picked up another. "I forgive you. To be honest, I was relieved that they decided to stay. They were hot to check out this morning and, I'm pretty sure, smear our name up and down Yorkshire." I glanced at Will. "Did they order from you yet?"

He sighed and leaned against the counter, crossing his arms and ankles. "Not yet. I would have attended the social but I don't want to pressure them."

"Lorna and Gavin chose your mead over the wine tonight," I said. "So that's probably a good sign." Unless their interest in mead had been an excuse to help Patrick Horn. I hoped not, for my brother's sake.

"We'll see." He inhaled through his teeth. "They have

twenty stores, so an order from them would be huge. It would take me to another level."

Imagining his mead available all over the UK, I had to agree.

"So what's going on with . . . ?" Will used his thumb to point to the garden. "They arrest anyone?"

"Not yet." As I continued to prepare the potatoes, I took him through it blow-by-blow.

He was horrified, aghast, and finally, worried. "Are you all safe here? Maybe I should come stay."

"No need." I rinsed the potatoes, drained them, and added more water. "It wasn't random. Hilda was the target." I turned on the gas under the pot. "And we have a lead. Today when Tamsyn and I went to Darby's—"

Will swallowed, his eyes suddenly vulnerable. "How . . . how is Darby?"

I frowned at him. "Fine. Why?" Then I got it. "Oh. You like her."

He turned away with a half shrug. "Maybe. Yeah. What if I do?"

"Because that's great news." A few months ago, Will went through an awful breakup. He'd been ready to propose and she'd dumped him for a friend. "You going to ask her out?"

He gnawed at his bottom lip. "Think I should? I mean, I don't even know if she's interested."

"Only one way to find out." I eyed my gorgeous brother. "Darby has great taste so I'm sure you'll be fine."

Another shrug and I dropped the subject. For now. "Anyway, while we were at Darby's, a friend of hers came in." I told him what Sandra had said about Joe.

"Joe did that?" Janet asked. "I don't believe it. He's such a lamb."

"A lamb with a temper," Will said. "You know why he was in jail? Assault. He got into a pub fight and beat up a man. Almost killed him."

"Ugh. How awful." My stomach churned with distress. Maybe Joe had killed Hilda after all.

CHAPTER 9

After dinner, Tamsyn and I took a stroll around the castle grounds. This had been one of our rituals when we were younger, especially in our teens. We'd amble along, confiding our deepest, darkest secrets, dreams, and worries.

Tonight I wanted to hear the details about her ex, Ben Morrison, and what had gone wrong. Tamsyn could be skittish so I couldn't ask outright. I'd need to work my way around to such a tender subject.

Rolf and Ruffian at our heels, our first stop was the vegetable garden. "I love fresh peas," Tamsyn said, plucking a couple of pods. She handed me one and we continued on, using our thumbs to open the seam and extract a row of bright green peas. I tossed a pea to Rolf, who gobbled it with enthusiastic slobbering.

We laughed. I shook my head. "He acts like that no matter how small the snack."

"Maybe there's a lesson there for us," Tamsyn said.

As we approached the gate to the main garden, my steps faltered. "I can't go that way . . . not yet." Rolf, expecting me to open the gate, butted his big head against it.

Tamsyn eyed me with sympathy. "Nora. You have to. Your plants need you."

And I needed them. My business couldn't exist without the castle garden's variety. Oh, I could buy supplies grown elsewhere but I wouldn't be able to speak to their quality or efficacy.

I reached for the latch. "Okay. I guess I should get it over with. Like getting back on a horse, right?" Rolf barged past me and was gone, galloping along the path.

"Exactly." Tamsyn gave me a none-too-subtle push.

"Cut it out. I'm going in." My gaze skittered around the garden, avoiding the fountain while taking in the familiar features that I so loved. Hawthorne, witch hazel, and willow trees. The rose garden. Elder, hops, and barberry. Stands of evergreens and, of course, the extensive herb and perennial beds.

Lengths of yellow tape tied to stakes fluttering in the breeze caught my eye.

"Let's go this way." I urged Tamsyn down a path leading between head-high hydrangea bushes.

"Baby steps," she said placidly. "You can start working again tomorrow."

"Tomorrow," I echoed. Hilda's death another day behind us. "Rolf, come." Naturally he was drinking out of the fountain. As he trotted away, water flapping from his jowls, Ruffian leaped up onto the rim. That was as far as he was going tonight.

The path ended in a small pool where yellow irises grew. A tiny summerhouse with marble benches sat on the far side but we didn't stop. Instead we skirted an ancient chestnut tree and entered the wildflower meadow, which bordered the water.

We stopped to take in the view while Rolf bolted through the field. Sweeping water and sky, the tints of sunset overtaking the blue. A huge sailing yacht was moored in the lee of the promontory, a deep-water spot favored by visitors. From here, the people moving around the deck were tiny black figures.

I pointed. "I bet that boat belongs to Patrick Horn. He said he was moored out here."

Tamsyn squinted. "I should have brought some binoculars."

"Next time." I continued toward a bench placed near the edge of the cliff. "Want to sit a minute?"

We sat and Rolf sprawled nearby, tongue hanging out as he kept watch on the seagulls and waves hitting the beach below. The comforting bulk of the castle loomed behind us, late sun gilding the battlements and peaked tower roofs.

"So," I started. "Ben." Disclaimer. "Unless you're not ready to talk about it."

Tamsyn stared out to sea. "I am. You know, the show being canceled is actually a plus in one way. I won't have to pretend I like Ben anymore."

Ben had played opposite Tamsyn, a dashing nobleman intent on winning her hand.

"I thought you two were getting serious." Judging by how they acted when I saw them, they had appeared to be marching toward living together, if not marriage.

Her mouth turned down. "Yeah, me too. When we first met to do the pilot episode, he had barely gotten divorced from Ainsley. So naturally I steered clear. Who wants to be the rebound relationship, right? Plus, guys who talk about their exes all the time are obviously not ready to move on."

The show had completed three seasons. "When was your first date?"

"Between series one and two. We happened to run into each other in London. Went for coffee, then lunch, drinks, dinner—all in one day." Her brow creased with anguish. "How did I get it so wrong? We were perfect together. I thought."

"You probably were. It's just that his ex has some hold on him, I'm guessing. I never got the sense it was one-sided. He looked smitten every time I saw him."

Tears shone in her eyes. "So I wasn't crazy. He did love me." Her lips trembled. "But I guess he loved her more."

"Or he felt guilty. If he didn't go back to her, she was going to share his dark secrets with the tabloids." I went from the possible to the ridiculous.

She dabbed at her nose with a tissue. "He didn't have any dark secrets. Well, except for staying in touch with his ex. She started contacting him again, calling or texting with all her problems. He tried to hide it but you know me." Her lips curved in a wry smile. "I wouldn't have snooped but I sensed something was going on."

Tamsyn did have good instincts. She could ferret out a secret faster than anyone.

"Is she the needy type?" I guessed. "He couldn't resist being the hero one more time?"

"Something like that." Her jaw hardened. "I would never stoop that low. I don't want a relationship unless we're equals."

"So he's a fop and she's a fool," I said. "A perfect match."

Tamsyn laughed. "Thanks. I mean, he is a really special guy and I don't want to trash him, even if he deserves it. But still . . ."

"It's better you found out now," I said. If only there was a way to prevent heartbreak. Sometimes it was obvious when someone wouldn't or couldn't be a good partner. Other times, people were blindsided by betrayal. So not fair.

"I suppose." She sighed. "I think I'll be single for a while. A real long while."

Based on her track record, I doubted that. But in the interests of sisterly relations, I kept my mouth shut. "It's his loss, for sure. Besides, he'll probably come crawling back."

"Uh, not this time." Tamsyn took out her phone and brought up a tabloid article.

The photograph showed Ben with his arms around his former wife. ACTOR BEN MORRISON AND HIS LOVELY WIFE, AINSLEY, SHARE GOOD NEWS.

"You've got to be kidding. This soon?"

"Yep. They're pregnant." A pause. "He is a wanker, isn't he?"

No comment necessary. I also held back my impulse toward gushing sympathy. She hated that, and I could tell that her prickly shell was snapping back in place.

She rose to her feet, startling Rolf, who leaped up with a woof. "Want to walk down to the beach?"

"Sure." The beach was another of our favorite haunts. Searching for sea glass. Examining tide pools. Swimming when water and air were warm enough.

An old set of stairs led steeply down, new rope slung along as a handrail. We'd defied death for years racing up and down hands-free, but with guests on site, I'd seen the stairs with a new eye.

The tide was still going out, revealing a length of packed, glistening sand. We took off our sandals and walked along the edge while Rolf romped back and forth, practically incandescent with excitement.

"I've missed this," Tamsyn said, squealing when a tongue of cold water covered her toes. "Remember how we used to play out here for hours? My new swimsuit faded in one day, practically."

Even the bare sand was cool enough that I shivered at the idea. "We were impervious to cold back then."

Marks in the sand above the high-tide mark caught my eye. I veered off to get a closer look. As I drew closer, I realized that they were from a boat pulled up on shore.

Tamsyn ran up to join me. "Whatcha looking at?" Understanding dawned. "Oh."

"Someone was here, obviously." Boaters sometimes landed and we didn't mind, long as they didn't go up the cliff and into the gardens. But it wasn't common and I hadn't noticed anyone during daylight hours. "I wonder if this has something to do with Hilda."

"It might." Tamsyn took a step back. "We should tell Finlay." She glanced around at the sand. "Look. Footprints."

The dry sand, deeper here, still retained impressions— leading right to the stairs. I pulled out my phone, hoping I could get decent pictures. Careful not to trample the tracks, I took a series of shots.

"Let me see." Tamsyn scrolled through. "Not bad." She aimed and took one more. "The shadows really define the footsteps now, see?"

"Good one." Her photo showed the clear connection of the boat and the prints. "They'll still have to gather evidence officially," I commented. "But just in case, I'm sending these to Finlay."

It was entirely possible that the marks would be obscured by an especially high tide—or on purpose, if the trespasser got worried.

Rolf, who'd been busy nosing around a pile of stinky seaweed, where I'd been happy to leave him for once, now began to gallop across the sand toward us.

"Stop him," I cried.

We ran toward him, shouting, "No. No, Rolf," trying

to head him off at the pass. After a few feints and darts, we got him safely away and headed back toward the stairs. For such a big, old dog, he was a nimble climber and reached the top first, looking back at us, tongue hanging, as though to say *What took you so long?*

Between pants, I said, "Want to keep going?" Our usual route led us along the shore and through dense woods to the tiny chapel and the sacred spring grotto.

"I'm game if you are." Tamsyn set off and I scrambled along to catch up. Like me, she was one to walk off her angst.

A clear whistle cut through the air. Guy, letting Rolf know it was time for dinner. The dog took off, racing for home, leaving us without a backward glance.

"Food always wins," Tamsyn said with a laugh.

"With that dog, yes."

The forest was dark and still, the sound of the ocean a distant murmur. An unseen bird trilled and something rustled in the bushes.

"I always thought these woods were so spooky," Tamsyn said with a laugh. "Now I love how peaceful they are."

"Me too. I have a favorite rock where I like to sit. Right up here."

The boulder was large enough for both of us to rest upon, legs dangling. Ferns clustered around its base and the branches of an ancient apple tree crooked overhead.

"Nice spot." Tamsyn tilted her head, staring up at the few faded blossoms still clinging on.

Footfalls thudded along the path from the direction we'd traveled.

Tamsyn's head whipped around. "Who could that be?"

"One of the guests?" That was something we'd have to get used to. Strangers rambling around the grounds, perhaps even hanging out in our favorite spots.

She put a hand on my arm. At first I didn't understand. Then I did. The footsteps had stopped.

"Maybe they didn't want to intrude," I said, sliding off the rock. "They're waiting for us to move on."

With a grumble, Tamsyn jumped down to the path. "All right. Let's get going."

We set off at a good clip. I glanced back now and then but I didn't see anyone. Maybe they had turned around and gone back.

The chapel was almost as old as the castle, small and stone and sheltered by a rocky promontory. Before St. Elmo's was built in the village, the family and tenants worshipped here, at Madonna of the Rocks.

Tamsyn turned the tarnished knob on the weathered door and we went in. With one stained window of the Madonna and slits for windows, the interior was dark. We usually lit candles if we planned to sit for a while. Right now, we just stood in the doorway to absorb the space's peace and tranquility.

A bouquet of sweet peas and cornflowers adorned the simple altar. My job now, inherited from Mum.

"She loved this place," Tamsyn said with a sigh, following my thoughts.

"I know. I feel so close to her here."

A footstep scraped on the stone path outside the chapel.

CHAPTER 10

Tamsyn and I stared at each other with wide eyes. "Someone's out there," she whispered.

Another scraping sound, closer this time.

Should I pull the door open and confront whoever it was? Then an image of a killer poised with a rock in hand flashed into my mind. Maybe I should throw my weight against the door and shut it instead.

Fervently wishing Rolf was still with us, I chose that course of action, making the door slam. "Go away," I shouted. "I'm calling the police." An overreaction, perhaps. After Hilda's death, I'd rather take the chance of someone thinking I was strange than risk a dangerous encounter.

Besides, they should have called out, to warn us. Not smart—or nice—to sneak up on two women in an isolated place.

I pushed the flat metal bolt closed, praying it wouldn't get stuck, it was so stiff with disuse. An inside bolt, on a church door? This probably wasn't the first time the building had been used as a refuge.

Tamsyn ran to the closest slit window, peering out. "I don't see anyone."

"Keep looking." Unfortunately, there weren't any windows on the wall near the door. As my pulse slowed, and nothing happened, I started to think we had panicked.

Even so, I didn't quite dare to venture out yet—nor did I want to be stuck in here all night. What if the person was still lurking?

Will. We could count on our brother to answer any SOS.

Tamsyn was peering out a different window. "Still don't see anyone."

My fingers were flying on the keyboard. "Hopefully they left. I'm texting Will to come meet us."

"Good idea. He was talking to Dad when we left so he's probably still at the castle."

My phone dinged. *Be right there.*

Awesome. Be careful, k?

He sent back a thumbs-up.

Now that help was on the way, we relaxed, sort of, and wandered along to our favorite seats in front of the altar. It was a shame we never used this place anymore. Not since my mother's funeral, a private service for us before the public one in town.

In the back of my mind, I'd always imagined getting married here. The ceremony would be small and intimate, with a large reception afterward at the castle. Now I just needed to find a groom.

Ah well, someday.

After about fifteen minutes, someone rapped on the door. "That must be Will." I jumped up and hurried down the aisle.

The knob turned and the door banged against the bolt. "Nora? Tamsyn?" My brother's voice was faint through the thick wood.

"Coming," I shouted. After a moment's struggle, I got the latch to slide back and opened the door.

Will strode in, looking confused. "Was it locked?"

Before I could answer, Rolf pushed past, tail wagging, and trotted up the aisle to explore. "Wish we'd had you with us a few minutes ago," Tamsyn said, patting his broad head.

I showed Will the bolt. "Someone was following us. We think." I told him about the footsteps we'd heard in the woods and again outside the chapel.

Will stepped back out to study the ground. Giving a disappointed grunt, he returned. "No footprints, which isn't a surprise on that hard-packed soil."

"Did you see anyone on the way over?" Tamsyn asked.

"Not a soul." Will stood, hands on hips, his eyes narrow with thought. "It might have been one of the guests. Or not. You two better be careful until they catch whoever attacked Hilda."

Tamsyn and I exchanged glances, both of us appreciating his concern but not interested in restricting ourselves out of fear. Our older brother's warning was a familiar refrain from our childhood. The fact that he'd often been right hadn't lessened our reluctance to listen.

"We'll keep Rolf with us," I said instead of making a promise. "He'll be our guard dog. Won't you, boy?" He panted in approval.

"Speaking of Hilda," Tamsyn said. "Before we came here, we went down to the beach. We found tracks in the sand. Someone dragged a boat onshore and came up the stairs."

"Really?" Will was taken aback. "Did the tracks look recent?"

"Above the high-tide line, so hard to say." I scrolled

on my phone and found the pictures. "Take a look. I've already sent them to DI Cole."

Will flipped through. "Well, it wasn't me. I haven't brought my boat over here for weeks. Too busy." Will fished from a small launch and sometimes made a stop on the beach to visit or just hang out. Once in a while, he cooked fish over a fire and we went down and ate with him.

He handed me the phone. "Ready? I need to get going." Will lived on the outskirts of Monkwell, next door to the meadery.

"Yeah, we're ready." I glanced around the chapel, thinking I should refresh the flowers tomorrow or the next day. "Thanks for coming to our rescue."

"Anytime. You know that." He allowed us to exit first, then firmly shut the chapel door behind him.

The sun was almost down and the grounds were shrouded in a shimmering, eerie twilight. As we hurried along the path toward home, Rolf in the lead and Will at the rear, I found myself alert for any noise, for any sign of someone watching or following us.

Yet another reason to figure out who had killed Hilda. They'd not only stolen her life, but also our sense of peace and safety on our own property.

When my cell rang the next morning after breakfast, I pulled off a dishwashing glove and answered. "Sandra. How are you?" Tamsyn, who was putting food away, glanced over and I nodded. Yes, Hilda's friend.

Sandra gave a big, shuddering sigh. "Still in shock, really. I keep picking up my phone to text her . . ."

"That is rough. I'm sorry." I'd lost someone close to me and I could sympathize.

"Did you find anything out yet?" Sandra asked. "About Joe, I mean? The police are useless. Useless, I tell you." She was working up a head of steam now. "Every time I call, they tell me there's nothing new to report. How long is it going to take?"

It had only been two days but I didn't think pointing that out would help. "I'm sure something will happen soon. They need to get their ducks in a row, just can't arrest someone willy-nilly—"

Tamsyn rolled her eyes at me. I held out the phone, asking through gestures if she wanted to take it. She shook her head with a smile. Of course not.

"You want a cat?" Sandra asked in an abrupt change of subject. "Hilda had a kitten and I've got to find a home for her. I'm allergic." She sniffed in perhaps a Pavlovian response.

"A kitten?" We had plenty of room. The question was, should we add another pet, with Ruffian and Rolf already, and now guests to take care of?

Tamsyn trotted to my side, eyes alight. "A kitten?"

Great. Problem solved. Tamsyn could take her.

"We're interested," I said cautiously. "Can we meet her first?" While all kittens were cute, some were feral or unfriendly. Considering this one's previous owner—well, enough said.

"Sure. She's still at Hilda's, so we need to meet there. You can take her box and toys and the food Hilda bought, too."

My pulse leaped. "At Hilda's? You mean you can go inside?"

"The police said I could. I mean, they understood that someone has to take care of the cat. They said they've finished searching the place."

"All right. Long as we have permission." Should I

tell Finlay? I wanted to stay on good terms with him, not have him think we were sneaking around behind his back. Although we were conducting our own investigation. I hadn't brought that up with him yet.

He was down on the beach right now, checking out the marks in the sand Tamsyn and I had found. Too busy for me to interrupt him.

I'd tell him later. "Where is Hilda's house? And when do you want to meet?"

Hilda had lived in Upper Monkwell, an area charac-terized by small bungalows and a few old farms. Her bungalow was one of several along a narrow lane with a view of the water. A small white sedan sat in the drive, and when we pulled up in front, Sandra emerged with a wave.

I was struck by a thought. "Where is Hilda's car?"

"In the garage, maybe." Tamsyn opened her door. Each bungalow had a small, one-car garage.

"Then how did she get to the castle?" Ravensea was over a mile from here, walkable yes. But at night? In the shoes Hilda had been wearing?

We met Sandra on the walk to the front door. "Thanks for coming." She gestured toward the front picture win-dow. "As you can see, she is getting anxious."

A curtain had been nudged aside and an adorable striped kitten face peeked out at us.

Sandra had the key in the lock when we heard a call from next door.

"Hello, there." A tiny older woman with white hair like a dandelion puff bustled toward us. "Sandra. Isn't it awful about Hilda?" Under a brow furrowed in concern, bright eyes regarded us with curiosity. "You're the Asquith girls."

"We are," I said. "And your name?" I was pretty sure I'd seen her around the village but couldn't quite place her. A member of the community helpers group, no doubt.

She patted her chest. "Mavis Boswell. Janet and I are on the summer fete committee together."

"Nice to meet you," I murmured. Thinking she was probably wondering what we were doing, I said, "We're taking Hilda's kitten home."

"Oh. Good. I already have three cats and they wouldn't be happy with another." She glanced around before leaning close. "Have they caught who did it yet?"

"Not yet," Sandra said. She pressed her lips together. "I have my theories."

I braced for questions, hoping we wouldn't have to shut down gossip about Joe. If he wasn't guilty, it was hurtful. If he was, well, too much talk might make him flee.

Mavis surprised me. "I know who it might have been," she said, scowling. After pausing to make sure we were sufficiently interested, she whispered, "A young man came to see Hilda the other night. She wouldn't answer the door so he pounded on it. 'You need to talk to me,' he said. 'You can't hide forever.'"

"What did he look like?" I asked, thinking this was probably Joe.

"Hmm. Medium height, short brown hair. Good-looking." She gestured down her body. "He was wearing a trendy windcheater with orange and maroon blocks and brand-new trainers."

Didn't sound like Joe, who was tall with longish hair and certainly not a fashionable type. Was there another suspect then? If so, who was he and what could be his possible motive?

"You should tell the police," I urged. "The officer in charge is DI Cole."

Mavis looked dubious. "You really think so?"

"Definitely," Tamsyn said. "We need this person off the streets."

"Oh." Mavis put a hand to her mouth. "You mean we might be in danger, too?" She seemed a tiny bit thrilled by the idea. Life was normally pretty placid in Monkwell.

Sandra snorted. "I doubt it. Whoever attacked Hilda, it was personal. Which is why you need to report this mysterious young man. He was obviously angry with her." She put her hand on the knob. "Now if you'll excuse us . . ."

Mavis backed away. "I'll talk to you later, Sandra. After I call the police."

I hoped she would. Maybe I'd mention Mr. Windcheater myself to Finlay, to put our new suspect on the radar.

The lock clicked and Sandra pushed the door open, releasing a gust of warm, stale air. Then she shut it almost all the way again. "The cat. Primrose is trying to escape."

"We won't let her," Tamsyn said. She crouched, ready to grab the fugitive and I did the same.

Sandra inched the door open as she stepped inside, using her legs to block the opening. With a cry of satisfaction, she grabbed Primrose and held her high. "Got you, you little scamp." Primrose began to purr frantically as she fought to get close to her captor. "Here you go." The allergic Sandra handed her to Tamsyn.

"Oh, she's so soft. Like thistledown." Holding her close, Tamsyn walked in behind Sandra.

I was right behind her, eager to view Hilda's abode. Straight ahead of us was a flight of stairs and to the left, a wide doorway leading into an elegantly furnished sitting room.

Which was in total disarray, as if it had been ransacked.

CHAPTER 11

"The police left it like this?" I assumed Hilda hadn't. Accent cushions were thrown around, books were pulled out of a bookcase, and a lamp lay on its side.

Sandra was staring around in disbelief. "Either that or someone broke in." She went to the fireplace, reaching for the crooked seascape painting hanging there. "She would be so upset at seeing her lovely little cottage this way."

"Hold it. Don't touch anything." I opened my handbag and rummaged for my phone. "I'm calling the police."

Meanwhile, Tamsyn had still been in the hallway, cuddling her new friend. Now she wandered into the room, cooing. Then she stopped short. "What happened in here?"

"That's what we want to know." I dialed Finlay's direct line, hoping he would pick up. If not, I would call the station to get someone here right away. We really shouldn't touch anything or retrieve the kitten's belongings until the police took note of this situation.

"Cole." His voice was raised, as if it was hard to hear, and in the background, I heard the pounding of waves. Still on the beach.

"Finlay. It's me, Nora." I braced myself for his displeasure. "I'm at Hilda Dibble's—"

"What are you doing there?"

"Her kitten. We're taking her home." I took a breath. "Someone broke in. Or else your team really made a—"

Again, he interrupted. "Broke in? Send me a picture, will you?"

I pulled the phone away from my face and took a video of the room, then sent it along.

"I'll be right down," he said after viewing it. "Don't touch a thing. Promise?"

"Promise." I disconnected. "The police are on their way." I glanced around, annoyed. Why hadn't the intruder waited until we were done in here? I'd planned a nice little snoop to look for clues. Tamsyn, still holding the cat, began to stroll around the room. "Don't touch anything," I warned.

She stopped in front of the mantel, which was lined with picture frames. "He didn't say anything about looking, did he?" She turned to Sandra. "Who is this woman with Hilda?"

The photographs were of Hilda at different stages in life—a child, teenager, and young woman—with another girl. The pretty pair looked bright and happy. Such a contrast to the dour, contentious Hilda of recent years.

"That's Celia Dibble, her sister," Sandra said. "She died about thirty years ago, in a car accident. Hilda adored Celia and still missed her."

My heart clenched in sympathy when I glanced at my own sister, who was intently studying the photos. I couldn't imagine life without my big sister. We were two years apart, and Celia and Hilda looked to have the same age gap. My first memories were of toddling around after Tamsyn, trying to keep up with her adventures.

"So sad," Tamsyn said. "Any other family members?"

"Not that I know of," Sandra said. "Their parents are gone and Hilda never married or had any children."

And Hilda hadn't exactly had a knack for making friends—we'd give her a good send-off, I vowed. I couldn't bear the thought of a lonely funeral.

I circuited the room, stopping beside the huge television. Hilda had been a film buff, I guessed, judging by the stack of older DVD cases. One was out and open, the disc probably still in the player. I used a pen from my handbag to flip the cover shut.

Thunder Road, starring Robert Mitchum. It was about bootleggers, I gathered from the blurb, action and adventure in 1930s Tennessee. Unusual choice, though Mitchum had been a hottie. I figured Hilda for a *Keeping Up Appearances* fan, modeling herself after Hyacinth Bucket.

I heard a vehicle and hurried to the window to peek out. No police, only a van, white with a painted logo cruising slowly by. *Cargill's Wine Shops*.

"I guess you're lost." There weren't any shops in this neighborhood. I thought about pulling the curtains open to let light in but refrained. Finlay probably wanted the place to look exactly the way the prowler left it.

"Where was this party?" Tamsyn was asking Sandra. "Do you know?"

The photo showed Hilda and Celia dressed in sequined dresses, party hats on their heads and arms around each other, laughing. A wide staircase rose behind them and other partygoers were living it up in the background. Balloons and streamers gave further clues. New Year's Eve?

"One of the house parties they used to go to. Horn House, I think. Celia's accident happened near there one weekend, I understand."

Horn, as in Patrick Horn, of Horn Hotel Group, who had made an offer to buy the castle? I took my phone and searched for Horn House.

There it was, a blocky, multi-winged stately home about fifty miles from here, on the other side of the moors. Further digging revealed that the place was now part of Patrick's chain, in fact the first property he'd transformed from a family home into a hotel.

At least he put his money where his mouth was. I had to give him that.

Another vehicle rumbled up. This time it was the police.

"I'll go," I said, figuring I could take the heat.

Finlay and Constable Emily Burns climbed out of the panda car. His eyes narrowed briefly when he saw me in the doorway. "Ms. Asquith," he said crisply. "Remind me what you're doing here?" He'd gone all formal on me again.

Emily smirked at me behind his back. We'd gone to school together and she was a good sort. Kind and fair, yet tough on the obnoxious and criminally minded.

Tamsyn shouldered through, keeping a tight grip on the kitten. "We're here for Primrose. Isn't she lovely?"

"She is." Emily patted the kitten's head gently.

My sister and I stepped back, allowing the officers to enter the house. "We were collecting the cat and her gear when we found this." I waved toward the sitting room as if I were a game show host.

"Uh, DI?" Emily's footsteps were hesitant. "It didn't look like this when we finished up."

Finlay's gaze swept the room, lingering here and there. "I don't imagine so." His attention fell on Sandra. "Was the door locked?"

"Yes, it was," Sandra said. "And it looked fine."

"Check the rear, will you, Constable?" Finlay requested. "I'll get the fingerprint kit." To us, he said sternly, "Did you touch anything? Anything at all?"

"The door," Sandra squeaked.

"The kitten," Tamsyn added. "Oh, and we need to get her things."

Finlay sighed. "Where are they?"

"The laundry room," Sandra said. "A carrier, food, a box, the usual."

"I'll help," I volunteered. Sandra couldn't carry all that and I wanted to see as much as I could before we left.

Emily's shout came from the back and Finlay headed in that direction. "The laundry room and that's it, understand? Then you three are free to leave. Ms. Snelling, I'll give you a call later."

Sandra led me to the kitchen, reached via a short hall. Although not especially large, the counters, cabinets, and appliances were new, the surfaces immaculate and gleaming. Bright as a new pin, Janet would say.

Finlay and Emily were in a tiny rear hall examining the outside door, the site of the break-in, I gathered. Through an open doorway, I saw a stacked washer and dryer, and Sandra continued in that direction.

Sandra emptied the cat box into a waste can. "There's a bag of litter you can take. The cat food is in the cabinet."

The cabinet held various canned and packaged goods and, on the bottom shelf, two bags of kibble, one open. I put them in a grocery sack and then used another to transport the bag of litter and the empty pan, which needed a wash. No time now.

Sandra had found the carrier in a closet. "All set?"

"Will you give us an update later?" I asked as we trudged back to the sitting room.

"Definitely." Sandra's face was troubled. "I wish I

knew what the intruder was looking for in here." Determination laced her tone. "I would have made sure they didn't find it."

"I hope she's all right back there." On the way home, my sister kept turning around to check on Primrose, who was in the carrier we'd strapped in with a seatbelt.

"She's fine." I smiled, touched by her utter and complete infatuation with the adorable kitten. "Almost home."

We were headed down the hill toward the harbor when a van pulled out of a side street and hovered right on my rear bumper.

Annoyed, I frowned into the rearview. The Cargill van again. Maybe he was going over to the island to talk to Gavin.

But after tailing us for two blocks, he peeled off right before the causeway. My shoulders lowered with an exhale of air. I really didn't like being tailgated.

Once we reached the castle, I pulled up in front instead of continuing through the arch to the stable yard where I usually parked. "You should probably keep Primrose in your room for a day or so," I suggested. "Let her get used to the place." And let our other pets gradually get used to the idea of another.

"Good idea," Tamsyn said with a laugh. "Rolf will probably slobber her to death." She paused, hand on the handle. "Do you think Ruffian will be okay with her?"

"We'll find out." Ruffian had been King Cat at the castle for quite a while.

Between the two of us, we got everything out of the car and inside. We were on our way up the staircase when Dad burst out of his study. "There you are, girls. You won't believe what just happened."

Thinking he'd stumbled upon an arcane bit of family lore, I said, "Can it wait? We need to get Tamsyn's kitten settled. Then we'll be right down."

"Kitten?" He rubbed his beard, taking in the carrier and the supplies I was holding. Primrose gave a sweet little mew and he grinned. "Cute wee thing. Go on with you, then. We'll talk about how I'm being framed for murder after."

The bag I was carrying slipped and I barely caught it, managing to prevent an avalanche of kitty litter and kibble. "You're being framed? How?" We'd been gone, what, an hour or two?

Tamsyn caught my eye. "We'd better find out." She turned, swinging the carrier, and headed back down the staircase.

My mind was spinning as I followed them into the study, making sure to keep a good grip on the bag of cat gear.

How could anyone frame Dad? He had been a bystander in the conflict between Hilda and me. Oh, he'd offered to wade in at times but I'd refused. The bed-and-breakfast had been my idea and it was my responsibility to see it through. He could go scorched earth if required, but I'd wanted to save him the toll such encounters took on him, especially with his high blood pressure and angina.

I gritted my teeth at the thought of anyone needlessly causing my father stress. If they hurt my father, they would regret it sooner or later.

All in an aboveboard way, of course, as justice served. The tearing of limb from limb and vicious reprisals were a thing of the past in this family.

Instead of sitting at the desk, Dad paced around the study, another sign that the unfair accusation had gotten under his skin.

"The police paid me a visit this morning," he began.

"Finlay Cole?" I was outraged. "We just saw him a few minutes ago and he didn't say a thing."

Dad shook his head. "Not him. Another officer. Following up, he said." He strode back and forth between the window and the door, hands clasped behind his back. "According to him, they got a tip. Someone reported that I'd tossed Hilda out on her ear and told her never to darken the castle door again."

That did sound like Dad, with his tendency toward drama.

"Hold on," I said. "When was Hilda here and why did you tell her that?" I didn't recall any visit to the castle recently besides her almost-attendance at the wine social. And her date with Death, of course.

Dad halted, staring up at the ceiling. "Hmm. Let's see." He tromped over to the desk and flipped through his calendar book, then stabbed it with a finger. "Two days before the guests arrived. I'd had a real breakthrough regarding Sir Percival's history and I was aggravated at being interrupted." His cheeks flushed with outrage. "Her abrupt arrival made me lose the thread I was chasing through the parish registers."

"I would have been annoyed even if I was sitting around drinking tea," I commented. "Why was she here anyway?"

Dad plopped heavily into his chair. "She wanted money." His expression was wry as he rubbed his fingers together. "Trying to put the touch on me. Good luck with that one."

"But we had all the permits and everything was a go," I protested. "Hilda lost."

I couldn't suppress a feeling of satisfaction. She'd fought me every inch of the way and the arrival of our approvals had been sweet victory indeed. I'd almost kissed the pieces of paper. Instead I'd framed them and hung them in a prominent location.

"She said that if I gave her money, she'd go away," he explained. "That she wouldn't cause us any more trouble."

"So she was going to continue the harassment." How, I wondered. Bad reviews? Complaints to the council?

"I assume so, yes," Dad said. "I didn't wait to hear the details. Soon as it became clear what she was up to, I demanded she leave." He ducked his head sheepishly. "I may have raised my voice a trifle."

I could imagine. Dad's shout was the bellow of an angry bull. "Tossed around a few insults, maybe?"

Head still ducked, he listed them. "Harpy. Quisby. Ronyon."

"*Dad*." Ronyon was the worst, meaning aged and ragged. Not that Hilda would necessarily have known that.

He mumbled on. "Might have tossed a *get thee behind me* as well."

"Ask the so-called witness," Tamsyn said sharply. "Sounds like they logged it all."

"Which brings me to the point: who was it? Janet and I were out, I'm sure Guy was working somewhere on the property, not that he'd ever rat you out . . . so who?"

Dad tugged at his beard. "The stonemason was here. Fixing a loose stone in the forecourt. You know, Nora, the one you worried would trip guests."

I did know. Casement windows overlooked the front and if one was open, as it was right now, Dad's shouts could easily be heard. "Was Joe with him?"

Dad frowned. "Let me think." He nodded. "Yes. I'm pretty sure he was."

"How convenient. Especially because Joe is a suspect." It all became clear to me now. Sandra had reported Joe as a suspect and, in turn, he had diverted suspicion to my father.

"What's this about Joe?" Dad asked.

"He threatened Hilda," Tamsyn said. She'd taken Primrose out of the carrier and was snuggling her. "He thought Hilda was trying to get his parole revoked. Sandra Snelling heard the whole thing so we urged her to tell the police."

"My, my." Dad's head shake was incredulous. "You can't trust anyone, can you? All the work I've given Shawn over the years."

"I doubt Shawn had anything to do with it," I put in. He'd grown up here, had a family and a long-standing business. "We're the biggest pile of stone for miles. He wouldn't want to lose us as customers."

"True." Dad laughed, followed by a deep, grunting sigh. "There's more. Some snoop saw me on the bluff the same morning you found Hilda."

"Communing with the ancient spirits?" Tamsyn asked. She also liked to spend time alone in a setting to imbibe the atmosphere and history. This had paid off in performances that were, according to critics, compelling and evocative.

"Exactly." Dad's gaze grew distant. "I trod the paths of our ancestors and try to imagine I'm back in their time. There's a spot on the bluff where the view hasn't changed for a millennia." He frowned. "Except for the gaudy behemoth that passes for a sailing ship these days. He's moored right in the way."

"Patrick Horn?" I edged forward on the chair. "Guess what, Dad? We found out from Sandra that Hilda knew Patrick Horn. Went to parties at Horn House with her sister. Who was sadly killed in a car accident near there."

Dad rocked back in his chair, hands laced across his middle. "Ah, yes. A very tragic event. Your mother and I were at Horn House that weekend."

CHAPTER 12

"You socialized with Patrick Horn?" I had faint memories of country weekends my parents had attended—and hosted. That all ended when my mother died and Dad buried himself in his books.

"Sometimes," Dad said with a shrug. "His brother, Dennis, was at university with me. Dennis owned Horn House, and Patrick was also living there. Big place."

"What happened?" Tamsyn asked.

"Dennis and Celia were leaving Horn House when he lost control of his sports car on a sharp curve and went over an embankment." Dad shook his head. "Talk about a freak accident. He drove too fast, yes, but he knew that road like the back of his hand."

Suspicious mind that I have, I immediately thought of foul play. "I assume Patrick inherited, which makes me wonder: Was it really an accident?"

"Yes, Patrick was next in line," Dad said. "And I agree, it stank to high heaven. The road was dry, it wasn't foggy, and the car had just been serviced. Far as I know, they examined the brakes, suspension system, and so on. The police chalked it up to excessive speed."

And poor Celia had been an innocent passenger. Was it more than a coincidence that Patrick Horn happened to be in Monkwell around the time Hilda, Celia's sister, had died?

Gavin Cargill also knew Patrick, claimed to be a close friend.

I had the sense that the pieces fit together somehow, in a shape that wouldn't quite come into focus. We needed more information about Hilda, about the players involved. If I hadn't been committed to tracking down the killer, this had certainly encouraged me to keep going.

And Joe. I needed to talk to him, face-to-face. He had to be the one who tipped off the police. That wasn't cool. Not at all.

The grandfather clock in the hall bonged twelve times. I jumped to my feet. "It's that late? I'd better go help Janet with lunch."

"It's only us today," Dad said. "The Cargills and Brian are out."

Finlay was busy investigating so he wouldn't be here. Too bad. I'd like to give him a piece of my mind. How dare he give any credence to supposed "tips" about my father.

Tamsyn held the kitten up and spoke to her. "And we need to get you settled."

Before I left the room, I sifted through the waste can for the letter and note from Patrick Horn. Not that I was planning to entertain his offer, whatever it might be.

Because he had known Hilda and her sister, his presence here might well require further investigation. If not by Finlay Cole, then it was up to Tamsyn and me.

After we confronted Joe.

I ate my sandwich—coronation chicken on homemade bread—on the terrace, under the shade of an ancient wisteria. Tamsyn was upstairs with Primrose, my father back in the study, and Janet and Guy were enjoying an afternoon out. Ruffian was pouting in my room, annoyed by the newcomer. Hopefully he'd get over the shock quickly.

Rolf whined at my feet, the crumbs not coming his way fast enough. "I know, boy." I tossed him a piece of crust. "I feel exactly the same way."

I took another bite, trying to stuff down my frustration. No arrest yet and now Dad was a suspect, along with me, who had the misfortune of finding Hilda—and being her enemy. What next? Finger-pointing at Tamsyn or even Janet or Guy?

This absurd thought made me snort-laugh and almost choke.

Besides the fact we were all innocent, law-abiding citizens, none of us were foolish enough to foul our own nest. No, if one of us had done it, we would have covered our tracks. I could have trundled her down to the bay in a wheelbarrow and dumped her in. There was more than one route down to the water. The cliff path happened to be the most direct.

Hopefully Finlay would see it my way. I planned to corner him at the first possible opportunity.

Trying to put aside distressing topics, I took another bite of sandwich, enjoying the taste of tender chicken spiced with curry powder and chutney and adorned with the first of the garden lettuce. Janet really was a marvelous cook.

Tonight the guests were on their own for dinner, she had said, although we were still holding the social. The rooms had been tidied, so I was off the clock until then.

My gaze fell on the garden, arousing a nagging discontent. I really should get out there and work. I also needed to assess inventory levels and check the batches of goat's-milk soap that were curing. My handmade toiletries should be fine for now, though. It was the garden that was a real concern. Plants needed to be harvested at the right time, whether used dry or fresh.

First, though, we needed to confront Joe. On impulse, I picked up my phone and placed a call. "Boswell Builders," a bright female voice announced. "How may I help you?"

"Think Primrose will be okay?" Tamsyn twisted around in her seat to study the castle as we drove across the causeway.

"You could have stayed home," I said. "I would have been fine on my own."

We were headed out to the roofing job where Shawn and Joe were working today. I'd told Shawn's wife I needed to talk about other projects at the castle. It was easier to grab the busy stonemason in person than wait for a callback.

I wasn't lying. We still had plenty of projects. My main mission today was to talk to Joe. Hopefully the element of surprise would provoke an honest reaction.

"There's that van," I said as the wine delivery vehicle blew through a stop sign and pulled out behind us. "Third time I've seen it today." Had it been lurking, waiting for us to cross the causeway? I scoffed at the idea. I was being paranoid.

Tamsyn turned around again, this time studying the van. "There isn't a wine shop in Monkwell, right?"

"No. The only places to get wine are the chain grocery and the general store." The chain would use centralized distribution and the general store was far too small a fish for Cargill's. They were mostly high-end, I'd noticed while perusing their website. "Whoever it is, must be here because of Gavin."

At the next stop sign, we continued straight and the van turned right. Good. He was gone.

"Have you thought about what you're going to say?" Tamsyn asked me. The day was getting warm and she unrolled the window, the sea breeze ruffling her hair.

"No, not really." I braked to let a woman with a baby stroller cross the street. Quite a few people were out, which meant we were basically crawling along. Pedestrians didn't always wait for the crosswalks.

We went by the Lazy Mermaid, which made my mouth water, and Tatiana's Bower. Darby was in front, watering her window boxes, and she waved.

Seeing Darby reminded me of Will. "Guess what? Will wants to ask Darby out."

Tamsyn gave an approving nod. "I can totally see them as a couple. He's so practical and grounded while she's imaginative and fun. They're perfect for each other."

Her analysis was spot-on, but to my surprise, I felt a pang. Of what? Longing and envy, I decided. "Think I'll ever meet someone who's perfect for me?" All I'd had so far were relationships that limped along, not that exciting to either party. Or an occasional crush on someone who was elusive and unreliable. Ambivalent relationships provided their own particular pain, one I never wanted to experience again.

Like the way Tamsyn's ex, Ben Morrison, had behaved? I wasn't the only one who had been unfairly jerked around.

Tamsyn was staring at me, I noticed. "What?" I brushed at my cheek. "Do I have something on my face?"

"What about Finlay Cole?" she asked. "I thought I saw a spark between you." She moved her index finger back and forth.

"He's really hot, no question." My mouth turned down. "But he's also a police officer who considers me a murder suspect. That sure puts a damper on *love*." I drew out the word with a roll of my eyes.

"All is not lost," Tamsyn said with a shrug. "That's why we're on this mission, right? To clear your name. And Dad's."

"Seriously? Proving I'm not a criminal before someone can consider me date-worthy kind of takes the fun out of it."

Tamsyn snorted a laugh. "Yeah, I get your point." She pointed to a side street. "Turn there."

Our destination was a hideous, three-story, yellow-stone Victorian heap called the Rectory, although no one of the cloth had lived there for a century. As we drew closer, I noticed pallets of slate roofing stacked in front and ladders leading upward.

I didn't see the work van. "They must not be here." I braked in front, wondering what to do. Call the office again? Maybe they were on break and would be back soon.

"Maybe they parked around back," Tamsyn said. "I see someone on the roof."

I turned off the engine and opened the door, craning my neck as I got out. As Tamsyn had said, someone was moving around up there, near one of the chimneys.

"All right," I said, taking a deep breath. "Here goes." I really didn't like confrontation so I mustered a sense of outrage and used it to propel me forward.

Joe accused Dad of murder. How ridiculous. What if Finlay believes him and Dad is arrested? I pictured my father wearing an orange jumpsuit in the dock, hands cuffed behind his back. Pictured him lead away, to spend the rest of his life—

"Hey, Joe," I shouted as I ran toward the house. "Joe Lumley, we need to talk."

"Not exactly subtle." Tamsyn was right on my heels. "He'll never come down now."

"So we'll wait." I took another breath before raising my voice again. "I'm not going anywhere until you show your cowardly face. Come down and talk to me."

Silence. A crow cawed in a nearby tree before taking off with a flap of his wings.

Then a strange scraping sound caught my ear.

"*Nora!*" Tamsyn screamed. She grabbed my arm and tugged. "*Back up!*"

CHAPTER 13

Several slates crashed to the ground, smashing into pieces. From that height, the heavy tiles could kill a person.

I let out a yelp. "Oh my God. Did someone do that on purpose?"

Still clutching each other, we backed away, retreating to my car. I didn't see anyone moving on the roof now, but an engine behind the house started up. Then, instead of a vehicle coming around the house and out, the noise died in the distance.

"Either they drove out a back way or that was someone else from a nearby house," Tamsyn said. She backed up farther, moving so she could better view the roof. "Looks like they're gone." Noticing that I was fumbling for my phone, she asked, "Calling the police?"

"No. Boswell's office. I want to find out where they went." My hands were shaking and I had to take a couple of deep breaths to calm myself. Screaming at Shawn's wife wouldn't do a thing to help the situation.

"Boswell Builders," she said pleasantly. "How may I help you?"

"Hi," I said, making sure to smile to inject good cheer into my voice—and hide my rage. Judging by

Tamsyn's look of bemusement, I was probably grimacing like a clown. "It's Nora Asquith again. I'm looking for Shawn at his job site and he's not here."

"Oh, they're having lunch at home right now. Swing by if you want."

"Thanks. We will." After I disconnected, I asked, "How did I sound?"

Tamsyn laughed. "Pretty intense. Chipper on steroids."

I reached for the car door handle. "I'm not the actress, you are. Next time, I'll have you do it."

"All right." She eyed me with concern. "You're doing great, Nora. This whole situation is crazy."

"That's for sure," I muttered as I slid into the driver's seat. "Ready?"

At the Boswell home, Shawn and Joe were sitting in lawn chairs inside the garage, the door wide open and music playing. Sandwiches in hand, they both glanced over when I parked behind the work van, in the street.

Shawn, wiry and muscled and tough, with a shaved head, put aside his lunch and rose to his feet when we approached. After glaring at his helper, Joe did the same. "What can I do for you, Nora?" He gave Tamsyn a friendly nod.

"This isn't about masonry work," I said, my heart pounding so hard I could barely get the words out. "Unless one of you tossed slates off the Rectory roof at us."

The men exchanged looks. "When did this happen?" Shawn asked.

"A few minutes ago," Tamsyn said. "We saw someone on the roof right before it happened." She patted her head. "The tiles almost hit us."

Shawn's face reddened. "Wasn't us, I promise. We've been here for, um, at least fifteen minutes." He pulled out his phone. "I'll call the owner right now. No one is supposed to be up there." As he scrolled, he muttered, "I'm so sorry about that. Really I am."

"Wait before you call," I said. "There's something else I want to say." Righteous anger flared as I leveled a stern look at Joe. "What's with the anonymous tip? If you're going to accuse people, at least own it."

Shawn put up a hand with a short, sharp whistle. "Nora, hold on. What are you talking about?"

"Someone called the police and said that my father had a bad argument with Hilda Dibble." My heart was pounding so much I could barely talk. "They think he killed her." Well, I was worried that they did. I hadn't talked about the situation with Finlay Cole yet.

Joe ducked his head, toeing the tarred driveway with his boot. "He told her off, didn't he? People shouldn't shout if they don't want to be overheard."

My face burned with heat. "You mean, like the way you threatened Hilda in front of her friend?" I retorted. "What you said was far worse."

Shoulders hunched, Shawn swung around to face his helper. "You reported a client's private conversation to the police? That's not cool, man. Our clients need to be able to trust us."

The other man's eyes were wild, his body tensed as though ready to bolt. "They were fingering me for the crime. I can't go back in, Shawn. I just can't." He began to back away, head swiveling as though seeking a way out.

Except for what he did to Dad, I would feel sorry for him. He was another of Hilda's victims. Unless he killed her, of course. Then I took back the sympathy.

"Come clean, Joe," I demanded. "Why were you so angry with Hilda?"

Shawn's gaze was curious. "Yeah. Exactly what went down?"

Joe hesitated for a minute, body swaying as though torn. Then he plopped down in his chair and scrubbed his face with his hands.

"I'm sorry I didn't tell you about this, Shawn. It was after we did some work at her cottage, remember? She sidled up to me in the pub and told me that she knew all about me. And that it would only take one complaint from her to get my parole officer involved."

"Did you do something?" Shawn asked.

Joe jumped to his feet with a roar. "No, of course not. How can you even ask that, Shawn? I've been staying sober, minding my own business, and working hard. You know that." He pointed to the garage. "I sleep right up there."

Shawn's forehead creased with doubt. "You were in the pub?"

"Having an orange squash. I was playing darts with some friends, actually starting to have a life." Joe's tone was bitter. "Ask them. They can vouch for me. Haven't touched a drop."

"What did she want from you?" I asked. "I mean, I'm assuming she wasn't just being a good citizen."

His eyes met mine and understanding passed between us. "Money, of course. Not that I have much. I did sell my truck recently. Been saving up for a new one. Made the mistake of talking about it to my friends."

Tamsyn barked a laugh. "Sounds like her MO. She was trying to do the same with our dad. Only in our case, she was promising not to harass us about our bed-and-breakfast. This is after we—Nora—finally got our

approvals and were all set for success. She was trying
to ruin it."

Shawn made a disgusted sound. "What a nasty piece
of work." Then he crossed himself. "God rest her soul."

Joe looked sheepish. "I'm sorry I went to the police.
It's my temper. Always getting the best of me."

"No," Tamsyn said. "In the past, maybe. But it doesn't
have to anymore." Her calm assertion was like a benediction. "Eyes front and keep moving." While I believed
she was sincere, I recognized the lines from one of her
shows.

After a light, cold supper of sliced ham and salads, I went
out to the garden to work. As soon as I stepped through the
gate, tool bucket and trug in hand, I felt the stress evaporate
off my shoulders.

I was in my favorite place in the world, surrounded
by greenery and flowers and birds singing. Ruffian ran
ahead of me and disappeared into a stand of purple irises,
the fronds brushing his body.

Surveying the plants, I decided to harvest some mint.
A bold, vigorous herb, it had been planted in a bucket so
as not to spread too much. Still, it was bushy and green,
the aroma sweet and refreshing.

Settling on the ground, I pulled on gloves and began
weeding first. Weeds were like life—it was better to root
out the unwanted before they grew too large. It was entirely unfair how weeds could choke out good plants while
being impervious to weather, cutting, and even burning.
They needed to be plucked out by the roots.

My analogy was veering a little too closely to a certain situation. Pausing my work, I took a moment to stare
at the glorious sights around me, to inhale fresh, salt-

tinged air. The air was soft, the late-day sun warm on my shoulders.

The gate creaked open and Finlay Cole entered the garden, Lady at his heels. He didn't see me at first so I frankly studied him, admiring his grace and strength and the confident movements of his body.

The way he watched his dog, fondly called to her when she strayed, told me volumes about his character. He was a good man.

He glanced over, noticing me, then made as though to retreat. I rose to my feet. "Please, make yourself at home. I'm just doing some weeding and harvesting."

Seeming hesitant, he hovered. Then Lady made the decision for him. She came trotting along the path, tongue lolling, and threw herself at me.

I hunkered down to pat her. "You'll have to come get your dog," I said in a teasing voice as I patted her head. She gazed at me adoringly. "Aren't you a good girl?"

Yes, her expression said. *I'm a very good girl.*

His footsteps crunched on the gravel. "Sorry. I probably should have leashed her."

"Absolutely not." I continued to focus on the dog. "You two are perfectly welcome to hang out here." He was a guest, after all. The fact that he was an officer investigating my family in the course of solving a murder on our property was entirely beside the point right now.

"May I?" he asked, indicating a nearby bench.

"Please do." Lady seemed done with me so I gave her a last pat and went back to work. I'd finished weeding so I found the snips and began clipping mint. Lady nosed around, trotting here and there to explore.

"What are you going to use that for?" Finlay asked.

I handed him a sprig, which he held up to his nose. "Mint is good for a lot of things. Digestion, relieves stress, boosts the immune system." I continued cutting. "As a flavoring for food and drinks as well. Mint jelly with lamb. Cold and hot tea."

He was still holding the branch of mint. "Being here reminds me of my mum. She's never happier than when she's in her garden."

It sounded like his mother and I were kindred spirits. "Where does she live?"

"Near St. Ives, in Cornwall."

"Oh, lovely." Cornwall was coastal as well, a beautiful area of England. "Did you grow up there?"

"I did." He began telling me about his childhood, his one brother, the loss of his father. How much Yorkshire reminded him of home. He'd been living in London but had jumped at the chance for a transfer, for what he hoped would be a more relaxed way of life.

"I plan on doing some hiking on the moors, maybe even buying a small sailboat," he said. "I also like visiting stately homes and historic sights." He glanced up at the castle. "It must be marvelous living here. Such a beautiful place."

I couldn't disagree. "I love it. And not only that, I'm truly grateful for the privilege. That's why I'd do anything to hold onto it." I reconsidered. "Well, almost anything."

He gave a little chuckle, indicating that he understood what I wasn't saying.

"When are you moving into your flat?" I asked, sidestepping the topic of Hilda. So far, so good. I was enjoying the break, enjoying time spent with a nice man who, at some point, might actually become a friend.

"Next week," he said. "I have movers clearing out my storage unit and bringing everything up."

I sat back on my heels. "You couldn't have picked a better landlady. Liv is one of my best friends." I felt myself smile as I explained, "She lives with her husband, Tom, on the cutest little dairy farm. With Jersey cows. They have three children like stair steps—ages five, ten, and fifteen. And they make the best ice cream."

"I know," he said. "I've had it a couple of times." He patted his midriff. "It might be dangerous to my fitness if I don't watch out."

Nothing could ding his attractiveness, I was pretty sure. He was handsome all the way around. "Well, that's why you have Lady. Walking her will keep you in shape."

We both gazed in Lady's direction right as she began to dig at a plant, front feet and soil flying.

He lurched to his feet. "No. Lady." Darting forward, he grabbed her collar. "She usually doesn't dig."

"It's catnip. Some dogs like it, too. Give her a piece, if you want."

Looking to me to be sure he was doing it right, he broke off a sprig and gave it to her. She lay down, leaves between her paws, perfectly content.

Ruffian, drawn by the commotion, came to check out the action. He stalked over to the bulldog and investigated, sniffing the little dog over. Lady didn't seem to mind at all. Then Ruffian went over to the catnip and lay down right on top of the plant.

We shared a smile. "His way of showing her who is boss," I said. "Animals are so funny."

I turned to see him studying me and he smiled. We gazed at each other and if he hadn't been a detective inspector and I hadn't been a murder suspect, I was pretty sure we were having a moment.

"Maybe when—" he said at the same time as I muttered, "I wish—"

We laughed and looked away, a fraught yet sweet silence falling. I had cut plenty of mint and our little bubble had popped, so I got up and sat on the bench beside him.

"I have some updates to tell you," I said. "Regarding the case." After taking a breath, I blurted, "Someone tried to kill me and Tamsyn this afternoon."

CHAPTER 14

"What?" Finlay drew back in shock. "Where? When?" He reached out to touch my arm, then, perhaps thinking better of it, dropped his hand. "Are you all right? Why didn't you say something earlier?"

My rather blunt announcement had gotten more of a reaction than I'd expected. "I'm sorry, Finlay. We're fine. It was a near miss, that's all." Why hadn't I said something before? I'd been enjoying the respite too much.

My thoughts scrambled as I pondered how best to explain. Basically we'd inserted ourselves into the case, which he probably wouldn't like. I could just say that we were looking for Shawn, to have him do some more work.

I shifted on the bench, strangely uncomfortable with the idea, even though Finlay had the power to arrest Dad—any of us, actually. No, being honest was the only way, if we were ever going to muddle through this mess.

"Dad told us that Joe ratted him out for shouting at Hilda. Well, he thought it was Joe. Because Joe's a suspect for shouting at Hilda as well." I glanced at him. "Are you following?"

Lips pressed together in a stern grimace, he nodded. "Perfectly."

My heart sank. If he was already annoyed, he'd be even more so in a moment. "It really made me angry that Joe did that to my father. It's obvious to me that he was trying to get himself off the hook." His mouth opened but I kept talking. I needed to get this out. "So Tamsyn and I went to confront Joe. Shawn's wife told us they were working at the old Rectory. When we got there, I approached the roof and yelled out for Joe. Next thing I knew, several slates came sliding off the roof toward us." I shivered. "Good thing Tamsyn noticed them. They almost hit us."

"Did you see anyone on the roof?" Finlay was on his feet, phone in hand and ready to make a call.

"Yes, we did. Not a clear view, though." He looked up from the screen. "Joe wasn't there. We called the business again and Shawn's wife said her husband and Joe were having lunch. So we went over there and there they were. The timing doesn't work for Joe to have been on the roof. We didn't see their van either, although we heard another vehicle start up and drive away right after."

Finlay took this all in. "I'd like you and Tamsyn to give me a statement, okay? Then I'll follow up with Shawn and Joe. It's possible it was only an accident." The grim expression returned to his face. "Or not. Be careful, won't you, Nora?"

What could I say except that, yes, I would be. We weren't going to stop investigating, though. We couldn't afford to. Not with Dad as a suspect. Which reminded me of the mystery man Hilda's neighbor had seen.

"One more thing. Another young man was angry with Hilda." That's what pounding her door meant to me. "He was wearing a very distinctive jacket—"

*   *   *

"Whatcha doing?" Tamsyn asked as she sauntered into my workroom the next morning. I had set up shop in the old stillroom, restoring its original functions of herbal apothecary and perfumery. Clusters of drying herbs hung from the beams and built-in drawers held packets of powders and teas. Bottles, jars, and wrapped soaps ready for sale sat on neatly organized shelves.

I placed a loaf of soap in the slicer and brought down the handle. "I'm cutting goat's-milk soap scented with lemongrass and verbena." After I made it from scratch using fresh goat's milk from a nearby farm, the soap had to cure for weeks. It was now ready to be sliced and wrapped.

She picked up a creamy bar and sniffed. "Oh, I love this. So fresh."

"Thanks. It's a customer favorite." I'd deliver the bars and other products to stores all over North Yorkshire soon. With summer finally here, sales were ramping up after the spring slowdown.

Tamsyn leaned against the counter to watch. "Need any help?"

"Maybe with wrapping. I use paper, attach a label, and then tie a piece of raffia around the bar." Although I used various colors of wrapping, labels gave me more flexibility in my packaging. I was far from producing the volume required to make preprinted wrappers financially worth it.

The wrapping station was nearby so I showed her what to do and then cut another loaf.

"This is fun," Tamsyn said, neatly centering a label.

"Feel free to volunteer anytime." She was being far more fastidious than me but I wasn't going to discourage her.

"What's next on the investigation front?" she asked, moving on to the next bar.

"Not sure. Finlay hasn't said. Not that he's going to give me updates." Actually, I was pleased about the rapport developing between us. He seemed to take me seriously and I appreciated that. I smiled at a memory. "He balked a little when I suggested tracking Hilda's visitor down by his jacket. I have the feeling he'd prefer more substantial evidence."

"I think I found the brand, by the way," Tamsyn said. "Going by the description." She named the maker, a high-end men's clothing company.

"So, expensive." I carried the new batch of bars over to the wrapping station. This was the last loaf today, so I began helping Tamsyn. "If the man hadn't been young, according to Mavis, then I'd think maybe it was Patrick Horn."

Tamsyn tied a piece of raffia with a bow. "Patrick did know Hilda; we've learned that much. I keep thinking about the fact that Hilda's sister died near Horn House. And his brother was driving the car."

"Me too," I admitted. "But it was decades ago. Why would it come up now?"

"'The past is never dead.'" Tamsyn quoted William Faulkner, then shrugged. "I don't know. It's another lead to investigate. No stone unturned, right?"

Patrick Horn. How could we get close to him, on his yacht? *His letter.* "I have an idea. Tell me what you think."

That afternoon, Tamsyn and I stood on the public dock awaiting transport to Patrick Horn's yacht. It was a warm if breezy day and we were dressed appropriately in Capri pants, T-shirts, and windcheaters. We wore neat white sneakers on our feet.

I'd placed the call to Patrick, telling him that my sister and I were interested in hearing about his offer, as representatives of our father. We'd told Dad, of course, and he'd been surprisingly sanguine about our plan.

"Just don't give away the farm," he'd warned us. "This is a fishing expedition only, right?"

"It's not actually about the castle," I assured him. "I want to find out if Patrick was still in touch with Hilda. He could easily be the person who landed on shore that night. Maybe he's the killer."

Dad's brows rose and he stared at me for a long moment. I'd worried that he was going to forbid us to go. Not that he actually could or would. I didn't want to worry him too much, though.

"There are two of us," Tamsyn said hastily. "We'll be all right." She pointed. "His boat is moored right there. We could swim home if we had to."

"He won't know we suspect him," I added. "It's an opportunity to poke around his boat." I grinned at my sister. "Maybe Tamsyn can charm info about Hilda out of him."

She made a face. "Please." Then she looked thoughtful and I guessed she was deciding how to play the scene. Having an actress help me investigate was very useful. I tended to be too straightforward and easy to read.

"Here comes the tender," I said now.

A small, white craft gleamed in the sun as it buzzed our way through the bay. Tamsyn and I walked down the floating dock to where we could board.

The boat cut its engine and floated up, guided expertly by a man wearing a brimmed cap. "The Misses Asquith?" he asked as a second crew member hopped out to secure the line.

"That's us," I said, strangely thrilled to be embarking

on this adventure. Tamsyn and I were pampered darlings being escorted to a yacht. How delicious.

Once the second man helped us safely aboard, we set off from the dock, the breeze making our hair fly. I waved to the fishermen and tourists on the wharf, some of whom waved back. The tender moved fast, yet smoothly, the motor surprisingly quiet.

The *Party Girl* was equally white and gleaming, with a wooden deck and trim. Modern yet tasteful. The name gave me pause. One caption under a photo of Hilda and Celia called them "popular party girls." Had Patrick named the boat in honor of them? Or another favorite?

We boarded at the rear, stepping up onto a platform. Patrick Horn, dressed cornily in a navy-blue jacket and captain's hat, was waiting to greet us above a four-step ladder to the main deck.

"Good afternoon, ladies," he boomed. "Welcome aboard."

When I accepted his extended hand, I got my first good look at him. He was only an inch or so taller than me, with a barrel-like build and a dark beard shot with gray. He wore wraparound sunglasses that hid his eyes and his hands were well-manicured.

Patrick especially lingered over Tamsyn, capturing her hand between both of his. "I do admire your work," he said. "*Highland Lass* is one of my binges." The way he said it implied that he would binge on my sister as well, given the opportunity.

"How lovely to hear," Tamsyn said, gently extracting her hand from his. "That role is one of my favorites." She said that about every role someone complimented, I'd noticed.

The hotel magnate gestured, ushering us forward.

"Please do come sit. Red or white wine? Or perhaps your brother's mead?"

I didn't generally drink during the day and I was tempted to refuse. But Tamsyn was saying she'd love a glass of mead so I concurred. We sat at a table midship, on benches under a canopy. Patrick filled glasses and handed them to us, then sat nearby, ankle crossed over his knee. He was wearing leather boat shoes without socks.

I took a sip of mead, barely tasting it. My stomach was clenched with anxiety. Now that we were here, how could we bring up Hilda? Or Celia?

"Here for the summer?" he was asking Tamsyn. "I'm thinking of making Monkwell my base for now. Much to explore on this coast." He grinned, teeth white in his beard. "Or maybe a jaunt to Amsterdam. Have you been?"

With this question, he was off on a sidebar about the delights of European travel. Tamsyn chimed in while I sat mostly mute, drinking my mead. Was this his tactic, ignoring the elephant on the boat until one of us brought it up? If so, it was working. I wanted to cut to the chase, make an assessment of the man, and go home.

The castle looked gorgeous from here, set among clustered trees with the field, bluff, and beach in view. It would have taken only minutes for Patrick to reach our property via the tender and hike up to the garden. He definitely had opportunity. Means, also. A rock from our wall. Motive was the missing piece here.

They were on to Paris now and I had to do something besides sit here and drink. I set my glass down and stood. "Excuse me. Where's the loo? I mean the head."

Patrick indicated the stairs to below. "Take your pick. Each cabin has facilities."

I looked to see if Tamsyn wanted to come but she didn't move. All right, then.

The stairs led into a seating area, everything polished wood and plush couches. Ahead was the galley and the cabins were to the rear, I guessed.

They were, three of them, so I had my choice. The master. I should poke around in there while I had the chance.

The decor was simple, a big bed, lots of built in cabinets, and a large-screen television. In the interests of being honest, I did pop into the en suite loo. Although it was compact, it was nicely tiled with elegant fixtures.

Two robes hung on the back of the door. A man's navy-blue terrycloth and something silky.

Oho. So Patrick did have a lady love. Where had he stashed her, I wondered. Then I took a closer look at the robe. I'd seen it before, the embossed peach silk and wide bands of lace. Size four.

Acting on impulse, I snapped a picture of it and sent it to Darby. *Is this from your store?*

She wrote back immediately. *YES. That's the style I sold to Hilda, in a 4. Where are you?*

On a sailboat. Thought it looked familiar.

The truth hit me like a slam to the belly. This *was* Hilda's robe. I'd bet my life on it.

Was there anything else of hers in here? I opened the medicine cabinet door. Fully stocked, with an assortment of first aid supplies and personal care items. A drawer held more of the same, brushes and combs, tubes of toothpaste and other creams.

A gold tube of lipstick. Chanel, a red called Passion.

After photographing the lipstick, I put it back and continued searching, squeamish yet determined. A robe and lipstick indicated to me that Hilda was more than a one-time visitor. I found nothing else in the bathroom and wondered if I should search the cabin closets.

Although I'd already been gone a while, and Patrick would be wondering where I was. He might even come looking for me. The last thing I wanted was for him to find me elbow-deep in his drawers.

A deep rumble began to vibrate under my feet. What was that?

I rushed into the cabin and looked out the window.

Instead of a static view, I saw water rushing past the hull.

We were moving. Patrick was taking us out to sea.

CHAPTER 15

Shock and fear held me rooted, my mind running wild. Had he figured out we were investigating? Was he going to kill us and dump us overboard? Or had he become infatuated with Tamsyn and was sweeping her away on a voyage?

My body finally thawed and I dashed out of the cabin and through the lower level. After taking the steps two at a time, I emerged on the deck, panting.

"What's going on?" I asked. "Where are we going?"

Tamsyn's posture was tense but Patrick merely smiled as he pushed his sunglasses on top of his head. "Thought I'd take you for a little cruise. It's such a lovely day."

"What? Tamsyn—"

"It wasn't my idea," she said, grimacing at me behind his back.

I whirled around toward the wheel, where one of the crewmen stood. He was staring straight ahead as if he didn't see me.

With a whirring sound, the mainsail rose, and for a moment, I was captivated by the sight of the gleaming white expanse. It caught the breeze and the boat immediately leaped forward, heeling slightly. Power and beauty working together.

I stared toward shore, the castle and village receding in the distance, the hills and moors beyond spreading in our view. We were headed due east, I guessed, toward Europe.

"Take us back," I demanded. "I . . . I have things to do."

Patrick's grin was raffish as he refilled our glasses. "Anything better than a little sail on a gorgeous day? Didn't think so. Besides, I want to talk to you without distractions."

My heart thumped. "About what?"

He gestured for me to sit. "About our partnership, of course. My plans to make Ravensea a signature property. Your lovely castle will be the centerpiece of my portfolio. Small yet exquisite and exclusive."

His eyes were on Tamsyn as he said this and I had to choke back a cry of rage. He'd better not make any moves on my sister or I'd—I'd what? I glanced frantically around the deck for a weapon.

Behind her glass, Tamsyn threw me a look of warning. She was right. A direct confrontation would only endanger us further. Perhaps we could play this out, string him along until he delivered us back to shore.

Someone needed to know what was going on. *Finlay.* I forced a smile as I sat and picked up my glass. "I should text Janet. She'll have to move ahead with dinner without my help." Patrick didn't need to know that we weren't offering dinner tonight for our guests.

"Ah, yes, Janet," he said. "I've heard from the Cargills what a fantastic chef she is." His tone grew speculative. "In fact, I would like her to stay on. At least to supervise the kitchen. The old girl could use a rest, don't you think?"

Very nice, Patrick. He was implying that our darling Janet would want to work for him instead of the brutes overworking her.

"Excuse me," I said, bending over my phone. Instead of Janet's number, I brought up Finlay's.

Help. Trapped on Patrick Horn's sailboat. He's taking us out to sea. Won't let us go.

There. A charge of unlawful detainment was in Mr. Horn's future, if not kidnapping.

I waited, nerves wound tight, for a reply.

Nothing. The huge sail above our head flapped and then steadied. Water skimmed with a hiss past the hull. Patrick worked a remote control and soft Celtic music began to play, eerily perfect and enchanting as we cut through the waves.

I sent another text. *I'm not joking. SOS. Mayday.*

Patrick had edged closer to Tamsyn, who sat with squared shoulders while using her glass as a barrier.

Keeping my phone in my hand, praying for a response, I moved closer as well, on her other side. We could probably take him, the two of us. But the crew—they were more like bodyguards than sailors.

I noted the sharklike gleam in Patrick's eyes, as if he scented chum and was about to bite. Flailing and screaming in protest would only encourage him, as it did real sharks. Better to stay cool and act as if we were considering his proposal.

Unless he touched Tamsyn. Then he wouldn't know what hit him.

"I've taken the liberty of designing mock-ups for Ravensea," Patrick was saying as he thumbed at his phone. "Take a look."

If he'd gone that far, he was very, very certain that we

would agree to sell. Too bad he would be facing arrest. After we were rescued.

He handed his device to Tamsyn. "Swipe right."

I looked on as she paged through the architectural renderings, based on our own photographs on the lodging website. This was Ravensea refurbished and tastefully updated while retaining historic features, as would be required for a listed building.

In other words, everything I'd want to do, if I had the funds.

Grinding frustration and anger gnawed in my belly. The castle was our home, always had been. We were never going to sell no matter how lucrative the offer.

I checked my phone. No text yet.

The yacht continued to plow through the waves, the mainland growing ever smaller. All I could see of the castle was the towers.

A fishing boat motored along off to starboard and I was tempted to wave my arms and yell for help. They'd probably think I was just being friendly.

I'd better call Finlay right now, 999 if I couldn't reach him, for HM Coastguard.

Near shore, something caught the sun. A boat, moving fast, almost skimming across the water. I put a hand to my forehead, squinting, wishing I had binoculars.

The man at the wheel did. Raising them to his eyes, he turned and scanned the water, then shouted to Patrick, "Company on our six."

I bent over, woozy with relief, when I recognized the fast-approaching craft as a red and white Coastguard Defender with mounted guns and dual two-hundred-horsepower motors. The sailboat would never outrun it and it was best not to try.

Patrick scowled. "Trim the mainsail," he called with a gesture.

The sail flapped and the boat slowed, its forward momentum lost.

Patrick rose to his feet, biting his lower lip as he watched the coastguard approach.

"I wonder what they want," Tamsyn murmured, earning a dirty look from our host.

Patrick adjusted his features into a display of amused tolerance. "Who knows? These provincial forces are always faffing about on some lame mission or other."

The Defender's engines racketed down and a bullhorn boomed out. "DI Cole, here," the voice said. "Permission to board?"

"Oh, yes," I cried, dancing up and down on my toes and waving my arms. "Finlay." I was practically swooning. He must have gotten my texts and raced to the rescue.

Patrick had put his sunglasses back on and now he turned my way, expression unreadable and arms crossed.

Something warned me not to reveal that I'd brought the police down on Patrick's head. I should let Finlay take the lead. Tamsyn and I were merely innocent bystanders, right?

I thought of the two photographs I'd taken. Evidence that Hilda Dibble had been on this boat, I was pretty sure. Of course, their relationship wasn't a crime by any stretch. It did, however, speak to an intimate knowledge of each other.

A tender went out from the Defender and soon Finlay was boarding, accompanied by a coastguard officer in uniform. "Mr. Horn. You're a difficult man to reach." Finlay displayed his identification. "I have a few questions for you."

Patrick took off his sunglasses, chewing on one bow. "Ah, I'm kind of in the middle of something here."

Finlay's polite smile grew wider. "I'm sure your guests won't mind cutting their visit short. I can have the coastguard run you home, Nora, Tamsyn, if you'd like."

"I'm ready." I looked at my sister. "You?"

She downed the rest of her mead and picked up her handbag. "Sure am." She put a hand on Patrick's arm. "Thank you for the lovely time. You've got a gorgeous boat here."

He relaxed slightly. "Anytime, dear lady." As we began to move away, he jabbed a finger at us. "We'll pick up our discussion at another time?"

Tamsyn twinkled, wiggling her fingers. "See you later."

We hurried to the stern, where another coastguard officer waited in the tender. "Get me out of here," I said under my breath.

The officer helped us aboard and we buzzed back to the main ship. "I wonder what Finlay is talking to Patrick about," Tamsyn said.

The two men were now seated under the canopy. Finlay was sitting back, relaxed, device in hand while Patrick leaned forward, hands clasped between his knees. Point to Finlay. Patrick appeared to be on the back foot.

"No idea," I replied. "Unless it's about Hilda. I think she and Patrick had a thing." We were almost at the Defender so I said, "I'll show you the evidence in a few."

"Great cliffhanger, sis," she said wryly.

As it worked out, we didn't have a chance to talk. As soon as we were on board, the captain throttled up the engines and we headed back to shore. The tender returned to the *Party Girl*, to wait for Finlay and the other officer.

In such a powerful craft, the journey was a matter of

minutes. What a contrast to the way out, the swift yet leisurely pace of the sailboat. Of course we were also frozen in fear that we'd never see shore again, which had made that voyage seem endless.

We watched as we approached Monkwell at speed, taking in the castle, village, headlands, and shingled shore. The individual figures of people soon became visible, including one on the bluff near the shore path, binoculars at his eyes.

He wore a maroon-and-orange windcheater.

I put a hand on my sister's arm. "Look. Up there, next to the benches." That section of the path was a popular viewpoint for ramblers and people having a picnic.

I fastened my gaze on the man, taking a mental note of exactly where he was standing. Once we were farther into the harbor, he wouldn't be as visible.

The Defender came alongside the wharf and a fresh-cheeked officer helped us to disembark. "Thank you so much," I said. "We appreciate the lift."

He touched his hat brim, smiling widely. "Anytime. Good day, now."

The Defender roared off again and we took the wharf at a trot. "We need to find that man before he leaves," I said between gulps for air. "It might be the same person who visited Hilda."

"I bet it is," Tamsyn said. "Not many jackets like that around."

We fell silent as we took the fastest route up to the bluff, a side street that ascended almost vertically. Not for the first time, I reflected on the hearty souls who had settled this area. Build on the flats above? Heck no. The steep cliffs fronting the bay were a far better choice.

Finally we achieved the top, stepping onto the winding route through gorse and moorland. From here, we could see the trail in both directions as it ran along the coast.

The man in the orange-and-maroon jacket was still birdwatching.

After catching our breath, Tamsyn and I ran along the path, slowing to a walk when we drew closer. Standing back toward us, binoculars still at his eyes, he didn't seem to notice our approach.

We were only a few feet away when he lowered the glasses and turned. "Oh. Hello there."

It was our guest, Brian Taylor.

CHAPTER 16

"Taking a little stroll?" Brian asked pleasantly. He gestured with his binoculars. "I've been working on my seabird list. I just spotted a black-headed gull."

"Nice," I said, my thoughts scrambling. Learning that it was Brian, our guest, who owned the maroon-and-orange jacket, flummoxed me. Why had he pounded on Hilda's door and demanded to talk to her?

Brian had seemed upset after Hilda's death, I recalled. He'd holed up in his room, and instead of being eager to leave like the Cargills, he'd wanted to stay.

Why? If he was the killer, why hadn't he bolted immediately? Of course that would have pointed the finger at him, but he didn't exactly seem the murderous type. I would have thought shock and regret were more likely to be the drivers of his behavior.

Of course, I was going by how I would react.

While I was thinking all this, Brian had been going on about how the black-headed gull turned almost all white in the winter. "An example of camouflage, I suppose," he was saying. "They won't be as easily seen by predators next to ice and snow."

Too bad for him he'd worn such a conspicuous jacket instead of blending in like that gull.

"Interesting," Tamsyn was murmuring. Resting her hands on her hips, she took the bull by the horns. "Why were you knocking on Hilda Dibble's door the other evening?"

Brian's mouth flapped a few times. "But . . . how . . . how did you—"

"Someone saw you." I had rallied enough to jump in. "She . . . er, they noticed your jacket." I didn't want to let him know it had been Mavis. "It's very distinctive." Then I frowned. "Why haven't we seen it before?" He'd been staying at the castle for days.

He brushed at his front. "It lives in my pack most of the time. I only pull it out when I go on rambles." He squinted toward the sky. "When it's breezy or the temps are dropping."

"Thanks for clearing that up," Tamsyn said briskly. "So, Hilda?"

His expression grew crafty. "What exactly did the person hear?" He nodded as realization dawned on his face. "I'll bet it was Mavis. She's always lurking about."

Sorry, Mavis. He guessed it was you. Thinking back to what she'd said, I quoted, "'You need to talk to me. You can't hide forever.'"

"Very good, Nora," Tamsyn said. "You memorized that beautifully."

Brian's expression relaxed. "Not exactly a confession of murder, is it?" He shrugged. "Yes, I wanted to speak to her. But she wouldn't answer the door."

Now we needed to find out why. I came at it indirectly. "You're another of her, um, boy toys? Isn't that right? Hilda was quite the man-eater, wasn't she? All slinky in her expensive negligees—"

"What?" As I hoped, this twist on the situation

alarmed Brian. "That's not the reason. I . . . she . . . Hilda was my aunt."

It was our turn to flap our mouths like fish. "Your aunt?" I muttered. "Then . . . Celia was your mother?" There hadn't been any mention of a child in the article about Celia's death.

Brian's eyes shone with regret and sorrow. "Yeah. She put me up for adoption. Don't get me wrong. I have great adoptive parents. They're the best. But still. After I found out my bio mom died and that she had a sister, I wanted to meet her." He swallowed hard. "That's understandable, isn't it?"

"Of course it is," Tamsyn said. "Anyone would do the same."

While I was glad Brian had decent adoptive parents, I wondered why Hilda hadn't taken the baby. If Tamsyn or Will had a child and couldn't take care of it, I'd be first in line.

"I wondered the same thing, Nora," Brian said. At my start of surprise, he laughed. "It's all over your face. Why didn't Hilda take me? That was one of the questions I had for her. Tactfully put, of course. I wanted her to tell me about Celia, to share pictures and memories, that kind of thing, first, before I asked the tough questions. All I have right now regarding my mum are newspaper articles about her death."

"She was a beautiful woman." I studied his face. Even going by memory, I could see a resemblance in the nose and eyes, the expressiveness of his eyebrows. "You also resemble your aunt."

Hilda had been very attractive, it was only fair to admit. My contentious relationship with her had tainted my impression.

His voice grew gruff. "Yeah, well, it's too late now,

isn't it?" He raised the glasses again, intent on whatever he was viewing. "Excuse me, please. I think I see a Mediterranean gull. Those are fairly rare around here."

Tamsyn tilted her head toward the path. "Head out?"

I nodded. "See you at the social, Brian? We'll have delicious appetizers again."

He didn't budge from his stance. "I'll be there."

"Birdwatching, my foot," Tamsyn muttered once we were out of earshot. "I'll bet he's in Monkwell because of Hilda."

"That makes sense. I'm definitely going to tell Finlay what he said." I liked Brian, but removing Dad and myself from consideration as suspects came first.

Janet was in the kitchen, feet up while she leafed through cookbooks. "There you are, miladies. Would you like a refreshing glass of mint water? Help yourselves."

I opened the fridge and pulled out the pitcher. Mint from the garden and cold, fresh well water—what could be better?

"How was your meeting?" Janet asked, leafing to another page. She jotted notes with a pencil on a pad. "I'm thinking of goat cheese and fig crostini." Janet made jam from our figs every year.

"Yum." I filled two glasses and gave one to Tamsyn. "We had quite the adventure. Patrick Horn tried to kidnap us. Well, sort of. Took us on an unauthorized sailing trip."

Janet put her pencil down. "What on earth?"

We took turns sharing the story. "Then Finlay Cole arrived with the coastguard," Tamsyn summarized dramatically. "Summoned by Nora's texts for help."

"Like a white knight riding in to save the day," Janet

said with a laugh. "Only the modern version." She reached out and patted my hand, because I was closest. "Don't do that again, please. You'll give me heart failure."

"We had no idea he would pull that trick," I protested. "It was supposed to be a business meeting. I also didn't have the faintest about *this*." I pulled up the picture of Hilda's robe and showed it to Janet and Tamsyn, who hadn't seen it yet. "Hilda bought that robe from Darby. I already sent her the picture and she confirmed."

"Oh, ho," Janet exclaimed. "So Mr. Horn and Hilda were an item?" Realization dawned. "He might be our killer. Do you think he was on to you investigating?"

"Don't think so. I mean, I wasn't until I saw her clothing." I hopped up to fetch a tin of biscuits. "I think his shenanigans were a show of power. He probably thinks he can intimidate us into selling to him."

Janet laughed. "He doesn't know my girls, does he?"

"No, he does not." Tamsyn took a chocolate-covered digestive. "Love these. Anyway, we have another suspect." She leaned forward, lowering her voice. "And he's staying here."

Before she could tell Janet about Brian, the house phone on the wall rang. "Let me get that." Janet bustled over. After a short conversation, she said, "Lorna Cargill would love a tray. Mint water and biscuits."

"I'll go," I offered. "Tamsyn, you give Janet the update."

Beyond brief encounters at breakfast or the social, we hadn't seen much of Lorna or Gavin the last couple of days. Today, Gavin was playing golf, he had said, while Lorna had decided to stay here and relax.

On the way upstairs, I was joined by the two cats, Ruffian and Primrose. After Ruffian's initial disdain for the kitten, they now seemed to be buddies. I had the feeling Ruffian was teaching Primrose all kinds of tricks.

All was still up here, and by habit, I put out my feelers, searching for any sign of ghosts lurking. Nothing so far. Only dust motes spinning in the colored light filtering through a stained glass window. The two cats curled up together in a patch of sun, another sign no spirits were lurking. Ruffian would bolt.

I continued on to the King's Chamber. As I reached out to knock, the back of my neck prickled. *Sir Percival.* When I turned to study the hallway, a sconce light flickered. I had just changed that bulb. I whispered, "What do you *want*?" It wasn't normal for him to show up so often. If having a ghost appear at all could be considered normal. Oh, how I wished he could talk.

Sighing in frustration, I turned and knocked on the door.

"Coming." Footsteps thudded and Lorna opened the door. Brushing a hand through her hair, she took in the contents of the tray. "Lovely. Thank you." Despite her stated plan to relax today, she seemed on edge.

I carried the tray into the room, heading for a table near the windows. A laptop sat open, stacks of folders and binders beside it.

"Let me get that." Lorna made room by moving a heap to a chair.

"Working?" I set the tray on the table, not too close to the computer.

She returned to her seat. "I am, unfortunately. Trying to keep on top of business stuff." She made a puffing sound of exasperation.

"I get that. Mint water?" At her nod, I filled a glass. "This mint is from our garden. Mint is not only tasty, it can improve alertness and relieve stress." Mint had many benefits and I chose the most appropriate at the moment.

"Exactly what I need," Lorna said with a laugh. She accepted the glass and took a long swallow. "Delicious." She put the glass down and took a biscuit. Then she waved the cookie at me. "Sit, if you have a minute."

If a guest wanted to talk, I would listen. Even if I wasn't on the trail of a killer. Basic innkeeping. I pulled out the other chair.

"How are you finding everything?" I asked, as a way to start a conversation.

"Fine." She shuddered a little. "No more encounters, if that's what you were asking."

I didn't mention that he was lurking in the hall. Instead I quipped, "No, about the mattress and the hot water supply, actually."

We both laughed. Lorna sat back, studying the room and the view out the tall windows as she chewed. "This place is just dripping with history. I used to be all about staying in brand-new hotels. Stately homes are definitely growing on me."

"Where else have you stayed?" I was curious to hear feedback about our competitors. In fact, it was on my list to visit some and see how they did things. Hopefully I could build a rapport with the owners or managers, a peer network of sorts.

"Horn House was the first place we tried." Lorna took a sip of water. "Which is natural, Patrick being one of Gavin's best friends. It's gorgeous. Four restaurants. Two swimming pools. Over forty bedrooms."

Impressive. Our little castle was pathetic in comparison. "My parents stayed there too, thirty years ago. It wasn't a hotel then."

She nodded. "Before my time. Gavin and I have been married for five years. Second time around for both of us, no kids."

"How did you meet?" I asked, to be polite.

"We actually met at a wine expo in France. I was working for another import company at the time. Gavin whisked me off on a Riviera holiday and the rest is history." She seemed troubled rather than nostalgic, and I thought about the conversation we'd had the night they arrived. She'd confided that she felt like more of an employee than a partner at times.

"Well, I hope you have a wonderful time here," I said sincerely. "My goal is to help guests create cherished memories."

"Hope so," she echoed. Then she added hastily, "Everything here is fine, honestly. It's just my husband . . ." She bit down hard on a biscuit.

I couldn't help in that department. They'd have to figure it out. I rose to my feet. "I'd better get back to the kitchen. We're putting together a lovely menu for the social."

Lorna was already staring at her computer screen. "I look forward to it. Thanks for the room service." She took another bite. "Fuel for the tasks ahead."

"I'll let you get back to work, then."

She was tapping away when I let myself out. Again, I wondered if Patrick had sent Gavin here to soften us up or to be an inside informant.

Will had invited them, I remembered. Still . . . pausing in a window seat nook, I sat and sent him a text.

Me: *The Cargills. Did you approach them first?*

Will: *Why do you ask?*

Me: *Just wondering how the whole thing came about. The comp stay.*

Will: *Sigh. I told you I was sorry. I'll never do it again. Without asking you first, I mean.*

Great. So there might be more freebies in our future. I let it go. Now wasn't the time to quibble.

Me: *So? How did it go down?*

Will: *Um, we met at a show. They stopped to try samples and he floated the idea of carrying the mead in their stores. Then we started talking about the castle and next thing you know, I was offering them a free stay. Oops.*

Me: *Thanks. No idea who brought up the castle first?*

Will: *Them, I think. Why? Did they do something?*

Me: *Not exactly. Patrick Horn, you know, the hotel magnate, tried to kidnap me and Tamsyn on his sailboat this afternoon.*

Will: *WHAT?*

I laughed. I knew that would get him.

Me: *He wants to buy the castle. Anyway, we're fine. Tell you the deets later. Wondering if Gavin is staying here on purpose to report back to Patrick. They're besties, according to Gavin's wife.*

Will: *I hope not. Grr. That's so . . . so . . .*

Me: *Underhanded and deceptive? I know.*

Will: *Should I refuse to sell to them, if they ever order?*

Me: *Of course not. I'd get the money up front, though. Or at least a good chunk.*

Will: *Definitely.*

Me: *Are you coming by for the social?*

Will: *Um, actually not. I'm taking Darby out for dinner.*

Me: *YAY. Have fun.*

She hadn't said a thing about their date when I'd texted earlier. I thought about teasing her, but decided to keep out of it. Maybe it wouldn't go anywhere with Will and I didn't want to damage our friendship by interfering. I'd feign ignorance for now. And keep my fingers crossed. I thought they were perfect for each other.

CHAPTER 17

"Hello, hello." Gavin Cargill strode into the drawing room, rubbing his hands together. Still in golf attire, all windblown and sunburned, he wore a hearty smile. "How was your visit with Patrick, Nora?" He pointed to a bottle. "I'll have the mead, please." He glanced around, looking for Lorna, I presumed.

"Lorna is on the terrace." I filled a glass for him. "Patrick has a beautiful yacht." *Plus an underhanded way of doing business, a sneaky friend in you, and a dead woman's robe in his cabin.*

Gavin took a noisy slurp. "He really does. I've started shopping around myself. We'll get something much smaller, of course. Perfect for the wifey and me to crew."

If she doesn't divorce you first. I told my inner monologue to shut up. "We've got some great appetizers this evening. Enjoy."

As I hoped, he moved on and started gorging himself at the food table. "Really worked up an appetite," he muttered, mouth full.

Finlay Cole entered the room, Lady jingling along beside him. I couldn't hold back a grin. "Glad you made it," I said as he approached the table.

He looked over the bottles. "Busy day. Red, please."

I sketched a little curtsey. "Certainly, sir."

As I poured the wine, I noticed that Gavin had gone out to the terrace and Tamsyn and Dad were chatting by the fireplace. This would be a perfect time to talk.

"Can I speak to you for a minute?" I asked Finlay, setting down the glass. "I have something to tell you." I amended that. "A lot to tell you, actually."

He smiled as he picked up his wine. "Sounds intriguing. Go on."

I hastily refilled my mead before heading across the room to a love seat and armchair in a nook. I took the love seat and he settled in the chair, Lady at his feet.

Where to begin? I didn't quite dare to ask him why he'd come out to Patrick's yacht. Did his visit have anything to do with Hilda or was it another matter? He'd stayed behind, which told me we weren't the only reason for his visit.

Whatever his reason, he needed to see what I'd found belowdecks. "I took this picture today on Patrick's yacht." I handed the phone to him. "That robe belonged to Hilda Dibble."

His brows rose. "And you know this how? Was her name written inside?"

"I wish. My friend Darby, who owns Tatiana's Bower, confirmed it. She sold that night set to Hilda."

"And probably dozens of other women as well?"

"No. Darby only carries a few of each item. Very exclusive and expensive."

"Good to know," he murmured, still studying the picture.

"Swipe to the next one. It's a lipstick," I added unnecessarily. "Maybe you can get DNA off it." I had just had this thought.

His expression was a study in amused bemusement.

"Two things, Nora. We'd have to have a reason to put that lipstick into evidence. Secondly, even if it did belong to Hilda, it doesn't mean that Patrick killed her."

I pleated the hem of my apron, thinking. "True. Although it might help establish her movements. And that she and Patrick were an item." I paused. "He could have killed her, you know. His mooring isn't that far from our land. He could easily have come over on the tender." I had another brilliant idea. "Match the tender's bottom to the marks in the sand. Its hull, I mean."

He gave me back the phone. "I assure you, we're looking into all possibilities."

Excitement tingled. He *was* investigating Patrick Horn. "Okay. I get it. You can't tell me what you were talking to Patrick about today." I took a sip to wet my throat. "Unless Tamsyn and I were the topic."

Finlay's brows rose. "I did ask for his version of events. He said it was all a misunderstanding on your part, that he'd floated the idea of a cruise before raising anchor."

"Liar. He did not. Ask Tamsyn." I drank more mead. "Maybe we should press charges. Kidnapping. Abduction. Unlawful detainment."

"You can do that, Nora. However, his crew confirmed that he'd mentioned the excursion."

Had he said something to Tamsyn? I'd been belowdecks, snooping around, when the engines fired up.

Tamsyn glanced over and I motioned for her to join us. After saying something to Dad, she put her glass down and sauntered across the room. Dad got up and turned on some classical music before moseying out to the terrace. Soon his booming laugh was ringing out as he spoke with Gavin and Lorna. Good move, Dad. Keep them distracted.

"What's up? Did you tell him what we learned today, Nora?" She perched on the love seat beside me.

"Not yet. We're talking about Patrick. Did he ask you if he could take us for a sail?"

She laced her fingers together and stretched them. "Sort of. He said something about sailing and I thought he meant at another time. Next thing I knew, he was having the crew raise the anchor and we were heading out of the harbor. Then he started talking about Ravensea, which is why we were there. I didn't want to cut the discussion short by acting like a nervous Nellie."

"You went on board to talk about the castle?" Finlay asked. "That was the reason?"

Not exactly. Discussing Patrick's offer was an excuse to see what we could find out about Celia Dibble's death.

"We were pretending to be interested," Tamsyn said. I elbowed her ribs. "Ouch. Nora." She rubbed the spot. "There's a connection between Patrick and Hilda's sister, Celia. Celia and Patrick's brother, Dennis, died in a car accident near Horn House about thirty years ago. Sandra Snelling said her sister's death never sat well with Hilda, that it continued to disturb her." She smiled triumphantly. "And we also found out that Hilda was close to Patrick. Her robe proves that. Maybe she was investigating him."

"The robe was in the master bathroom, which means to me they were intimate," I added. "Celia wasn't the only one to die, don't forget. The original heir to Horn House was at the wheel."

The bemused expression had returned to Finlay's face, but he didn't try to get us to stop talking. He was listening intently.

Tamsyn leaned forward. "And wait. There's more." She turned to me. "Lay it on him."

"Brian Taylor is Celia's son. He told us that himself this afternoon."

He rubbed his chin. "Hmm. How does he fit into the case?"

"Not sure, except he was angry with Hilda. A witness saw him pounding on her door and demanding to talk to her." I smiled in triumph. "Remember I told you about his jacket? He was wearing it today."

Finlay didn't move. "So you think he killed his aunt?"

"Maybe," I said. "He must have been frustrated with her when she wouldn't answer his questions. He's been wondering why she didn't take him in instead of letting him be adopted, he said." My heart ached for Brian. He must feel so rejected.

"He was staying here that night," Tamsyn put in. "So maybe they arranged to meet in the garden. It all fits together."

"Not that I want him to be guilty." I shifted uneasily. "He seems like a nice guy." I was definitely too soft for police work. I even felt bad about pointing the finger at Joe and he'd tried to do the same to my own father.

"That's why we focus on the evidence," Finlay said. "Personal feelings can't come into it or we couldn't function. That also goes for people we don't like."

"'Off with your head,'" I quipped, thinking of the Queen of Hearts from *Alice in Wonderland*. "Would you like a refill, Finlay? I'm thinking about adjourning to the terrace."

On Hearing the First Cuckoo in Spring by Delius was playing and his light, uplifting music was perfect for a warm summer evening.

"Thank you, but I think I'm going to take Lady around the garden. For a w-a-l-k." Despite the spelling, she scrambled to her feet, claws scrabbling, and we laughed.

We filled our glasses, grabbed plates of goodies, and stepped outside. Dad was still talking to the Cargills at one conversation grouping so Tamsyn and I chose another.

"I'm going to make a circuit of Yorkshire stores tomorrow," Gavin was saying. "Come with, Lorna?"

She tilted her head in question. "Did you rent a car?" They'd arrived in Monkwell by train.

"I had one of the lads run a van over," Gavin said. "It's parked in the forecourt."

We'd seen one of his shop vans around town, I recalled. Now there was an explanation for why.

"Look," Tamsyn said, drawing my attention away from the Cargills. She pointed toward the bay.

The sweep of water was empty except for a late fishing boat, ripples on the water catching the late afternoon sun. Finlay and Lady were out on the bluff and, as I watched, he sat on the bench, picked up Lady, and placed her beside him. Fragrance from wisteria climbing a lattice wafted our way.

"Nice view." Leaning back, I rested my feet on the terrace wall.

"No, silly. What *isn't* there, I mean?"

"Ummm . . . what isn't—" I sat up clumsily as realization struck. "Patrick's yacht. It's gone."

Tamsyn smiled. "Chased off by the police, do you think?"

"Maybe. I'm glad. With any luck, he won't bother us again." We'd told Finlay about the Hilda connection and he could take it from here.

"Speaking of Patrick." Tamsyn picked up her phone. "I had an idea."

Maybe we weren't quite finished.

"I've been thinking about the other properties he's bought. I know one of the owners. Harold Sutcliffe. Met him in London at a party. He went to school with Ben." She grimaced at the mention of her ex. "Anyway, take a peek."

The webpage displayed Sutcliffe Hall, located farther north along the Yorkshire coast. A charming Elizabethan manor with pointed gables, it had been in the same family for hundreds of years—until sold to the Horn Hotel Group last year.

"What a shame," I said, thinking that Harold must have been devastated to let such a beautiful place go. "How do you think he can help us?"

My sister pushed out her bottom lip. "I don't know if he can. It's just a hunch. At the very least we'll learn more about Patrick and how he operates."

"I'm game if you are," I decided, handing back the phone. "Where is Harold now?"

Tamsyn began to tap on the screen. "He bought a house in the same area. Ah, found it. I knew I had his number." She busily composed a text, the phone whooshing when it sent. "Wow, that's loud." She turned the volume down.

Down the terrace, Gavin slapped his knees. "I think we'd best get on, love. I made reservations for us at the White Rose."

Lorna drank the rest of her mead and then pulled a pashmina up around her shoulders. She still looked drawn but the fresh sea air had brought some color to her cheeks.

"The White Rose does a very nice menu," Dad said. "I recommend their leg of lamb." Before we opened as a bed-and-breakfast, I'd coached Dad on how to help concierge. He'd taken this task seriously, going so far as to sample food from most eateries within a twenty-mile radius.

"Sounds good. We'll see you in the a.m., Arthur." Gavin gave Dad a few hearty pats on the back. "I'll want a big feed before heading out on the road."

"We can do that," Dad said with good humor. "Rashers of bacon and whatnot."

Lorna looked apologetic on her husband's behalf. "Lovely social. Thank you."

"You're very welcome, madam," Dad said gallantly. He ushered them off the terrace and into the drawing room. Then he pivoted and began picking up the used glasses and plates.

"I'll help with that, Dad." I reluctantly hoisted myself out of the chair. Glancing into the drawing room, I saw Brian standing in front of the drinks table. "Tamsyn, want to help Brian?" I was glad he had finally shown up after spilling his guts to us earlier.

"Right away." She scurried inside.

Holding the dishes, Dad and I stood gazing out over the garden. The shadows were long and black now, the garden features, hedges, and trees touched with gold.

"Your mum would have loved this," he said. "She so enjoyed making people feel comfortable and at home. You have her knack, Nora."

Careful not to drop anything, I leaned against his arm. "Aw, thank you. I'm honored you think so." Being told I resembled my mother in any way was the best of compliments.

"It's a shame about the . . . ah, difficulties we're facing at the moment, but we'll get through them. Have a little faith, my girl."

"I'll try." After soaking up his warmth for another minute, I straightened, moving toward the door. Time to tidy away the social leftovers and help Janet with dinner.

Inside, Tamsyn and Brian were chatting, glasses in

hand, looking quite friendly at a casual glance. I placed the dishes on a tray, making room for the ones Dad held.

Dad trundled toward Brian. "Hello, young fellow. Any luck with your list today?"

Tamsyn threw Brian a grin and ducked away, coming along as I gathered a stray glass or two around the room. "I've got news," she whispered.

"Oh. Did Harold get back to you?" I glanced around the room for that one dish that would inevitably be overlooked.

Her phone beeped. "That's probably him now." She stayed on my heels, thumbing at the screen. "Hold up a sec." I stopped moving. She whispered in my ear, "Brian asked me out to lunch. Do you think I should go?"

That explained the cozy atmosphere. "Why not? He might tell you more about Hilda." I noticed that Dad and Brian had gone out onto the terrace so it was safe to talk. "What did you say?"

"Nothing yet. Dad interrupted." She was frowning at her phone. "Listen to this. Harold said, and I quote, 'We need to talk.'"

CHAPTER 18

Morning found me zooming along Yorkshire's lanes in my car, delivering Castle Apothecary products up and down the coast. I hadn't slept well so the car windows were open, fresh air laden with scents of green growing things and flowers flooding in.

Living so close to the water, boat engines were a common sound, especially early in the morning when the fishermen went out. Last night, though, I'd startled awake several times, imagining someone landing on our beach. Climbing the stairs to the garden. Breaking into the castle.

Were there more boats than usual last night or was I now overly aware of them, thanks to Guy's mention of smuggling? I wasn't sure. Patrick's yacht was still gone. I'd checked out the window first thing.

We were meeting Harold Sutcliffe tomorrow, so Tamsyn had said yes to Brian's invitation. They were having lunch at the White Rose, and my plan was to drop in casually for a bowl of soup at the bar. I wanted to keep an eye on my sister, just in case Brian was the killer.

Driving often helped me clarify my thoughts and today was no exception. This case was like a maze, I realized. The farther we traveled, the more lost we became.

All we could do was keep going, hoping that we found the clues that brought everything into focus.

Who killed Hilda? And why? Was the location relevant—or a coincidence?

In my view, Joe, Patrick, and Brian were the leading suspects. As guests at the castle that night, the Cargills also had access to the scene. I hadn't found any particular reason to suspect them yet.

A memory flashed into my mind. Hilda, so intent on crashing the wine social—until she saw someone in the room. Then she'd backed up, almost trampling her friend, and practically ran out of the castle.

Had it been *Brian* she didn't want to face?

The more I thought about it, the more sense that made.

I had stopped for a coffee in a tiny, adorable village, the boot of my car finally empty. Seated outside in the sunshine, I sent Tamsyn a text. She hadn't seen Hilda's reaction at the social and I wanted her to know about it. Before her date with Brian.

She sent back a thumbs-up and a note that she was halfway through tidying the guest rooms, thank you very much.

So I responded the same way, with a thumbs-up. If she was going to be here for the summer, then it was only fair she help with the chores. I also had my herb business to run.

Another text came in. Darby. Oh good. I was so curious about her date with my brother.

Darby: *You around today?*

Me: *On the road. Back soon.*

Darby: *Want to swing by? Liv and I will be having tea shortly.*

Me: *Fifteen minutes?*

Darby: *See you then.*

I crammed a lid on my paper cup and hurried to my car. A session with the girls was exactly what I needed.

They were seated behind the counter when I arrived. "There you are, lovely." Darby got up and gave me a hug and kiss. Gesturing for Liv to stay seated, I embraced her as well.

"What are you having?" I asked, peeking into their teacups.

"Orange spice," Darby said. "Want a cup?"

"Sure." That was one of my blends, black tea with orange peel, clove, and ginger. It was invigorating and tasty.

I joined Liv at the table while Darby made me a cup. "How's everything, Liv? All ready for the summer season?"

To my surprise, her face paled and she made a sudden dash to the back.

"Was it something I said?" I called.

Darby set the cup in front of me. "It's not you. Liv had some very surprising news yesterday."

News that seemed to be turning her stomach. Oh, how I could sympathize. While during the thick of it with Hilda's opposition, I lived on mint and holy basil teas.

I dunked my teabag, waiting until the liquid colored sufficiently before adding milk.

Liv staggered out of the back room, hand to her stomach. "I've forgotten how much fun this is."

"Stomach flu?" I asked, thinking she was being sarcastic.

She sat down, still holding her belly. "Not exactly." A deep breath. "Remember that little procedure Tom had a couple months ago?"

"The big V?" Uh-oh. I had a feeling where this was going.

"Yeah." She sighed. "We love having kids, but with three, at fifteen, ten, and five, it seemed like a good place to stop." She laughed. "Think we can sue?"

"You're pregnant?" I studied my friend for a cue to how she felt about this unplanned event.

Liv's face broke into a huge grin. "Yes. After the shock wore off, we were pretty excited." She patted her stomach. "Little Tom is hoping for another boy, of course. I think he wants to even the playing field."

I went over and gave her a hug. "Congratulations. I definitely want to be on the babysitting list."

"Of course," Liv said with a snort. "It will be all hands on deck, I'm afraid. Between the other three, the farm, and the ice cream shop . . ."

"What are friends for?" As I returned to my seat, I recalled what Finlay had told me. "On another topic, I heard that you rented your flat to DI Finlay Cole."

"Ooh, what a dish!" Darby exclaimed. "I wouldn't mind following him home." She gave the raucous laugh that was always a surprise from someone so tiny and delicate.

"Now, now," Liv said. "You've got your own dishy man to ogle. Leave Finlay for Nora."

"Me?" I pretended to be surprised but inwardly I was thinking *yes*. Assuming we got through the murder investigation with our friendship intact. "He can't date me. I'm a witness in a case."

"After it's closed," Darby said comfortably. "He's totally adorable. And a police officer, which means he's good at being protective."

"This isn't one of your bodice rippers," I said with a laugh. "I can take care of myself." Then I recalled the frantic texts from Patrick's yacht. Well, I could take care of myself most of the time. "On another topic, how was your date?" I paused. "In general terms. Since he's my brother."

Darby's eyes sparked with excitement. "It was really lovely. We had a very nice dinner. I got all dressed up." Getting out of her seat, she went to a rack. "I wore this style." The floral chiffon dress was long and draped, with a deep V-neck and flowing sleeves.

"Beautiful," Liv said with a sigh. "You must've looked like a queen."

Darby hung the dress back up. "Felt like one, too. Will is just the sweetest man. I feel so peaceful and happy when I'm with him."

Since Darby tended to fall for unavailable bad boys, this was very good news. "He doesn't bore you?" I asked, having heard all about the tedious dates she'd suffered while detoxing from the latest heartbreaker.

"Not at all." Darby put a hand to her chin, musing. "We have such similar outlooks on life. Plus he keeps me in stitches. All we did was laugh."

"A good sense of humor is an absolute must," Liv, our resident authority, declared. "That and kindness. Doesn't matter how good-looking he is, how much money he has, or anything else if he's not kind."

Was Finlay Cole kind? I thought of how he treated Lady, his adopted dog, and the answer was yes. He'd passed a test he didn't even know had been set. The Liv Becket test of masculine fitness.

I burst out laughing and the other two stared at me. "What?" Darby asked.

"We're going to call it that," Darby declared when I shared. "Will Asquith gets passing marks. So does Tom Becket."

My hand tentatively went up. "I think Finlay does, too, although we haven't laughed much. It's been all murder and forensics so far." And riding to my rescue. Which I hadn't told the girls about. "Remember that picture I sent you yesterday, Darby? I was in the master bath on Patrick Horn's yacht."

Over tea—decaf for Liv—we hashed everything over. The visit to the yacht. Brian's sad story. Celia's death. Almost getting killed by roof tiles.

It felt good to get it all off my chest. Even though Tamsyn and I were in this together, my friends provided another layer of support. I trusted them implicitly to keep everything I told them in confidence.

"So Tamsyn is having lunch with Brian?" Liv's brow furrowed. "Is that really a good idea?"

"I'm going to be there," I said. "At the bar. And I should get going." As I looked around for my handbag, I noticed a Cargill's van stopped out front. Lorna was on the sidewalk talking to the driver.

At first, I thought it was Gavin, but then I noticed the driver had light hair and a beard. One of the employees?

"What are you looking at?" Darby asked.

"Lorna Cargill." They knew who I was talking about. "Wondering what she's up to. That's a company van."

Liv shrugged. "Probably nothing, then."

Lorna opened her handbag and rummaged around. Then she handed the driver an object that I couldn't see from here. Crossing the shop, I peered out the plate glass window, hoping she wouldn't notice me.

What was that in his hand? Something small and black. He closed his fingers around it and put it somewhere, giving her a nod. Then he put the van into gear and pulled away.

Lorna turned and stared right into the window. I gave her a little wave. She hesitated a moment, then made for the door.

I slung my handbag strap over my arm and pasted a smile on my face. "Hi, there," I said as she came in. "How are you?"

She glanced around the shop. "Great, thanks. Thought I'd do a little shopping."

"You've come to the right place." I nodded toward my friend. "Darby will take good care of you." I was tempted to hang around for a few minutes but Tamsyn and Brian were supposed to be meeting right now. Even if I ran down the street, I'd be late.

Darby hurried forward to greet Lorna. "Good morning. Or should I say good afternoon? Welcome to Tatiana's Bower."

I gave Liv and Darby a wave before slipping out. The White Rose was a couple of blocks down, a rectangular white stucco building with black shutters and window boxes filled with red geraniums and ivy. They also rented rooms and before opening our bed-and-breakfast, I'd spoken to Tegan, the owner, to be sure she was okay with it.

"The more the merrier," she'd said. "We don't offer enough holiday lets in Monkwell as it is." Tegan already stocked her rooms with my products and, in turn, we promised to recommend her restaurant to guests, as Dad had with the Cargills.

Inside, the pub was dim and cool, the large room made cozy by aged wood wainscoting, booths, and a long *L*-shaped bar. Potted plants and stained glass lamps added color, as did antique prints and paintings hung on smoke-darkened plaster.

Tamsyn and Brian were sitting at a two top in the window, studying menus. I tried to sneak through to a seat at the bar, but Tamsyn looked up and caught me. She frowned and shook her head slightly. *What are you doing here?* With a shrug, I scampered on, hoping to reach sanctuary before Brian noticed me.

Sandra Snelling was seated by herself on the short end of the bar, which faced into the room and was perfect for my mission.

"Mind if I sit here?" I asked her, hand on the adjacent stool.

She glanced up from her phone. "Nora. Hello. Go ahead." Her mouth turned down. "Hilda and I often had lunch here. This is my first time without her." She lifted her wineglass and drank. "Here's to you, old friend."

"I'm so sorry," I murmured. Sandra missed Hilda. Did Patrick? I wondered what Sandra knew about their relationship.

Tamsyn and Brian were now ordering so I grabbed a menu. "What are you having?"

"Our favorite meal was the cullen skink with a baguette," Sandra said mournfully. "I'm having it today in her honor."

"That does sound good." I loved smoked haddock soup. The bartender came over and I ordered the soup and a half pint of bitter.

The ale arrived immediately, nutty and brown with a nice backbite. I lifted my glass. "To Hilda." *To the woman who made my life hell. May she rest in peace.*

"To Hilda." Sandra finished the wine and signaled for another.

Not sure where to go from here, I swiveled on my stool, unwrapping my utensils and arranging them on the paper place mat. Heads close together, Tamsyn and Brian were talking. I should have had Tamsyn call me and leave the line open so I could eavesdrop.

"That's your sister," Sandra said suddenly.

I made a sound of assent.

"Why aren't you eating with her?" Sandra turned toward me, her gaze curious.

"They're, um, on a date," I explained. "Didn't want to be the third wheel." I forced a laugh. "Plus coming in was kind of on the spur of the moment. I've been making deliveries this morning. For my business. Castle Apothecary."

Gaze still on Tamsyn and Brian, she nodded absently. "Good-looking chap. He resembles his mother."

I pulled back. "You know who he is?" She hadn't said anything when Mavis told them about Brian's volatile visit to Hilda.

"Hilda's nephew." Sandra rested her chin on her hand. "She showed me a picture of him once, compared it to Celia's."

It was odd she was admitting this now. When we were picking Primrose up at Hilda's, I distinctly remembered Sandra saying that Hilda didn't have any relatives. Why didn't she say anything then?

I wasn't quite brave enough to confront her about that, so instead I asked, "Remember what Mavis told us about a young man showing up? Did you know it was Brian?"

She didn't meet my gaze. "I thought maybe . . . wasn't sure, though. Didn't want the lad to get in trouble. Hilda wouldn't like that."

Indignation made my ears burn. "Did you know she refused to talk to him? That doesn't sound very concerned to me." My voice was louder than I intended, drawing attention from others around us. With a wince, I lowered the volume. "I'm confused, that's all. Brian does seem like a nice guy."

"It was complicated," she finally said. "Hilda said he

was angry the first time they met. Made some hurtful accusations. I think she was afraid that he blamed her."

"For not taking him in?" He'd said as much to us.

"No. For his mother's death."

CHAPTER 19

The soup and bread were delicious. The lunch conversation, less so. After Sandra's revelation, she'd basically shut me out, attending to her phone and meal. It left me to ponder what she'd said. Did Brian blame Hilda? Or had Hilda worried that he would?

Over at Tamsyn's table, all seemed well. My sister's laugh rang out now and then and Brian was beaming ear to ear. At least someone was having fun.

While I spooned up creamy, smoky soup, the questions I had for Sandra stacked up like airplanes on a runway: Why would Brian blame Hilda? Had she been there when Celia died? Dad hadn't said so, and he was there that weekend. Was it her involvement with Patrick? Or maybe it was more subtle than that. Maybe Hilda had introduced Celia to Patrick's brother, thereby leading eventually to her death.

The place was beginning to clear out as the lunch trade dwindled. Tamsyn and Brian lingered over a shared chocolate cake. I refused dessert, instead nursing my beer with the plan to follow them out.

Sandra balled up her napkin and placed it on the counter. Unclasping her handbag, she pulled out a pack of cigarettes, a lighter tucked in the cellophane. "I'm going to step out for a minute if the barkeep asks."

"I'll tell him." I swiveled gently on my stool, watching as she made her way toward the back hallway, which led to the restrooms and the alley where smokers congregated.

The pub door opened and Lorna entered, big shopping bag in hand. She stood near the entrance, scanning the place, then made her way across the room to the bar.

"Hello again," I said as she placed her bag on the floor and hoisted herself onto a stool around the corner from me. "Buy out the shops?"

She smiled. "Darby was very persuasive. I bought a couple outfits, skin care products, and some jewelry. And this." She pulled a red, packable beach hat out of the bag and plopped it on her head. "What do you think?" she asked, turning this way and that.

"Red suits you." The vibrant color set off her blond hair and tanned complexion. She should wear lipstick the color of Hilda's to complete the look.

"Very fetching, madam," the bartender said as he slid a coaster across the bar. "What can I get you?"

Still wearing the hat, she glanced at the menu. "Glass of white wine and a veggie personal pizza, please."

After he put in her order and poured the wine, he came over. "Another?"

My glass still had an inch of beer. "No, thank you. I'll pay up."

Tamsyn and Brian were still talking, the cake plate scraped clean. Hopefully they would leave soon. Otherwise I'd have to call it a day and head back to the castle.

Sandra came sauntering along from the rear. To my surprise, Lorna waved. "There you are. Thought I'd missed you."

Hmm. Interesting. I'd had no idea that the two women knew each other.

"Just indulging my bad habit." Sandra's laugh was throaty. "One of them, at any rate." She winked at the barman.

He gave her a cheeky grin. "Top off?" He held up the wine bottle.

"Don't mind if I do." Sandra picked up her glass and carried it around, then sat beside Lorna.

I drank my last inch of beer, wincing. I hated the warm dregs.

Tamsyn and Brian were finally getting up from the table, Tamsyn fussing with her phone and handbag while Brian put on his jacket. Plain blue, not the maroon-and-orange one. He probably wouldn't wear it again after he found out we'd told Finlay Cole about it. Not to mention Mavis, who had probably spread her sighting of Brian at Hilda's far and wide. He might as well wear a neon sign reading "murder suspect."

As they strolled toward the door, I hopped down and followed. "Have a nice day," I said, my smile encompassing the bartender, Lorna, and Sandra. When I walked past the women, I listened intently, curious why they were meeting up.

"Gavin was always part of the gang," Sandra was saying. "Patrick's loyal sidekick. A real party animal." She touched Lorna's hand. "That seemed to change when he met you."

"Oh, they're still thick as thieves," Lorna said wryly. "When Patrick calls, he jumps. That's one reason we're staying in Monkwell, actually. Because of Patrick."

I'd dated someone who often prioritized his friends over me and it wasn't great. Rather irritating, actually. No wonder Lorna was discontented.

Reluctantly moving on, I hurried outside to catch up with my sister.

They were standing outside the pub. "Nora." Tamsyn's smile was sly. "Fancy meeting you here."

Brian regarded me with amusement and I felt my cheeks flame. "Watching out for your sister?" he asked.

Of course I had been. Rather than admit it, I mumbled something about the delicious haddock soup.

Tamsyn put her arm through Brian's. "Shall we get ice cream and go for a stroll?"

I stared at her in amazement. Not only had she shared a dessert with Brian, she wanted ice cream? While not obsessed about avoiding sweets, this wasn't her typical behavior.

She threw me a look, brows raised, and I got it. Ice cream was an excuse to prolong their date. Maybe they really had hit it off.

"I'm not following you," I said as we all started down the sidewalk in the same direction. "My car is parked near the Lazy Mermaid."

"You're welcome to join us," Tamsyn said. "Unless you have to rush back."

So my theory was wrong. They were still in the friend zone.

"We were having a very interesting chat over lunch," Tamsyn went on. "Do you mind filling Nora in, Brian?"

"Not at all," he said. "I'm grateful for your help in getting some answers."

"After we get our ice cream," Tamsyn said. "We'll go down to the waterfront."

After buying cones while fielding a few curious looks from Liv, the three of us ambled down to the harbor. The tide was low, the air heavy with salt and seaweed, red and blue and yellow fishing boats rocking gently along the wharf. Farther out, a thicket of sailboat masts bobbed in the mooring area.

"What a great little town," Brian said, lapping at his three-decker cone. "You must love living here."

"We do." I gave Tamsyn a sidewise look. "Or did."

She pulled a face. "Why don't we sit?" Beyond the wharf, a grass promenade fronted the seawall, with benches set here and there.

After checking the empty benches for seagull poop, we chose one. This end of the promenade was fairly quiet, only a few people walking past or sitting on the seawall. An artist had an easel set up a distance away, fully engrossed as he painted the view.

"Brian, do you want to tell Nora what we discussed?" Tamsyn asked. She neatly nibbled at her baby-size cone.

"Only if you're comfortable," I said hastily while thinking, *Please do.* I would rather hear it from him rather than secondhand. Although I would settle for that if need be.

Brian tossed the end of the cone into his mouth and crunched, then wiped his mouth and hands on a napkin. "Okay," he said. "You already know about me being adopted. It was an open adoption, like most in the UK, I've learned. So I could have grown up knowing my mother. Except that she died before I reached my first birthday."

"Oh, that's awful," I exclaimed. "I'm so sorry."

He nodded in acknowledgment. "Could have been worse. I have wonderful parents. Anyway, a few months ago, I came across a mention of my mother's name and a photograph. I won't bore you with where, exactly."

His comment made me intensely curious, naturally. I didn't ask, though.

"I started looking into her death, and when I read her

obituary, I found out she had a sister." His fists, resting on his thighs, clenched. "I asked Mum about Hilda, why I'd never met my aunt. You might have thought, under the circumstances, that she would step in." Visibly upset, he took a moment to compose himself. "Mum said Hilda never responded to her overtures. Not a word. I didn't even get a birthday or Christmas card, let alone visits."

"I don't understand that." The situation was even worse than I'd thought. Hilda had been contacted by the adoptive parents so she couldn't claim ignorance of his whereabouts.

Brian's face was pure misery. "Neither do I. She did agree to meet up with me and at first it went really well. Until I started asking the difficult questions. I probably pressed her too hard . . . I just wanted to know . . ." He rubbed his hand up and down his pants legs in distress, as if wiping it clean.

Tamsyn put her hand on top of his, stilling it. "Totally understandable. Especially with the tragic death of your mother. Tell Nora what she said about Celia."

"She said—" He swallowed hard. "She said that my mother was murdered. And she was working on proving it."

Seagulls wheeled and cried overhead, landing with flapping wings to gobble stray chips left by a picnicker. One pecked at the greasy cardboard.

I'd had my suspicions about the accident, mainly because an heir to a fortune had died, but hearing them stated so bluntly took my breath away. Hilda had been grappling with a very disturbing situation—and bravely, by the sounds of it. I had to give her that much.

Is that why she, in turn, had been killed? To stop her? It made sense.

"Hilda actually said that?" I asked, to confirm. "She was investigating Celia's murder?"

Brian let out a breath, as if relieved to share this troubling information. "Not in so many words but she implied it. Said something was rotten about the accident and she was going to get to the bottom of it."

"Why now, I wonder?" I mused. "Why not sooner?" Had something happened recently to make her rethink the accident? I had answers to an earlier question, I realized. It didn't seem like Brian blamed Hilda for his mother's death. For not being in his life, definitely.

"Have you seen the police report?" Tamsyn asked. "I assume there was one."

"Already on it." A return to the practical seemed to energize Brian. He pulled his phone out and began tapping. "I made a digital copy."

"Do you mind sending it to me?" I asked, curious to read it carefully at my leisure.

"Not at all." I gave him my cell number and he entered it. "It doesn't say much. Mainly that the car didn't navigate a sharp corner and they crashed."

My phone dinged when his text arrived. "Anything wrong with the car?" Dad had said he thought they'd checked.

"Not according to the report. They chalked it up to speeding." Brian made a face. "I thought I'd try to follow Hilda's trail. So far it's been a dead end. The car is long gone and the investigating officer has passed away."

A dead end, exactly the way I'd been feeling about solving Hilda's murder.

"Some witnesses are still alive," Tamsyn said. "My dad, Patrick Horn . . . whoever else was a guest at Horn House that weekend."

Confusion creased Brian's brow. "Arthur was there?"

"Yes, with my mother," Tamsyn said. "He remembers it well. We can ask him who else was there and see if he remembers any more details. Actually, why don't you sit in on that conversation? I'm sure Dad would love to help any way he can."

Brian reached for Tamsyn's hand and squeezed it. "I really appreciate your support." He glanced at me. "Yours as well."

We shared a moment until interrupted by the ring of Brian's phone. He grabbed it off the bench and studied the number. "Sorry, but I'd better take this. It's Hilda's executor. We've been playing phone tag."

He took the call and Tamsyn and I walked back to my car. As soon as we were out of earshot, I said, "Hilda's executor? Do you suppose he's her heir?"

Throwing me a glare, Tamsyn started walking faster. "What if he is? Does that put him back on the suspect list?"

"Maybe," I puffed, hurrying to catch up. "I agree, he's a nice guy. And I feel very sorry for him, losing his mother that way. Hilda's behavior was shameful. You have to admit, though, he has plenty of motive. Plus, he was staying at the castle that night."

She stalked along, arms swinging, frowning.

"Do you like him?" I asked softly. "Is that it?"

She grunted, sister language I easily interpreted. *I might. So what? Don't make a thing of it, please.*

I changed the subject, vowing to keep any rumination about Brian's guilt to myself. "We should go to Horn House soon, check out the scene of the crime. Patrick will think we're still contemplating his offer and want to see his operation."

Tamsyn visibly softened. "Maybe tomorrow after our

meeting with Harold. We can swing by there on the way home."

I looked up the route on my phone as we walked. "That should work."

Maybe tomorrow we would get more answers. Right now, I had to get back to the castle and work through my list of chores.

"How far did you get this morning?" I asked my sister. She was supposed to tidy the guest rooms.

Her expression was apologetic. "Queen's and Knight's are done. Didn't get to King's. I had an unexpected call with a producer."

"You did? A good part?" Much as I loved having her around, I'd been hoping that Tamsyn would get another role soon.

"It's awesome. I'm up for the lead in *Mist on the Moors*, a gothic series inspired by *Wuthering Heights*." She held up both hands, fingers crossed. "They'll be filming in Yorkshire."

I copied her movement. "Fingers crossed. That would be spectacular. Love the premise."

She began to tell me about the part and the pilot script, which they would shoot first. Murder, mayhem, ghosts, and ancient buildings. Sounded an awful lot like home.

By the time we reached the castle, the script had arrived by courier. I left Tamsyn to her reading—curled up in the solar, Primrose and Ruffian as audience—and went up to clean the King's Room.

In the linen closet, I added fresh sheets and towels to the cart. We only changed the beds every few days and it was time. As I was checking over the supplies, the door to the hall gently swung shut.

A tingling sensation ran down my spine and it was as if the room was suddenly full of another presence. Invisible but looming, if that makes sense.

"Who's there?" I whispered.

No answer, but the bobbles on a bedspread hem swayed in sequence, accompanied by a lute strum.

Sir Percival, once again showing up unscheduled.

"Is this going to be a regular thing?" I asked him. "After four hundred years, you're expanding your repertoire?"

The presence deepened, somehow conveying a sense of urgency.

Again, I got the feeling he wanted to communicate something. I waited, but nothing else came. As always.

"Okay. Have to get to work now." I opened the door and tugged the cart out, walking backward. After parking the cart, I switched off the closet light and shut the door.

Conscious of being followed, I pushed the cart down the hall to the King's Room. I knocked, waited, and let myself in.

"Are you good with a scrub brush?" I called, tongue in cheek. "If you're going to hang around, at least make yourself useful."

The casement window burst open, the curtains fluttering in a strong gust.

"Great. We could use a little fresh air." I began by stripping the bed and gathering the used towels and stuffing them into the hanging laundry sack. The room was pretty tidy, only a few personal belongings around and clothing hanging in the wardrobe. This was going to be simple and easy.

A short while later, I was seated on the edge of the

tub, scrubbing, when I felt his presence looming again. "What is it?" I asked. "What are you trying to tell me?"

The ghostly lute played again, this time a melancholy succession of notes.

Sir Percival had broken protocol by showing himself the night Lorna arrived, instead of waiting for the full moon. I'd gotten the impression then that he felt some sort of kinship with her. His life had been marked by betrayal and sorrow. Was he implying that hers was as well?

"Is it Lorna?" I asked. "Are you concerned about her?"

One long plucked note vibrated. That sounded like a yes to me.

Then Lorna called from the bedroom, making me jump. "Hello? Is anyone in here?"

The sound of an exploding lightbulb was followed by a flash and he was gone.

"Nicely done," I said. Sir Percival was really stepping up his game. Leaving the scrub brush on the tub ledge, I went to the doorway. "I won't be much longer. Have to finish the bathroom and run the sweeper, that's all."

Lorna had set her shopping bag on the carpet and she picked it up again. "I'll put this out of the way, then." She placed the bag on a chair and tucked her handbag next to it. "Let me grab my tablet." She went over to the bedside table.

"Did you have a nice lunch?" I asked, wishing I could more directly indulge my curiosity about her meeting with Sandra. "The food is pretty good, isn't it?"

"We like it." Tablet in hand, Lorna came across the carpet, heading toward the door. "Enjoyed catching up with a friend as well." She paused to add, "Sandra is Gavin's ex-wife."

"She is?" That reveal jolted me back on my heels.

She laughed at my shock. "Surprising that we get along so well, isn't it? They were divorced ages ago and neither holds a grudge. So we see her quite often, especially at the holidays."

"Wonderful," I muttered. "How it should be. One big, happy family."

Sandra laughed again. "I wouldn't go that far but, yes, it's preferable to drama." She strode out of the room, leaving the door ajar.

I returned to the bathroom, my mind turning over this new information. Sandra and Gavin had been married. As I scrubbed away, making the porcelain gleam, it occurred to me that Sandra might have known Hilda for longer than I'd realized. Somehow I'd gotten the impression that the friendship was fairly recent.

Because Hilda had moved here after Sandra's arrival. That was why I'd assumed they'd met in Monkwell. Had Sandra also known Celia? She hadn't mentioned it, if so.

Her involvement was probably a sidebar. The important thing to focus on was the tragedy at Horn House. Had Dennis and Celia been murdered? Was Patrick responsible, and if so, how could we prove it?

CHAPTER 20

Late that afternoon, while the castle grounds drowsed in the day's warmth, I slipped out into the garden. At my insistence, Janet had put her feet up to listen to an audio book, knitting in hand. Tamsyn was pacing about reciting her lines and Dad was deep in the family papers, as usual.

Carrying a wire bucket, I passed through the walled garden, where Guy was turning over soil for a new bed. "Good day, Miss Nora. Where are you off to?" Rolf, who was lazing nearby, leaped to his feet with a scramble of paws and came over to butt his head against my leg.

I moved the bucket to my other hand and patted his head. "Out to the point to collect some seaweed."

Guy stopped digging, foot resting on the shovel. "Seaweed, eh?" His expression was curious. "For the garden?"

Seaweed made great compost but that wasn't my mission. "I'm going to try using it in skin care products. Creams and salves, to start."

He threw back his head and guffawed. "Seriously? Ladies want to put seaweed on their faces?"

"Not just women." I gave him a mischievous smile.

"Men will use them, too. I have an idea. Want to be my guinea pig?"

Guy patted one tanned cheek. "Maybe I will. Got to take care of this handsome visage. Keep my youthful good looks." He winked.

"I'll give you the first sample." As I started moving again, Rolf tagged along. "Mind if he comes with me?" Hopefully he wouldn't find any decaying carcasses on the beach today.

"Fine with me. He could use the exercise." By the time we reached the gate, Guy was already digging again.

Rolf and I meandered through the garden, with frequent pauses to examine the progress of various plants. How I loved monitoring the growing season, watching leaves bud and blossoms emerge. Later, I'd be watching for berries and seed pods to ripen.

Instead of going down to the main beach, I took a different route, winding along the bluff and down to the next cove. Here a strip of beach ended in a mucky, rocky area where seaweed grew in abundance like patchy green hair. The cove itself was embraced by two arms of striated chalk cliffs. The one to the south had a deep cave partially accessible at low tide, nicknamed the Dragon's Lair for the way heavy surf sprayed into the air like snorts of smoke.

When we were kids, we'd come down here and tromp around in our wellies, enjoying the way they squelched in the wet sand. Seaweed then was for throwing at each other, especially when well-rotted. We'd chase each other, holding our bellies and hooting with laughter when we scored a direct hit.

Smiling at the memories, I turned my attention to

my task. Trying new flora in my work brought a different sort of joy. An important part of the ritual was entering the plant's environment and coexisting there for a while. Stilling myself, breathing the air, using all my senses.

Today's environment was whiffy mudflats at low tide, the waves a distant roar, and, despite the arch of blue sky overhead, scudding clouds massing in the west. We'd have rain by tonight.

I could buy herbs from reputable companies. Even seaweed was available dried or powdered. It would be easier but not nearly as satisfying.

We squished over to the first band of seaweed, where I hunkered down with my shears. This was bladder wrack, identified by its air-filled bladders. I snipped fronds of live plants, careful not to pull so more would grow. Bladder wrack was edible and a source of soda, potash, and iodine. In skin formulations, it could calm inflammation, ease dryness, and improve texture.

I filled half the bucket with bladder wrack and then walked farther out, to the kelp bed. Water covered the fronds waving in the pools and I was grateful for my boots. I set the bucket on a rock and bent over to harvest, not wanting to get my shorts wet. Rolf was paddling around, lifting his head every now and then to sniff.

Sugar kelp fronds were wide, with a ruffled edge. I snipped a frond and placed it in the basket. Kelp was very good for skin, especially excess oil and acne. Some people applied the rehydrated sheets directly on the skin for full body or facial treatments. I'd blend mine with herbs to make products.

Rolf let out a woof and began to run, big paws splashing. He was headed right to the edge of the cove, where

I now noticed that something was huddled on the sand next to the cliff. A tarp? Or a ripped sail?

I sighed. He usually didn't get so excited about canvas. There must be something else there attracting him.

"Rolf. Come." Still trucking, he didn't even flinch. Leaving the basket and shears, I stumbled along behind him, calling fruitlessly for him to stop, to wait. My foot slipped and I lurched into a pool, cold water flowing over the boot top. Now I was squelching along, wide-legged for stability, gritting my teeth, wishing I had time to stop and empty my boot.

"You're staying home next time," I yelled. Not that he cared. He was already nosing the bundle, pushing as though to turn it over.

It was canvas, grubby white cloth wrapped with multicolored braided rope.

What could be so fascinating about that for a dog?

Then I saw the hand.

Spots danced in front of my eyes and my knees buckled, dropping me to the sand. "Rolf, come," I managed to call.

Miracle of miracles, he did, maybe because I was clutching my legs and whimpering in shock. His big head bumped my shoulder, his huge tongue slobbering my cheek.

"Love you but no." I pushed him away and felt around for my phone. Rolf collapsed on the sand and leaned against me, wet and smelly and comforting.

Nine-nine-nine or Finlay? Finlay was closer. He'd been at the castle when I left.

The phone rang once. Twice. The hand was still. Waves hissed and roared. Or was that my ears?

"Hello? Nora?" He must have my number stored with my name.

"It's me," I said. "I'm down on the shore." The knowledge of what I had to share pressed in my chest and I shuddered, my teeth beginning to chatter. "Uh, uh—"

"What is it?" His voice was sharp with alarm. "Are you all right?"

"I am," I managed to say. "He's not. I'm in Dragon Cove." Hot tears stung my eyes. "I found a body. Please come."

A stunned silence. Then, "Dragon Cove?"

"Ask Dad. Tamsyn . . . Janet. Anyone." I couldn't muster the ability to give him directions. I closed my eyes and tried to breathe. I couldn't get enough air, it seemed.

"Hold tight. I'll be there shortly."

I'm not sure how much time passed before I heard his shout. Finlay, carrying his murder investigation bag, was with Guy, and once they came down the path, they hurried across the cove. Rolf lurched to his feet and trotted toward them, whining.

When they got closer, I started to struggle to my feet. Finlay set the bag down and extended a hand, his clasp warm, and tugged upright. Without thinking about it, I collapsed into his arms, which went around me. He pulled me close to his chest—or was it me, snuggling up?

Either way, I wanted to stay there for a long, long time. Which we didn't have.

Hands on my shoulders, he pulled back. "You okay?"

I nodded. Wrapping my arms around my middle, I used my chin to point. "He's over there." I looked down at the dog. "Rolf, stay." For once, he was obedient.

The two men trudged over to the sodden length, Guy

standing back while Finlay put gloves on before pulling back a corner of the canvas. He looked up at Guy, who nodded.

"It's him, all right. Bloody hell." Grimacing, Guy turned away, a hand to his chin. Finlay asked him a question in a low voice and Guy shook his head. "I'll be all right."

"Who?" I called. "Who is it?"

Guy glanced at Finlay, who nodded. He came over, staring down at me with concern. "It's Joe. The bloke who was working with the stonemason."

"Joe? Really?"

"'Fraid so." Guy looked over his shoulder. "Looks like he was dropped overboard from a boat, wrapped in canvas like that."

Unfortunately, I could picture it, the bundle of sailcloth bobbing in the waves, eventually deposited on shore by the tide. Patrick Horn had a sailboat. Did he have something to do with this?

He might have killed Joe and then taken off. The *Party Girl* was still gone. The question was—why? Because of Hilda? She had tried to extort money from Joe. Maybe Patrick had gotten revenge for her murder.

Or had Hilda's killer done it? Maybe Joe had figured out who it was. They would have had to have access to a boat. Not that those were hard to come by, here on the coast.

Finlay was still examining the body, moving back and forth, bending close at the head. He took out his phone and made a call, speaking with crisp authority.

After disconnecting, he strode over to us. "Team is on their way. I'll need a statement from you, Nora. We can do that up at the castle, if that's more comfortable."

I realized my bottom was soaking wet and cold from

sitting on the ground. "Definitely." My bucket was over by the kelp bed. I'd better retrieve it while I remembered.

Finlay and Guy were conferring, pointing at the bluff. I guessed they were talking about the best route down here. There was a lane that led to this cove, little used and gated. It would be much closer than going through our property and along the clifftop.

Rolf came with me to get the bucket. "You're a good boy for finding Joe," I told him. How long would the stonemason have been lying there otherwise? My stomach turned at the thought. We rarely came down here and there weren't many visitors. The rambling path didn't run close and with all the seaweed, it wasn't exactly pleasant for a picnic or swimming.

I studied the contents of the bucket, deciding I had enough to work with. The next step was hanging the seaweed out to dry, on the clothesline, perhaps. Janet's probable reaction made me smile. It might be best to string a separate line for plant matter.

Rolf and I wandered back toward Finlay and Guy. The first officers were already arriving, making their way down the path. When they got closer, I recognized Constable Emily Burns. The other officer was Constable Advick Kumar.

"We were on patrol nearby," Burns said. "The rest of the team is right behind us."

Kumar, who was new to the force, stared at the body with a mix of fascination and dread. "This anything to do with the operation the other night?"

Operation? I slid a glance at Guy, who widened his eyes.

"Constable," Burns said with gritted teeth. She tilted her head toward us.

He shrugged his shoulders in apology. "Sorry. I've

been studying the topo and there is a sizable cave near here—"

"The Dragon's Lair," I said. "It was used by smugglers way back. Boats can get inside at high tide." I pointed to the rock face. "Reaching it on foot is more difficult and it's safe only at low tide." Despite the steep climb and treacherous footing, smugglers had managed to carry goods out of the cave and up the bluff, I'd read in a local history.

The three officers were staring at me. "What?" Then I got it. "Oh." The boat engines I'd heard. A body wrapped in sailcloth, so likely dropped into the water. A cave used by smugglers hundreds of years ago—and now? What could they be smuggling?

"It might be worth checking out, DI." Kumar said, poised as if ready to scale the rock face. "When you're finished with me here."

Finlay studied the cliff, the body, the encroaching tide. "Constable Burns, I'd like you to help me set a perimeter and then take photographs." He looked at his phone. "Medical examiner is on the way and so is the forensics team."

Kumar was practically vibrating with eagerness, as if waiting for the starting gun.

"Ms. Asquith, do you know the way to the cave from here?" Finlay asked. "And can you walk in those boots?"

I was always *Ms. Asquith* in front of others. Had I been *Nora* when we hugged? I thought so, and my whole body blushed at the memory.

"I do, yes," I said. "Been in there many times." I held up a foot. "These will be fine." We'd played smuggler and excisemen with friends, chasing each other around with pieces of wood for swords. And flinging seaweed, of course.

"Take evidence markers and bags with you just in case," Finlay instructed Kumar as he opened his murder investigation bag. "Photographs, too. It's a long shot but we'd better take advantage of the window." He tucked supplies into a smaller bag and handed it to Kumar, who looked thrilled.

So was I, at being included in an investigation. A front row seat, so to speak. Tamsyn would be so jealous.

"Ready, Ms. Asquith?" Kumar asked with a gesture of his arm. "Lead on."

After placing my bucket of seaweed out of the way, I headed toward the cliff. We clambered up to an opening in the rock face, one of many along this section of coast.

Kumar gave a grunt of dismay as we ducked our heads and entered the cave. "Trust me," I called. "It gets better."

Blocky walls of rock enclosed us on all sides, which was definitely claustrophobic for an adult.

"You're sure this is right?" Kumar asked.

"Positive. Feel the wind? It's blowing through from the other entrance."

The tunnel gradually opened up, the ceiling lifting into the darkness. Kumar switched on his torch. Within five minutes, we emerged onto a ledge, a doorway of sorts to the main cavern. Beyond the opening, we could see the ocean glinting blue in the distance. Edging closer as the tide turned.

"At high tide, the whole floor fills up," I said. "Our parents never let us come in here then. It was too easy to slip and fall in and get battered against the rocks."

Kumar squinted. "The opening is large enough for a boat to come right inside."

"Definitely. Perfect for smuggling." I pointed to a piece of rusty metal set in the stone. "Mooring ring." I explained to Kumar how smugglers rowed into the cave, tying off and unloading to waiting helpers. Or, alternatively, stored goods here and moved them later by boat.

"I'd better get searching." Kumar edged past me, lowering himself down to the cavern floor.

"Check the back of the cave above the high-tide mark," I suggested. "Anything that was dropped would wash up back there, maybe." If pulled out to sea, it would never be found.

Sweeping his flashlight back and forth, Kumar began trudging toward the rear, pausing now and then to study something.

The area was sizable, so we'd be here a while if he worked alone.

"Want me to help? I can use my flash app on my phone."

"Please do. Don't touch anything, okay?"

Choosing a different spot because it was easier, I lowered myself off the ledge.

Something crunched under my foot. Which wasn't totally unexpected. We found sea glass all the time.

Leaning over, I turned on my phone light. As I'd thought, glass glinted. Thick green glass, like from a wine bottle.

Again, not unheard of. People partied in the caves all the time. The usual debris was more along the lines of beer cans or bottles, though.

"Kumar," I called. "Come look."

He turned and made his way back, the light bobbing. "What is it?" he asked when he reached my side.

"Wine bottle glass, I figure." Other shards lay here and

there, enough to make a standard-size bottle. "Fairly recent. The edges aren't worn by the water."

He bent close, moving the light slowly over all the pieces. The light paused on the bottom of the bottle, which had a deep ident. He made a noise of satisfaction. "Ms. Asquith, you are brilliant."

CHAPTER 21

I couldn't take any credit for stepping on the glass but I accepted the compliment anyway. At least we'd found something of value in the cave, or so Kumar believed.

He hummed happily to himself as he photographed, then bagged up the shards, scanning the area several times for stray pieces. "We will be able to tell what kind of wine it was," he said. "From the shape. Did you know that, Ms. Asquith?"

I did, thanks to my brother, Will. He'd explained it all very thoroughly while choosing bottles for mead. He used the hock style—narrow with a gradual slope to the shoulder.

Although Kumar didn't tell me anything about the case, I could guess. The smugglers must be bringing in wine. Alcohol smuggling was certainly traditional around these parts, mainly gin and rum in the old days. As then, taxes and duties were the incentive to cheat.

Naturally my devious mind went right to a possible suspect. Gavin Cargill. He owned wine shops all over England. Did his visit to this section of coastline have a devious purpose? If so, what were the implications for Will? Was Gavin really interested in carrying his mead?

Another thing. If Gavin was involved in smuggling, Will needed to stay far away.

Ugh. I didn't want to be the one to break it to him.

After the bottle was bagged, a marker was placed on the ledge above due to the water that would soon encroach. Then Kumar and I explored the rest of the cavern. The only item of interest was one crushed cigarette butt above the high-water mark.

Kumar used tweezers to pick it up. "Never know," he said as he dropped it into a bag. "We might get DNA from this." He carefully set a marker to indicate the spot.

"Belonging to any one of a hundred teenagers," I said.

He sealed the bag. "That is true. Regardless, we must be thorough."

The investigation was in full swing when we returned to the cove. Officers were swarming around the area, doing a fingertip search. I recognized the medical examiner, who was talking to Finlay. Joe's body had been bagged and was awaiting transport to the morgue. They'd have a devil of a job getting him up the cliff path.

Finlay saw us coming and excused himself. "Any luck?"

"Yes, sir." Kumar was beaming. "We found a broken wine bottle and a cigarette butt. The bottle was near the ledge for foot access so I believe it might be significant. Dropped while carrying cargo out of the cave."

Finlay lay a hand on his shoulder. "Good job, Constable." Turning to me, he said, "Guy will accompany you home. I'll see the two of you later, once we're done here."

"Is there any extra clothesline kicking around?" I asked Guy when we reached the castle grounds. Until then, we'd walked in silence, even Rolf seeming subdued. "I don't think Janet will appreciate me using hers."

Guy eyed the bucket of seaweed. "Don't think so either. I'll fetch the line and a post, how's that? We'll set something up for you."

Neither of us was rushing into the house to share the news about Joe, I noticed. We'd have to tell the others soon enough. Right now we could pretend that putting the seaweed out to dry was the most important task.

While Guy foraged in the shed, I carried the bucket over to the clothesline frame in a back corner of the walled kitchen garden. The lines were empty except for a bag holding the clothespins. I'd use those, I decided. All we needed was the wind blowing seaweed strands all over the garden.

"I figure we'll tie off the main frame," Guy explained when he joined me. He handed me a length of line and began pounding a post into the grass.

While he set the pole, I tied one end of the line to another in the frame, near the end. Then I extended it out tightly and he made a solid knot around the post.

"Perfect. We'll take this down after the seaweed dries." If I ended up drying seaweed frequently, I'd have Guy build me a dedicated spot. Right now, this was all experimental.

"I'll be in the shed if you need me." Guy carried the sledgehammer back, to put it away, Rolf at his heels.

Pungent aromas rose from the slippery fronds as I plucked each out of the basket and hung them by the widest end. From what I'd read, the plants would need several days to dehydrate.

I tried to imagine life three or four days from now. What else would explode in our faces? We'd had two murders in the past week.

Had we been transported back to the Dark Ages somehow? What I did today would have fit right in. Seaweed was valued in that era, a diet staple, in fact.

I lifted the last strand of seaweed out of the basket. Murder and mayhem were par for the course in Sir Percival's day. How did people function? One day at a time, I supposed.

Task finished, I inhaled deeply. It was time to share the bad news. "Guy?" I called. He put his head out of the shed. "Are you ready?"

We sat around the kitchen table, clutching mugs of my Calming Chamomile tea. As expected, the family had been shocked by Joe's untimely death and my discovery of his body close to our property. Janet was watching Lady for Finlay and the bulldog was dozing at her feet.

"Does this mean he didn't kill Hilda?" Tamsyn mused. With hair piled high, wearing a striped cotton sundress, she looked fresh and pretty for the wine social. Which was supposed to start in fifteen minutes.

"Not necessarily," I said. "Maybe his death was revenge for Hilda's murder."

Guy shook his head. "I think it was related to the smuggling. Something went wrong the other night, and Bob's your uncle, he was tossed overboard to feed the fishies."

A grim image, indeed.

"What do you mean, Guy?" Dad fingered his beard. "Were you aware of the shenanigans offshore?"

"I heard a lot of boat engines," I put in.

"So did I." Guy turned to Janet. "Remember I was up and down like a jack-in-the box? All the commotion kept me awake."

Janet groaned. "Sure do, love. I didn't sleep a wink either."

We all looked at Guy, waiting for him to elaborate. "I distinctly recognized the sound of the coastguard cutter engines," he said. "Another boat was moving really fast, must have been a speedboat. After that went by, I heard another coastguard vessel. They were looking for someone, I figure."

"They didn't check the cave," I said. "A constable and I found a broken wine bottle in there. Recent breakage."

"Smugglers in the Dragon's Lair," Dad mused. "Our ancestors used that cave to bring in tobacco, silk, tea, and brandy, which was then transported around the countryside, horses' hooves and carriage wheels muffled with cloth."

I wasn't surprised. Our family tree had its share of scoundrels, although, in those days, smuggling was an accepted way of life in remote coastal areas. The English government and its representatives were heartily distrusted, even despised.

Janet glanced at the clock. "I suppose . . ." She slid her chair back.

"We'll take care of it." I glanced down at my salt-stained shorts and sweaty T-shirt. "After I change."

"I won't say no." Janet pulled back up to the table. "I've got a nice ratatouille in the slow cooker and homemade rolls for dinner."

"One of my faves." I finished the tonic wine and stood. "I'll be ready in a few, Tamsyn."

To my surprise, she followed me to the back stairs. Figuring that she needed to get something from her bedroom or to freshen up, I charged up the steps.

"Nora," she said when I reached the top. "Wait up."

I halted while she climbed, thinking about what I

was going to wear for the social. Maybe a decent pair of jeans. I really needed to go out to the garden after dinner.

"What's up?" I asked. "Something else happen?"

She shook her head. "Not exactly. You know the role I'm up for?"

"Heard you rehearsing some lines. You sounded great. Filming right here in Yorkshire, too." Maybe she and I could remain close even after she left again. The usual pattern was that we hardly ever heard from her while she was filming. Understandable, as it was pretty all-consuming, being on location and all.

Tamsyn nibbled at her bottom lip. "The part is perfect. No doubt about it. It's just that . . . Ben is up for the male lead."

"What? Ben, your ex? You're kidding."

"Wish I was. Yeah, he's in the running." Tamsyn's eyes filled with misery. "How can I do it? We'll be working together every day."

"As romantic partners? On film, I mean?" This was appalling.

She nodded. "Kissing and everything."

"What does your agent say?" Surely he would go to bat for Tamsyn. "Oh, and what about Ben's wife? She can't be happy either."

"My agent is on it." Her face creased with anxiety. "But if I turn it down, my career is dead in the water. There's nothing else right now."

I searched for the right thing to say, the approach or reassurance that would ease her mind. All I could summon on short notice were platitudes and pep talks. Lame and unhelpful, to say the least.

In a swift reversal of mood, she brightened. Now that she'd heaved her troubles onto my shoulders, she felt better, which was typical of my sister. "On another topic, are we still on for tomorrow? I want to confirm with Harold."

I started walking toward my room, conscious that I needed to hurry. "I think we should still go. I want to hear more about Patrick's tricks because, far as I know, he still wants this place."

She was right behind me. "I agree. We also need to keep investigating Hilda's death in case Joe didn't do it."

"And Celia's, which Joe couldn't have been involved with. He probably wasn't even born yet." I opened a bureau drawer and pulled out a pair of jeans. "I have a thought. Remember how Hilda was trying to extort money out of Joe?" I used my knee to close the drawer.

Tamsyn snorted. "And Dad."

"What if she knew about the smuggling? Maybe that's what she was holding over his head. He would have gone back to jail if he'd been arrested." In another drawer, I found a three-quarter-sleeve T-shirt in one of my favorite colors, periwinkle. That would do.

"Then she was killed and he didn't have to worry about paying her off."

"Or he did it and someone took revenge on him." I glanced at the bathroom. "I'd better get cleaned up. You want to head down? Guests will be showing up any minute. Well, except Finlay. I'm sure he'll be tied up for the evening." I recalled our hug, a visceral memory that made me flush with warmth. If we'd been alone, if Guy hadn't been there, not to mention a dead body, what would have happened? I pictured him tipping my chin back and kissing—

"Nora." Tamsyn's tone was teasing. "What are you thinking about?"

"Nothing. See you in a few." I went into the bathroom

and shut the door. My sister knew me all too well. She might not know who for certain, but she could probably guess.

Finlay arrived back at the castle late. I'd been watching for the car and Lady and I went out to meet him. "He's home," I told the sweet dog. "Your daddy is home." Her little legs churned even faster and she let out a woof.

Finlay got out of the police car with a word to the driver, who drove off. Crouching down, he began to pat Lady. "You miss me, girl? I missed you."

"Are you hungry?" I called. "I can make you something to eat."

He glanced up and even in the dim light from the outdoor bulb, I could see how weary he was. "If it's not too much trouble."

"Not at all." I had an ulterior motive. Actually, several motives. First and foremost, feeding a tired traveler. Second, finding out what was new about Joe's murder. And third—

"Sorry I didn't make it back for your interview," he said as he walked toward the door, Lady running ahead. "Got caught up."

I stood aside to let them enter first. "No problem. We can do it tomorrow." I closed the door and locked it, then led the way through. "Do you mind eating in the kitchen?"

He made a gentle scoffing sound, teasing me. "Not up to my usual standards but I suppose it will do. At home, I eat standing up over the sink. Can we do that?"

Looking over my shoulder, I said, "If you like. Anything for our guests." That last sentence echoed in my mind and I almost blurted a disclaimer. *Almost anything.* Thankfully, I managed to keep my mouth closed.

Why draw attention to what might be considered innuendo?

In the kitchen, I directed him to a chair. "Would you like something to drink? Glass of wine? Beer? Sparkling cold well water with mint?"

"A beer wouldn't go amiss." He stretched out his legs with a sigh. "Sounds like heaven, actually."

"Bitter or ale?"

"Bitter, please."

We liked the same beer. I fetched him a can from the larder. "We have ratatouille or I can make you a sandwich."

He popped the top and took a long drink. "Ratatouille sounds great, thanks."

"Coming right up." I took the container out of the fridge and spooned some into a pan. After turning the gas on, I took out a couple of rolls and the butter and set them on the table.

Finlay was sitting slumped in his seat, sipping beer and staring into space. "I'm thinking about putting in a transfer back. Monkwell isn't the quiet retreat I was hoping for."

I gave him a sharp glance. "Really?" Then I noticed the humor glinting in his eyes. "Oh, you. You are totally right, though. There haven't been this many murders at Ravensea for over a hundred years."

"All streaks must end, I suppose."

His deadpan delivery startled a laugh. "Suppose so." I sighed as I gave the pan a stir. "Unfortunately, it's under my watch."

"I'm sorry about that, Nora," he said softly. "I can see how hard you're working to make the bed-and-breakfast a success."

I went over to the cupboard for a pottery bowl.

"Thanks. No cancelations yet, thank goodness." The next guests were scheduled for the end of the month. This first batch was our soft opening, as they call it, with time to adjust between bookings. "It might help that you're telling the public that Joe drowned."

To my surprise, Gavin and Lorna Cargill had said as much at the social. Apparently neither the press release nor the rumor mill included details about the condition of his body or the possible connection to smuggling. Brian hadn't even known about it, or so he said when he arrived late, having been "chasing down a rare bird."

"The actual words were"—he looked at his phone—"'A man's body was found today washed up on the beach in Dragon's Cove, Monkwell. The police are investigating and the name of the deceased and the cause of death have not yet been released.'"

"We won't say anything here. We clued in to your strategy when the Cargills told us the story." I certainly wasn't going to tell anyone outside the family circle that I'd found Joe. Not even my best friends. Not until we solved these murders. "By the way, what *was* the cause of death?"

Finlay hesitated and I thought he'd refuse to tell me. "Head injury," he finally said. "Not drowning. No water in the lungs."

"The same MO as Hilda." I ladled the hot stew into the bowl. "Although that's a very generic method." I carried the bowl to the table, made sure the salt and pepper were within reach. "Not the same murder weapon, though. Unless someone carried off one of the garden stones, which isn't likely. Who wanders around with a big stone ball?" He was staring up at me. "Need anything else? Another beer?"

"All set, thanks." He looked down at his meal. "This

looks excellent." As he dipped his spoon into the bowl, he asked, "Sit with me? I'd enjoy the company."

He didn't have to ask me twice. I poured a glass of mint water and joined him at the table. No more murder talk tonight. This was our time.

CHAPTER 22

The promised rain was lashing against my windows when I woke up the next morning. My first thought was the trip Tamsyn and I were taking today. Driving in the rain on Yorkshire's winding, narrow roads wasn't ideal.

I sat up in bed, nudging a disgruntled Ruffian aside, and brought up the radar map on my phone. The green blob was over us right now, projected to move out in a couple of hours. My garden would get a lovely drenching and then the sun would make everything take off.

Putting the phone aside, I went over to the window. A figure in a black rain slicker was moving through the knot garden. Who was that, up so early? Then I noticed the small white dog. Finlay and Lady, taking an early morning stroll.

I perched on the windowsill, gazing at the view—and Finlay. Last night had been really nice. We'd chatted about this and that, nothing really earth-shattering. Books we'd read lately, recommendations for binge-watching on television, summer activities we liked.

Our conversation had been totally normal, as if we were on a date, one that was going particularly well. Except that we were in the middle of two murder investigations, the results of which might derail my family's future.

Yeah, all good except for that difficult detail.

In the garden, man and dog disappeared out of view, my cue to shower and dress. We had breakfast to put on and clear and then Tamsyn and I were leaving for most of the day.

"How was dinner?" Tamsyn stood in the doorway, adorable with her rumpled hair and wrinkled floral pajamas. "With Finlay, I mean."

"Fine. We had a nice chat." I decided to wear the same jeans again, at least for breakfast. "Should we dress up for our meeting?" We were meeting Harold at a restaurant and then stopping by Horn House. I didn't want to dress too casually.

"I think so." Tamsyn went to my closet and began pawing through the hanging clothes. "Perfect." She pulled out a sleeveless print crepe dress with a cowl-neck. "Easy and stylish."

The tags were still on it, I noticed. Easy I'd been doing. Stylish, not so much. I dug around and found a pair of mules. "These will work, right?"

She examined the shoes, nodded, and selected another dress. "Mind if I borrow this?"

When we drove through the gate later that morning, the sun was already glinting off the raindrops edging stonework and foliage. The sky was a tender blue and the day had a fresh-washed feeling.

"How are you doing?" Tamsyn asked. "After yesterday, I mean."

I slowed for a puddle, the water whooshing on both sides like a boat wake. "I'm okay. Trying not to think about it too much." The shock of realizing that there had been a body lying on the beach while I ignorantly collected seaweed would take a while to fade.

"Sorry to bring it up." Tamsyn turned to stare out the window.

We crossed the causeway and continued straight up the hill, through the village.

"Don't apologize. Although it was pretty gruesome, the sailcloth covered everything except his hand. Poor Guy had to actually identify the body."

"Poor *you*. I can't believe that you've stumbled over two bodies."

"Me either. Maybe you should do the honors next time." I threw her a mocking smile.

She put a hand over her face with a shudder. "No, thank you."

Finlay had done brief interviews with us after breakfast. He'd taken me through yesterday, the decision to go down to the cove and my movements while there.

At the top of the hill, Tamsyn directed me to turn north, toward Whitby and points beyond. We were meeting Harold in Parva-by-the-Sea, a beautiful village popular with tourists. What Monkwell aspired to be when it grew up.

"Main road or back way?" I asked at an intersection outside Whitby. The main route led inland and then we'd cut back toward the village. The other way edged the water, passing through farms and hamlets.

Tamsyn checked the time. "Back way. It's actually shorter and there won't be as much traffic."

"The coast route it is." With a little flutter of excitement, I flipped the indicator. Traveling off the beaten path was one of my favorite pastimes.

Less than an hour later, we reached Parva-by-the-Sea

without incident, except for a brief stop to let a herd of sheep go across the road. My favorite type of commuters.

The village was fronted by a long beach and cliffs, the buildings tightly packed in a grid of streets. "Where's Harold's home in relation to here?" I asked as we looked for a parking spot.

"A few miles inland, inside the park."

The North York Moors National Park encompassed over five hundred square miles, much of it still wild and home to many birds, wildlife, and plant species.

We found room in a car park, paid, and walked a few blocks to Gilbert's, where we were meeting Harold. The front of the restaurant looked classic with its painted wood panels, large glass windows, and gold lettering. Inside, it was sleek and modern, with tables lining each side of the narrow space.

The hostess flicked her long ponytail back as she gathered menus. "Two for lunch?"

Tamsyn craned toward the rear. "We're meeting someone."

A man sitting by himself had raised his arm in greeting.

Following her gaze, the hostess started walking. "Right this way."

Harold Sutcliffe rose to his feet as we approached. Tall and thin, with receding sandy curls and pale blue eyes, he wore an air of morose ennui.

"Tamsyn!" he cried, rousing himself enough to embrace her with air kisses. "How are you, love?"

The hostess left the menus on the table and ducked away.

"I'm fine, Harold." Tamsyn's smile was wide. Her public face, I called it. Any observer would think that she adored Harold and wouldn't want to be anywhere else.

Perhaps that was true. Harold looked all right if a bit clubbish.

He turned to me now. "This must be your sister." He put out a hand. "Harold Sutcliffe. Lovely to meet you."

"Nora Asquith," I murmured. "Nice to meet you as well."

Harold gestured to the chairs and we sat. A brief silence fell and we all picked up the menus. We were here to discuss the distressing loss of his family property and it was hard to pretend it was merely a social occasion.

"What's good here?" Tamsyn asked.

"Everything." Harold was still studying the menu. "They do a decent scampi." After a pause, "My treat. Have anything you like."

Tamsyn ordered a smoked salmon salad and I had the scampi, as did Harold. The server also brought us lemonade. Harold had wine.

"Well," our host said, spinning his glass by the stem. "Patrick Horn. He's approached you?"

"He kidnapped us," I said.

That made Harold sit up. "What? You're joking." He frowned. "How?"

We both laughed. "He invited us onto his yacht," Tamsyn explained. "We got our signals crossed and he lifted anchor. No worries. We didn't get far."

"Our voyage was interrupted by the coastguard." Making a sudden mental connection, I gasped. Harold and Tamsyn stared at me. "I'm okay. Just wondering why they stopped him, that's all."

Tamsyn got it. "Hmm. So do I."

Harold looked back and forth between us. "Sorry. I'm lost."

I inhaled, wondering how much we should tell him.

"Can we trust you to keep whatever we say under your hat?"

He patted his bare head. "Of course. I'm completely trustworthy."

"You are," Tamsyn said. "You've kept a secret or two of mine." Her dimples flashed and he reddened.

Interesting. No time to probe, however. "We've heard there are smugglers operating in the Monkwell area . . . and we've had two deaths recently." If the police weren't revealing Joe's cause of death, I wasn't about to, not even to Tamsyn's friend.

"Deaths?" Harold's nose wrinkled. "Is Toot-Your-Own-Horn escalating his methods?"

"I hope not," I said. Although . . . if Hilda's murder brought enough bad publicity, our business would fail and then Patrick could try to swoop in with a low-ball offer. That would be risky in more ways than one.

"Good name for him," Tamsyn said. "The ego on that man."

"Truly." Harold sat back. "Our food is arriving."

After the server brought our lunch, we took a moment to dig in. The langoustines were fresh and large, the wine-and-butter sauce delicious.

"Have one," I said to Tamsyn, who was eyeing my meal.

"Maybe I will." She stabbed a piece of seafood and, for good measure, took a hot, salty chip.

Once we'd satisfied our initial hunger, Tamsyn smoothed her napkin across her lap. "Harold, you mentioned Patrick's methods. What were they, exactly? We need to know."

Between bites, Harold told us the story. "I inherited the place ten years ago after my father died. As you can imagine, there were some difficulties straightening out the estate. A larger problem was what to do with the place. Too large, really, for just me. So, I had a brilliant idea. I would convert it to a hotel."

Sutcliffe Hall was huge, a sprawling manor with thirty bedrooms, a banqueting hall, conservatory, and acres of parkland.

"I began on a small scale, adding en suite bathrooms in one wing, leasing space to an upscale restaurant for dinners. Hosting weddings and so on. I was able to plow the profits back in for renovations and expansion. Even got a silent partner or two interested." He stared into space, obviously caught up in memories.

Far as I could tell, Harold had a sound plan. He'd developed the business gradually, making sure he was on firm footing before proceeding.

"What went wrong?" Tamsyn asked softly.

Harold took a moment to answer. "This is still hard for me to talk about."

Tamsyn touched his hand. "Don't feel you must, if it's too difficult."

Inwardly, I groaned. While I certainly didn't want to trample his feelings or make him relive a difficult experience, I hoped he wouldn't leave us hanging.

"We appreciate whatever you can share," she went on. "Ravensea Castle means everything to me. Us. I'm sure you understand that."

Harold's gaze was somber. "Of course. You've been there since what, the eleven hundreds or something? It's criminal what Horn is doing. Even worse, he's regarded as a hero for dumping money into stately homes."

My pulse jolted. "Criminal? Like, actually illegal?"

His lips twisted in a rueful smile. "Nothing overt, I'm sorry to report. He hires agitators to oppose plans, to rouse public opinion against a project. Then, once he's firmly at the helm, all opposition melts away." He made a brushing motion with his hand. "Like magic."

Pieces came together in my mind. "That sounds familiar," I said with foreboding. "Our project is tiny compared to yours. Only four bedrooms. Breakfast and some dinners. Should have been a shoo-in, as they say, what with our local standing and good reputation."

Harold tapped his fingers on the table. "Let me guess. Local residents came out of the woodwork to object, oppose, and argue every step of the way."

"Yes. Led by one woman, a newcomer to town." I wrinkled my nose. "To be fair, she complained about plenty of other things as well. Quite a crank in general."

"Smoke screen," Harold said. "I'm convinced that my crank was hired by Horn to wear me down, to discourage me. I almost went mad with frustration at times." He mimed tearing out his hair. "Now she's gone and the hotel is doing well. I'm much richer, sure, but have to live with the fact that I sold my family legacy."

"Who was your crank?" I asked, my heart thudding as I waited for the answer.

"A woman named Hilda Dibble. Have you heard of her?"

CHAPTER 23

"Oh, yeah," I managed to mutter. "Sure have." Had Patrick Horn paid Hilda to move to Monkwell and make my life miserable? That put a whole new spin on the situation.

"Tell him about Hilda," Tamsyn urged.

The server came by to check on us, offering drink refills. After Harold's startling news, I would have loved something medicinal. I had to drive, however, plus keep my wits about me for our visit to Horn House.

"Please do. I'm very curious." Harold scrolled on his phone. "Here's a newspaper article where she's quoted. Take a look."

We leaned close together to read the story. Hilda had ranted on about "preserving our history" and "preventing tasteless renovations to historic properties."

I gave Harold his phone. "She used the exact same wording talking about us." I gave Harold an overview. "Like you, I wanted to find additional revenue to support our property. We're not huge, never will be, but renting out bedrooms would be a low-impact way to bring in extra cash, I thought. I also have have an herbal products business, including bath and body, which was a nice crossover."

"Nora makes wonderful products," Tamsyn put in. She patted her cheek. "I owe this complexion to her."

I stared at my sister, a sudden idea striking me. "Want to make some adverts for Castle Apothecary?" Then I thought of another totally obvious tactic. "And reels about the castle? You'll be a huge draw." We could film a video tour.

"Great idea," Harold said. "You're very well-known, Tamsyn. Not to mention gorgeous."

Tamsyn blinked and blushed, flattered and a little taken aback. I hadn't forgotten that, right up until opening day, she'd been against my scheme to take in paying guests. What a twist to have her doing an endorsement.

I gave her a warm and knowing smile. "We can talk about it later." Turning back to Harold, I said, "So there I am, plugging away with my plans. I take them to the local council expecting, if not a rubber stamp, at least minimal objections. Then Hilda Dibble showed up at one of the meetings. A year later, here I am, finally with permits in hand and open. I had to fight every step of the way."

Harold picked up his second glass of wine and sipped. "I'm truly glad that you were able to succeed despite Hilda's machinations. Where is she now? Moved on to a different town to wreak havoc?" When we didn't say anything immediately, he frowned. "What's wrong?"

I swallowed, reluctant to share the bad news. "Hilda has, um, passed away."

He made a sound of disbelief. "I'm sorry. I didn't like her but I certainly didn't wish her ill." He paused. "Not much, anyway. Perhaps poverty and shame."

She'd gotten much worse than social humiliation, that was for sure.

"Hilda wasn't that old," Harold said. "Early fifties? What happened?"

I pondered how to answer. Harold was a good sort but was it wise to confide in him? If he hadn't heard about her murder, why spread the news? Tamsyn didn't say anything, leaving the decision up to me.

Then I thought, maybe he has an insight into Hilda's life. Knows something with bearing on her death.

"Hilda was murdered," I said baldly.

Harold yipped, pushing back in his seat at the same time. The diners around us glanced over with curiosity. Waving his hand, he smiled an apology before pulling his chair in again. "Sorry. You startled me. I was expecting a medical condition or a car accident." He leaned forward, speaking in a low tone. "When did this happen?"

"A few days ago," I said. "In the castle garden. No arrest yet."

He rubbed his chin, eyes distant as he mulled over this information. "Think someone was trying to pin it on you? Odd location, wasn't it? Surely she wasn't welcome there, after the trouble she gave you."

"I think the same." I was relieved that a person of obvious good sense so quickly came to that conclusion. "It happened in the middle of the night, so she was lured there somehow by someone with a grudge."

Harold's smile was sly. "It wasn't me, I can promise you that much. I would have done it in a, uh, more neutral location." He mimed pushing someone. "A long walk on a short pier." He leaned forward again. "Any other local enemies?"

"A few, I'm sure," I said. "The main one, well, he's also dead." I bit my tongue, not wanting to reveal Joe's death as a murder.

Tamsyn smoothly stepped in. "A local man has passed away. Police haven't released the cause yet."

"Oh. Right. The other death you mentioned." He went

on. "They say it's usually the love interest. Did she have one? Hilda was quite the heartbreaker, you know." He closed his eyes briefly. "Even came on to me one night after a few too many drinks. Not that she was unattractive physically. Ugly personality."

I didn't want to reveal the Patrick Horn card yet. We had learned that Hilda worked for him, or so Harold believed.

"No one that we know of for sure," I said.

Harold put up a finger. "How about her friend? Sonia . . . Sadie . . . no, Sandra. She might be of help."

"Sandra Snelling?"

"That's it. Maybe she would have some insight for you." He made a face. "She and Hilda used to be joined at the hip. Like Tweedledee and Tweedledum."

"Still were. Did Sandra live in Parva-by-the-Sea, too?"

Harold nodded. "They were neighbors. Maybe you can track her down."

"We already have," Tamsyn said. "She lives in Monkwell now."

"Odd. They followed each other around? Maybe Sandra was on Patrick's payroll as well, though she was more the cheering section." Harold glanced at our empty plates. "Who wants dessert?"

"That was really nice," I told Tamsyn as we drove away from Parva-by-the-Sea. "I really like Harold."

Although we'd declined dessert, we lingered over cups of tea and coffee and chatted about lighter topics. Harold had plenty to say about Ben's perfidy, which pleased Tamsyn, and they promised to keep in touch much better going forward. I invited him to come by the castle any-time. He said he'd promote Ravensea to his friends, so our lunch was an all-around success, I thought.

"He's great," Tamsyn agreed. "I feel so sorry for him, though. What a terrible blow it must have been to lose Sutcliffe Manor. I can't imagine."

"Neither can I. We are going to hang onto Ravensea, come hell or high water."

Tamsyn regarded me with approval. "You are fierce. I like that about you."

"Except when we both want the same thing," I joked. I gestured toward my phone. "Want to update the directions on GPS?"

Horn House was north of here, also close to the coast.

"Ooh, they offer afternoon tea," Tamsyn said. "Shall I book us in?"

Although my full belly objected, I said, "Sure. That will give us an excuse to hang around."

"Done." Tamsyn set the phone in the holder. The robotic voice gave us the first direction and we were on our way.

Horn House was set upon a rise overlooking the water, announced by a discreet brass sign on one of two massive pillars guarding the main entrance.

"I guess if you have to ask, you don't belong here," Tamsyn quipped.

We drove slowly along the wide, winding drive, taking in acres of rolling lawns, groups of trees, and garden areas.

I had to admit being impressed, almost intimidated. This was truly a stately home. One thing, though. "I don't see anywhere along here that's dangerous to navigate."

Tamsyn studied her phone. "They must have gone out

the back way. That route is very steep and narrow, with switchbacks." She peered at the image again. "It's actually a shortcut to the village and main road so that's why people use it."

"That makes sense."

We rounded a final corner and Horn House came into view. Constructed of age-darkened yellow stone, a central tower overlooked a fountain in a circular forecourt. Wings extended in both directions, three stories of windows capped with a peaked pediment at intervals and numerous chimney pots.

The building loomed over the countryside, much like the Horn family had over their so-called inferiors, dominating the economy in the area.

Much like Patrick Horn was attempting to do to us.

We pulled around to the front door, where valets waited to assist. As we got out, I gave my keys over, thinking that my Saab 900 had to be the humblest in the lot. At least it was a classic.

"Just here for the day," Tamsyn said to explain our lack of luggage. She swept inside, nodding regally to the attendant holding the door for us.

"I can't believe Mum and Dad used to hang out here," I whispered to her when we entered the lobby, an enchanting space of cream-painted arches and wainscoting offset by pale green walls and delicate gold hanging lights and chandeliers.

"It probably didn't look like this," Tamsyn whispered back. "This is all very up-to-the-minute."

I'd pictured us discreetly poking around the place but Tamsyn had other ideas. She walked right up to the front desk. "Hello," she said, smiling until the desk clerk did the same. "I'm Tamsyn Asquith." She paused, allowing the name to sink in.

The young woman's eyes grew wide and she gave a tiny gasp. "Ms. Asquith. I love your show." She spoke in a low voice, her body language still controlled. Probably trained to treat celebrities and other notables with restraint. After ten seconds of starstruck goggling, she said, "How may I help you today?"

I wondered what Tamsyn would say. That the hotel owner was trying to wrest our property from us probably wouldn't be fruitful. At best, the clerk would think we were off our rockers.

"I'd love a tour, if it's possible. If someone is available." Tamsyn smiled again.

"Are you thinking of holding an event here?" The clerk filled in the blanks for her. She reached for her phone. "I'll see if the manager is available."

After a moment, she put the receiver down. "He'll be right with you. Please feel free to have a seat."

Another guest was approaching the desk, so we got out of the way.

"This place is gorgeous," Tamsyn said as we wandered around the lobby. "Five-star rating."

"Wow. That's impressive." What were we? Half a star? Oh well. We offered an authentic experience, I told myself.

Still waiting, we were peeking into the adjacent room—little seating groups with tiny round tables—when Tamsyn nudged me hard. "Patrick. Walking through the lobby." She took my arm and pulled me through into the sitting room and off to one side.

From here, I could see Patrick swaggering along, all bluster and pride, talking to the woman beside him.

Recognition hit me like a dash of cold water. "Sandra Snelling. What's she doing here?" Suspicion churned. "Is she taking over for Hilda?"

"Or maybe she's been on the payroll all along," Tamsyn said darkly. "She seemed so nice, too. Even gave me a kitten."

"Well, not wanting to take Primrose might have been a clue." What kind of person could say no to a kitten, especially one belonging to a late friend?

I watched as Patrick and Sandra disappeared through an arch on the other end of the lobby. "They're gone."

Tamsyn gritted her teeth, hands fisted. "I hope the manager doesn't mention my name. How are we going to explain what we're doing here?"

Good question. "Bluff it out, I suppose. We have every right to check out his operation before entertaining his offer."

"True." Tamsyn gestured toward the desk. "Is that the manager, do you think?"

"Looks like it." A balding middle-aged man wearing a suit was speaking to the desk clerk. She pointed this way.

We went through the lobby to meet him. "Ms. Asquith?" he asked, extending his hand. "How lovely to meet you. I'm Mr. Smith, the hotel's general manager."

Mr. Smith took us through the hotel, showing us the drawing room and library, each of the three restaurants, the indoor pool and spa, the most luxurious suites, and, finally, delivering us back to the sitting room for tea.

"If there is anything I can do . . ." he said with a little bow as he showed us to a table. Most of the others were already full. A hotel packet already sat at one place setting, an anticipatory touch I thought went above and beyond.

"Thank you so much for your time." Tamsyn shook his hand. "Everything is very impressive."

He shook my hand as well and then was gone, speaking to staff as he made his way through.

"Well," Tamsyn said as we settled at the table. "I'm impressed."

"Me too." A jumble of images from the tour floated through my mind. Every last detail was impeccable and in the best taste. "What could he do with Ravensea, I wonder."

"Bite your tongue," Tamsyn said tartly. She smiled up at the server who naturally came over right then. "Hello. How are you?"

The server said she was fine, then asked what kind of tea we wanted, explaining that we'd get individual pots and share tiers of sandwiches and sweets.

One side benefit of walking miles around the hotel was that my appetite had returned. "Everything looks incredible," I said, reaching for a smoked salmon sandwich.

"Hold on," Tamsyn said. "Take pictures. We might do teas at some point."

"Great idea." I took several photographs, then dug in, using two plates—one for the savory, one for sweet. They had given us the cutest little cream puffs and tarts.

"I want to go back to the library before we leave," Tamsyn said. "Did you notice the wall of old photographs? They reminded me of the ones Dad showed us. Same era."

I poured more tea from the (real) silver teapot. "I did. Unfortunately, Mr. Smith whisked us right through."

"The suite with the upstairs bedroom was divine," Tamsyn said with a sigh.

"We have spiral staircases, too," I pointed out. Ours were gloomy and stone, with arrow-slit windows, but still.

Tamsyn took a bite of sandwich. "We need to lean into our unique selling proposition. 'Staying at Ravensea is an adventure. Step back to medieval times with us.'"

I laughed. "People are enchanted by castles and contentious noble families, don't forget." I thought of a certain television show that had been extremely popular.

"True." Her tone was casual when she informed me, "I'm going to put Ravensea forward as a location for *Mist on the Moors*, if that's all right with you and Dad."

I didn't know what to ask first: how much it paid or if she'd decided to take the role, so I merely said, "Fantastic. Let me know when and we can block off the dates."

"I will." She paused. "Even if I'm not in the show, Ravensea can still be a location. I'll connect you to the scout they're using."

"They'll probably want a package, right?" I immediately began to think about which photographs to use and what I'd say in a write-up.

In addition to the extra revenue, the cachet of being a filming location would really boost our status. Maybe they'd let us share stills from the production on our website.

Tamsyn was being really helpful and positive about the new venture, I'd noticed. "Thanks for your support, sis," I said. "You're really encouraging me. Maybe we'll make it after all."

She waved a hand. "I wish I'd come on board sooner. I feel like such a brat for letting you struggle alone." Then, to play down the soft side she'd risked revealing, she pointed to the stand. "I call dibs on the last chocolate tart."

After tea, we made our way back to the library, a long room with floor-to-ceiling bookcases and inviting armchairs placed at intervals. As Tamsyn had noted, there was an extensive grouping of photographs on the only available wall, an old painting of Horn House in the center.

"It's a history exhibit," I said when we got close enough to study the photographs.

Typed labels under the pictures gave year, event, and in some cases, names. Many were family portraits, others showed the vast staff the hall had once needed. The most recent showed Patrick and his brother, Dennis, as adults.

"Ah, here we go," Tamsyn said. "New Year's Eve."

"Hilda had a photograph from the same night." I took a closer look. "She's in this one, next to Patrick. There's Celia and Dennis. And who's that?"

Tamsyn bent toward the photo. "I think it's Sandra. With . . . Gavin Cargill?"

"They used to be married." Again, something struck me as odd. "Sandra was around back then, obviously. But when she was telling us about Celia at Hilda's house, I didn't get that impression at all."

Tamsyn straightened a frame. "I thought she and Hilda were recent friends, like you mentioned to Harold. Maybe she doesn't like to talk about the ex." She set her jaw. "Who does?"

"Well, having lunch with the new wife is really weird, then." I took a picture of the New Year's Eve photograph. "I'm ready if you are."

Our last task was to check out the place where Dennis and Celia had crashed all those years ago. To get to the rear exit from the estate, we drove around the house and through a parking lot. As we approached the back gate, a delivery van came through. This route must be used by tradesmen and employees.

Beyond the gate, the lane immediately began to head downhill. The Saab handled corners well but I had to slow to thirty kilometers per hour to make it around the first curve, which was edged by trees and thick undergrowth. This wasn't the spot.

The next curve had to be it: long and sharp with a steep drop-off on one side. A mistake here and a vehicle would tumble down the slope until it hit a tree.

"Pull over," Tamsyn said. "I want to take a look."

I parked on the narrow shoulder and we got out. Thirty years on, there wasn't any sign of the deadly accident. No tire marks through the scrub or scars on the trees.

"He'd driven this road hundreds of times before. Maybe thousands." Tamsyn edged closer to the drop-off. "What was different that time?"

"He and Celia were fighting? Or all lovey-dovey?" I suggested. I took a few photographs with my phone for later reference.

"Maybe. I think there's more to it, don't you?"

I certainly did, with an inheritance at stake. How could we ever prove anything, though? The wrecked car was long gone and no trace remained of the accident.

Hearing the purr of a motor, I glanced up the road, then at my car, making sure it was far enough over.

A black luxury sedan soon nosed into view, moving at a snail's pace. A man was at the wheel. Patrick Horn.

CHAPTER 24

"Hell's bells," Tamsyn exclaimed. "Talk about bad timing."

Seriously. Another minute or two and we would have been on our way with no one being the wiser.

The car window rolled down. "Is everything all right?" Patrick asked. "You're not having car trouble?"

We glanced at each other. Here was an easy out. "We're fine," I said. "Worried about overheating so I stopped for a moment."

"Enough water in the radiator?"

"Yes, already checked. I'll have our local mechanic take a look later."

"If you're sure. I can call for help. Not much fun being stranded in the countryside."

Will you leave already? "Any sign of trouble and we'll be right on it," I said, displaying my phone.

He didn't respond. Neither did he roll up his window and continue driving. "You should have told me you were coming," he said, smiling. "I would have given you the grand tour."

"We appreciate that," Tamsyn said. "It was a spur-of-the-moment thing. We didn't even know you were here. Delicious high tea, by the way."

"We thought you had sailed away, maybe to Holland

or France." I winced at his scowl. He hadn't liked being reminded of our ill-fated excursion, I guessed.

"No, just came up the coast to spend some time here." He gave us and the Saab another once-over. "Are you sure you're all right?"

"Perfectly," Tamsyn said. "We'll be fine."

"Good day, then. See you later." The window rolled up and the car began to move forward.

We watched until the taillights, flashing as he navigated another steep curve, vanished out of view.

"Phew," Tamsyn said. "Let's get out of here."

We hopped into the Saab and continued down the hill, my heart still pounding from the nerve-racking encounter.

"I was so worried he'd guess what we were doing." I had the car in a lower gear to keep control. The lane had a few more curves before the rear gates came into view.

"How could he have any idea?" Tamsyn took out her phone and began checking messages. "He doesn't know we know about Celia's death."

"True. Unless Sandra mentioned it." I braked at the intersection with the road. "Which way?"

She told me, briefly explaining the route back to Monkwell. "I was surprised to see her with Patrick. Although I probably shouldn't have been. He and Hilda were close."

I thought of the silk robe. "Yeah, really close. I was floored when I learned Sandra was Gavin's ex-wife, too."

"I wonder if Sandra has also been working for Patrick, hassling property owners."

"If so, she might take up Hilda's mantle." I groaned. "I was hoping all the opposition was over." To be honest, I'd been relieved that Hilda's relentless campaign against the bed-and-breakfast had stopped permanently with her death.

"We'll confront her. Tell her we won't put up with it."

"Now that we know money is involved, definitely. Before, I was trying to manage public relations and not make too many enemies." I'd had to maintain a professional decorum and watch every word I said or put in writing. Refrain from responding to nasty social media posts. It hadn't been easy.

"Don't worry. The villagers will probably run her out of town with pitchforks and torches. No one likes a cheat."

I smiled at the image. Monkwell folks were very loyal to their own.

A phone rang. "That's mine." Tamsyn studied the screen. "It's Brian. I'll put him on speaker." She placed the phone between us. "Hello, Brian. I'm with Nora, in the car. We're heading back from Horn House."

"Hello, Nora." Brian's voice was tinny but clear.

"Hey," I called, feeling as though I was shouting down a well. Using speakerphone was always a little strange.

"Horn House, huh?" he asked. "Learn anything interesting?"

"Not really," Tamsyn said. "There's no sign of the accident now. It is a supersharp curve, though. Nora can send you pictures."

"Besides it being a corner that you don't want to miss, nothing stood out," I added. "What gets me is that Dennis knew the road. Why did he crash that day? According to reports, it was clear and dry."

"Driving too fast, distracted . . . no cell phones back then, right?" Brian's voice held humor despite the serious nature of our discussion.

Speaking of distracted, I was keeping my eyes on the road while we chatted. Our route was taking us along the edge of the moors and traffic was light.

"I've come up with a theory," he went on. "Thanks to an old movie I remembered. *Thunder Road*. Ever heard of it?"

We both squealed. "Yes," Tamsyn said. "Hilda was watching that. So tell us, Brian. What did you figure out?"

"Spike strips. Someone put them out and Dennis hit them. The tires popped and he careened off the road. Then someone removed the strips before anyone showed up."

And no one was the wiser. The ruined tires would have been chalked up to the accident.

Hilda must have figured it out as well. Had that knowledge led to her death?

Tamsyn's face creased in distress. "How horrible. I'm so sorry, Brian."

His voice was muffled. "Yeah. Well. Figuring it out is helping me deal, believe it or not." He cleared his throat. "What will really help is bringing the bastards to justice."

"Absolutely." Tamsyn's jaw set with resolve. "That needs to happen."

How, though? After all this time, the culprits weren't likely to suddenly confess. Had Patrick acted alone? Or did he have help? Judging by the way he handled property extortion, I guessed he'd had a henchman or two. It would have been incriminating if he'd been seen on the back lane that day. He'd probably stayed well away, made sure that he had an alibi.

My stomach twisted. Our parents had been his alibi. Part of it, anyway, along with the other guests.

"We'll talk more when we get back," Tamsyn said. "We'll be there within the hour."

"Unfortunately, I won't be here," Brian said. "I have . . . um, something I need to do. Just came up."

"Oh, okay. See you later, then." Barely waiting until

he signed off, Tamsyn disconnected and practically slammed the phone down.

"What's the matter?" I asked, thinking her reaction was rather extreme.

"I must have read his signals wrong." My sister's lips were tight. "I feel like such a fool."

"Why? He called you, remember?"

"About his mum." Tamsyn shifted in her seat. "I feel like he's hiding something from me. Not just now. A couple other times as well." She scowled. "He's probably married."

I thought Brian was a nice guy and she was probably overreacting. Not that I could blame her, after Ben Morrison's betrayal.

"Have you stalked him online? To find out if he *is* married?"

Her head shake was firm. "No, I'm not doing that. It's totally pathetic."

Had to agree, not that I hadn't indulged a time or two. "I'm sure it will all work out." No, I actually was not. My sister deserved better than lame platitudes. "Sorry. I don't know what's going on with him. I hope it's totally innocent and he tells you more when you see him."

"Me too." Tamsyn sat back with a sigh. "I really hate dating. It's such a minefield nowadays."

"Maybe so. It's still better than having Dad arrange marriages for us, like way back." I riffed on, describing imaginary suitors vying for her hand from all around the land.

As I hoped, this flight of fancy made her laugh. The rest of the way back to the castle, we bantered and joked, shared memories—and confided in each other.

"I'm so glad you're home," I said impulsively as we pulled through the castle gate.

"Me too." Tamsyn sighed. "I can't wait to pour a glass of wine and sit on the terrace."

Bees were buzzing joyfully in the warm, fragrant garden when I arrived, carrying a bucket for weeds, a basket for clippings, and a metal bottle of water. Rolf was padding along behind me after promising to be good and not trample anything.

We'd see.

Tamsyn waved at me from the terrace, where she was reading a magazine and drinking wine. Today's social had been canceled because all the guests were out, Janet had informed us. Hence my foray out here, to do some weeding—which never ended—and harvest limeflower and sweet cicely for tea.

We'd updated the others about the results of our trip, of course. Dad had said he was going to contact our attorney and have him write a cease and desist should Sandra try any tricks. Enough is enough, he'd thundered.

I quite agreed with him.

Weeding first, to get it out of the way. I sat on the ground and began plucking out the invaders by hand or using a cultivator. Weeding was a chore, but a strangely satisfying one. I imagined the plants sighing in relief, able to spread out their roots once the parasitic growth was gone. Rolf, after an exploratory sniff, lounged on the grass, panting.

After cleaning up a couple of flower beds, I moved over to the lime tree, also known as a linden tree. Standing among the clusters of creamy flowers, I closed my eyes and inhaled, enjoying their sweet, strong scent. Bees loved limeflower blossoms and they made delicious honey.

Thundering paws ripped me out of my reverie. I ducked away from the tree to see Rolf dashing along the path toward the summerhouse.

"Rolf, come," I yelled, knowing it was futile. He wasn't coming back. I tried to whistle, like Guy. My attempt sputtered out like a wet tweet.

Although tempted to let him run, I went after him. No telling what trouble he might get into, what unsavory discoveries he might make.

Another body? The thought made me miss a step and I tripped over a lifted brick and almost went flying into a rugosa rose shrub.

He couldn't have scented a body. At this rate, there wouldn't be anyone left.

"Come back, you annoying dog," I shouted. "Don't you run off on me."

His hindquarters disappeared into a dense stand of rhododendrons.

Ever valiant, I pushed through. Nothing. No dog either. I heard panting up ahead and realized he'd taken a shortcut to the trail that led to the chapel and the sacred spring.

Okay. We were going to the chapel.

Now that I knew the destination, I stopped to send Tamsyn a text.

Chasing Rolf to the chapel. Send help if we're not back in a half an hour.

She replied with a thumbs-up.

At least someone knew where I was. This was too large a property, with too many hazards, to wander around without telling anyone. Even before the murders.

I trotted out of the woods into the clearing where the chapel stood. No Rolf. The door was shut, so he wasn't inside.

The sacred spring it was, then. Sacred springs, also known as holy wells, dotted England, and were often thought to have mystical and healing powers. Ours had been discovered by a monk, and for many years, local people believed the water had beneficial properties. I wasn't sure about that, but it was fresh and pure and cold, delightful on a hot day.

The spring was in a glade of hawthorne and ash trees, inside a natural cave where steps had been carved at some point.

Rolf was trudging up the steps when I approached. He stopped and shook, his wet muzzle flinging droplets.

"What? You were thirsty?" I couldn't believe that he'd run all the way over here to drink. Besides the fountain being available in a pinch, Guy kept a dish of water out for him in the walled garden.

His answer was to come over and push his big head into my hand. "All right, boy. I forgive you. Ready to go home?"

Instead of moving toward the path, he went back toward the spring and trotted down the steps.

Rather than wait for him to emerge, I followed him down. I hadn't been to the spring for a while and I wasn't quite sure why. It had always been one of my favorite nooks, dim and cool, water gurgling out of the rock face into a small basin. As kids, we'd pretended that the water could cast spells: invisibility, strength, or make someone fall asleep like Snow White.

Rolf was standing in the chamber, looking toward the far corner, where a couple of cartons sat. That was odd. We didn't store anything down here. Had someone been bottling the water?

I switched on my phone light to read the writing on

the sealed cartons. *Wine.* Someone had left wine here. Six bottles in each box, according to the description.

If this was a smuggling haul, it was pretty small.

Rolf's head went up and a moment later, I heard a sound. Footsteps scraping on the rocky path, followed by a muffled exclamation.

What to do? Set Rolf on them? That was over the top. If they attacked me, then, yes.

I grabbed hold of his collar. "Stay," I warned. "Stay." He growled low and menacing, in his throat.

The footsteps came closer, moving tentatively down the first steps, which were out of my view.

Then I saw a foot, clad in a woman's trainer. Followed by another foot, a pair of jeans-clad legs, and the rest of Lorna Cargill.

CHAPTER 25

Lorna flinched when she saw me. Rolf, recognizing her, gave a woof of joy. I almost did as well, I was so relieved. Not the big, bad smuggler I was expecting. "Hi, there. Exploring the spring?"

"Sort of." Her eyes darted around the cave, finally landing on the cases of wine. "Those yours?"

"I found them here. We keep our wine in the castle cellar." I let go of Rolf's collar and he sat, panting.

"Of course." Her shoulders sagged. "Stupid question." She went over to the cases and examined them, reading the printing on the boxes.

"You carry that brand?" The question popped out of my mouth. If anyone would know vineyards and wine, it would be Lorna. She was co-owner of a chain of wine shops.

"We do." She straightened, still staring at the crates, one hand resting in the small of her back. "You have any idea how these got here?"

I did, but it might not be wise to blab about smugglers. What if I messed up the coastguard's case? "Someone's private stash? We hardly ever come down here."

Lorna folded her arms. "You think maybe someone stole them?"

"Could be." I thought of the Cargill van I'd seen tooling around town. Like any business, the wine shops probably had a problem with inventory leakage, as they call it.

She didn't say anything for a long moment. Figuring I'd ask Will to come get the wine when he could—it was on our property—I started toward the steps.

"I'll see you later," I said. "I just came over here after this rascal. Rolf, come." As I herded him toward the steps, I glanced at Lorna, expecting to see her following us.

She was watching me, an expression on her face I couldn't mistake. She couldn't wait for me to leave. In a flash, I realized why that might be. "Are you involved in the smuggling?" I asked. "Is that why you're down here?" Maybe she'd been tracking goods missing from the shipment.

Her mouth dropped open. "Me?" She shook her head. "I didn't . . . I had nothing . . ." Her eyes were pleading. "Honestly, Nora." She gestured toward the cases. "I'm just finding out about this."

"Right. I'm supposed to believe your husband has been smuggling wine and you had no idea." I probably shouldn't have said that. I took a couple of steps toward the stone stairs, ready to bolt.

"Remember those numbers I was working on?" Her tone was frantic, as if she was trying to convince me. "Things weren't adding up so I started digging. Then I discovered the duties are way below what they should be." She pointed at the cases. "That wine is some of our most expensive. When I heard the coastguard was after smugglers around here—it all came together."

Why was she telling me this? Surely she must realize I would go to the police.

"I want you to file a report," she said, taking me totally off guard. "It can't come from me, understand?" She stepped toward me, urgency in her voice. "If Gavin finds out I've been sneaking around behind his back, investigating him—"

A chill washed over me. "Are you afraid of him? Has he hurt you?"

"No." She sounded almost offended. Then her face crumpled. "He'll think I betrayed him, which I have. I can't face that."

Of course she'd rather keep her hands clean. I didn't blame her. "What were you going to do with the information?"

Lorna shrugged. "Divorce him. Without too much fuss, hopefully. Take my settlement and move to Spain or Capri. Somewhere warm and sunny. Live a simple life."

She probably had wanted to leave him already, before she found out about his criminal activities. This way her conscience was eased, I suppose. Although a spot of blackmail might help get her a better settlement, I cynically thought.

"All right," I finally said. "It's not my business. Your marriage, I mean. The cases of wine, yes. I will be reporting them." I wasn't quite sure I fully believed her, but I'd let the authorities figure it out.

"Rolf, come," I said as I started up the steps. Naturally he barged past, almost knocking me over. "See you later."

Rolf bolted toward home and dinner and I hurried along behind him. That had been a confession that Gavin Cargill was involved in smuggling. It really made sense, considering the fact that he owned a chain of shops. The inventory could be added to the shelves very discreetly and a fiddle with the books would hide the irregularities.

Maybe Gavin had killed Hilda.

If she knew about the smuggling, then she could have

done more than try to blackmail Joe with it. She might have gone to the top dog, so to speak.

Gavin Cargill's pockets were a lot deeper than Joe's, that was for sure.

I could imagine the whole thing. A secret meeting in the garden. Hilda, thinking she's going to receive a fat envelope of money. Instead, Gavin beaned her on the head.

Problem solved.

Or it might have been Joe. The perfect fall guy. He had a bad temper and a strong arm.

And then Gavin had killed Joe. A loose end tied up nice and neat.

The same method, though. Hit on the head. That detail made me doubt Joe's guilt in Hilda's death.

I started running, eager to find Finlay and tell him everything. Was he even at the castle? He'd been returning late every night. I jolted to a halt and took out my phone.

Me: *Where are you?*

Finlay: *At the wharf. Just bought a sailboat. Want to help me take her for a spin?*

He'd mentioned wanting to buy a sailboat during our first real conversation in the garden. Good for him.

Me: *Congrats! I'd love to go. Want me to bring food and drink?*

Finlay: *Would you? That would be lovely.*

Me: *Be there shortly.*

I started running again, this time with the aim of changing my clothes and packing a picnic basket. Being out on the water alone with Finlay would be a perfect opportunity to talk without interruption.

Was this a date? Again my steps slowed. Then I firmly rejected the idea. We couldn't date. He was the investigating officer on two murders where I was a witness. That all had to be cleaned up before we even thought about dating.

Assuming he was interested.

I thought he was. I'd certainly felt a spark. And we got along so well, the conversation flowing easily as it did with the best of friends.

I came down to earth with a thump. Maybe that's all we were. Friends.

Okay. Great. We were friends. And right now we had a couple of murders to solve.

"Janet," I puffed as I burst into the kitchen. "What do we have for a picnic?"

Ensconced in her armchair, cup of tea at hand, she looked up from her knitting. "We have some nice cold coronation chicken for sandwiches and leftover new potato salad. A bottle of wine or beer and Victoria sponge for dessert. Oh, and a thermos of tea or coffee, for later."

I was already grabbing items out of the refrigerator. "Thanks. Finlay and I are going sailing. He just bought a boat. Not sure how long we'll be gone." A thermos of hot drink was a good idea. The sea air chilled quickly in the evening.

"How nice. He'll have a lot of fun with that."

And, if all went well, so would I. Finding a loaf of bread, I placed slices on the cutting board. "Oh, and I ran into Lorna Cargill. Her husband is involved with smuggling, she told me. Don't say anything, okay? I'm going to tell Finlay."

Janet's brow was furrowed with thought. "That makes sense, doesn't it? He's got the perfect setup to move smuggled goods."

"That's what I think, too. Who knows? Maybe that's why the Cargills came here in the first place."

"Poor Will," Janet said. "He has his hopes pinned on a big order from them."

"I know. It totally stinks." Then I remembered my marking idea. "On another topic, I had a huge brainstorm today. We should film ads with Tamsyn for the bed-and-breakfast, my apothecary business, and Will's mead." We could film them all here, at the castle.

"That is a good idea," Janet said with enthusiasm. "She has so much name recognition, plus she's incredibly photogenic. What does she think of the idea?"

"She's considering it. We all have our strengths to contribute, right?"

Janet had started knitting again. "That's certainly true of you three. So different yet remarkably talented."

I darted over to give her a hug. "What would we do without you, Janet?" She'd always been our cheering section, especially important after Mum died.

"Aw, go on with you," she protested. But her smile was pleased. "Do you mind switching on the kettle? I could use a fresh cup of tea."

"'Course not." I made her tea in between the tasks of putting together our picnic supper. I packed everything, including two cans of bitter, in a padded cool box. Then I hurried upstairs to change. Layers, that's how you dressed for sailing.

I found Finlay on one of the floating docks off the wharf. He was coiling line on the deck of a really beautiful pale blue sailboat with a low-profile cabin.

"Ahoy, there," I called. "Permission to come aboard?"

He glanced up with a grin. "Permission granted." He dropped the coil and came to help me with an extended hand. "What do you think of the *Intrepid*?"

I set the cool box and my backpack on the deck. "Totally awesome. What's the length? About thirty feet?"

"She's a 1974 Nicholson 32. Big enough to sleep on, small enough for me to handle alone." His eyes twinkled. "Though better with a mate."

"Speaking of mates, where's Lady?"

Right as I said that, she trundled up from below, wearing a doggie flotation device. She came over to say hello. "What does Lady think?"

"So far, so good. It's nice to have the cabin in case the seas get rough." He pointed at my things. "Shall we put your bags below?"

"Sure. Hold on a sec." I opened my pack and pulled out a windbreaker and a brimmed cap. Better to have them up here if it got windy or cold later.

I carried the pack and he took the cool box and we stepped through the hatch to belowdecks. He showed me the seating area, galley, head, engine, control center, and cabins. The space was compact yet functional and, despite its age, obviously well cared for.

"I love it," I declared. "It's perfect."

"The main thing is, it's stable and reliable." He gestured for me to return to the main deck. "And simple to maintain."

I thought of Patrick's yacht, which was incredibly luxurious and roomy. I preferred Finlay's boat, I decided. Simple was better.

Finlay made a few more preparations, checked the weather and radar charts, then started the engine. We had to leave the harbor and get out into open water before raising the sails.

The motor hummed and the breeze tossed my hair as Finlay expertly steered us with the tiller through obstacles of moored vessels, buoys, and channel markers. As we slowly moved past, I waved at people on the wharf, on other docked sailboats, and fishermen readying their boats for the next day.

The castle loomed to our right, guarding this section of coastline. No one was on the bluff or the beach.

When I spotted the chapel among the trees, I felt a pang of misgiving. I should have told Finlay about the wine stashed at the sacred spring and Lorna Cargill's startling admission before we set off. In case he wanted to cancel our excursion and investigate. Was smuggling actually his purview, though? Didn't that fall under coast-guard jurisdiction?

We were clear of obstacles now, almost out into deep water. I went over and sat beside him. He smiled. "Having fun yet?"

"I am." My guilt forced the words out of my mouth in a rush. "I'm so sorry, Finlay. I should have told you before we left."

He regarded me with humor. "Told me what? Are you prone to seasickness?"

"No. I found two cases of wine at the sacred spring this afternoon. But that's not the important part. Lorna Cargill told me her husband is a smuggler."

My shoulders went up as I braced for a possible explosion of displeasure. For questions as to why I hadn't told him immediately, before we left the harbor.

Instead, he continued to regard me with a thoughtful gaze. He finally nodded. "That fits with what we already know."

"What? You know? Why is he still walking around, then?"

"Everything has to be done by the book," he told me, eyeing the mast. He cut the motor back to a trolling speed. "Besides, it's not my case. The coastguard has it all well in hand."

"I'm sure they do," I muttered, even though I wasn't. So far it looked to me like the smugglers were getting away with, well, murder. If they had killed Joe.

"Gavin probably killed Hilda," I blurted. "That's my latest theory, anyway. She knew about the smuggling, I figure."

Finlay threw me a look. "It's possible. Right now I'm about to raise the mainsail. We're going to start moving pretty fast so hang on, all right?"

Swells were lifting the boat, pulling us back toward shore, so we needed to get underway.

He tugged on the lines, raising both fore and aft sails. Loose, they flapped in the breeze and then, after he cleated and trimmed the lines, we shot off across the bay.

"Yahoo," I cried, caught by the thrill of movement. I braced myself against the tilt of the boat as it heeled, still well under control.

"She handles nicely," Finlay said, staring up at the sails, so white against a deep blue sky.

We skimmed across the water, nothing between us and Europe except water. Once everything was trimmed to his satisfaction, he pulled out his phone. Passing along my information? Catching me watching, he shrugged. "Sorry. Work. I've gotten used to the idea that I'll never completely get away."

"It's the same thing owning a small business." Castle Apothecary didn't involve issues of life and death but it was difficult to totally disconnect. The to-do list was endless, customers contacted me anytime they felt like it, and problems or new ideas were always on my mind.

The bed-and-breakfast was shaping up to be equally consuming. The plus side was, I loved both businesses. My work was my life.

I wondered if Finlay felt the same way. "Do you like being a detective inspector?"

He took a moment to answer. "'Like' is perhaps the wrong word. It's . . . a calling?" He winced. "Sounds a bit woo-woo, doesn't it? All I know is, whenever I think about quitting—and I have, believe me—something in my gut says no."

He gave a self-deprecating shrug. "Plus, life would be really, really boring if I left the force. I can't imagine what else I could possibly do that would be anywhere near as absorbing or satisfying. Guess I'm a glutton for punishment."

I respected his passion for his profession and I felt fortunate that I'd found mine. To me, the idea of spending my life clocking time at a job I hated was a fate worse than death. Despite the difficulties and risk.

"We're lucky," I said. "Both doing what we love."

"We are," he agreed, throwing me a smile.

Our direction was northeast, the shore still in view to our left. From here, I could see tiny toy cars zipping along the coast road.

"Tamsyn and I drove that route today," I told him. "To Parva-by-the-Sea. We met up with someone who sold their property to Patrick Horn. And Hilda was involved."

Interest lit his face. "Really? What did they say?"

As we cruised along, a wake creaming along the bow, the sails taut and full, I filled him in on our day. The revelation that Hilda had been paid by Patrick, Harold believed, and the possibility that Sandra had as well. Then our visit to Horn House and our viewing of the crash site.

"Brian Taylor—you know, Celia's son—thinks that the killer used spike strips—"

Finlay was rummaging around in a duffel. He pulled out a pair of binoculars and pointed them north.

"What is it?" I asked, squinting over the water. The late-day sun was glinting on the water, making it hard to see. Oh, I could see the container ship on the horizon. That thing was huge. He wasn't looking in that direction, though.

He handed me the binos. "Take a look. Brian suggested spike strips? That would work. No evidence once they're removed unless you're specifically looking for it."

I put the glasses to my eyes, making a slight focal adjustment. "I bet they didn't. Especially if Patrick greased palms."

If he would pay people to try to force a sale of a desired property, I had no problem accepting that he might have murdered his brother. Again, a valuable property was at stake.

"See it?" he asked.

Moving the binoculars again, I picked up another sailboat traveling south. "Think so. Were you looking at that boat?" Even from a distance, I could tell it was much larger than ours. I handed the binoculars back to him.

"We are," he said cryptically. He slung the strap around his neck and picked up his phone.

Patrick Horn's sailboat had been berthed up the coast near Horn House. Was Finlay out here to keep an eye on his movements? The sailboat looked about the right size. We were still too far away to make out details.

Was Finlay planning to arrest Patrick for murder and had brought me along? This was an unusual, er, not-a-date.

I wanted to ask questions but instead I tried to play it cool. "Are you hungry? I can go get the food."

"I could eat something," Finlay said. Lady had hopped up at the word *food*. "Do you mind if she goes with you? Her dish is below."

"Of course not. Lady, come." Her nails skittered along behind me to the hatch. Once we got there, I had to help her through and down. She looked back up at me, licking her lips. "You know it's dinnertime, don't you?"

Her folding dish already had kibble in it so I added more. I made sure she had water as well. She'd want to go back up, I figured, so I sat on a cushioned bench to wait.

While Lady crunched away, then lapped at the water, I thought about Patrick Horn. His misdeeds were about to catch up with him. The murder of his brother. The extortion of property. Hilda's death? I couldn't quite believe that he had killed her. Although if he was ruthless enough to kill a sibling, why not a lover?

Greed did terrible things to a person.

Lady came over, signaling that she was finished. I grabbed the cool box and helped her back out through the hatch. Once on deck, she ran over to a piece of carpet to pee. I'd been wondering about that.

"That's her spot," Finlay said. "First thing I showed her."

I sat down beside him and unzipped the bag. "We have coronation chicken sandwiches, crisps, cake, and beer." As I spoke, I handed out the portions.

"A veritable feast." Finlay held up his beer can and popped it. "Toast?"

"Sure." I opened my can and lifted it, waiting.

"To a good ship and friendship, may we ever sail free." He touched his beer to mine.

"I'll drink to that." The first sip of beer was always the best.

We sat in companionable silence while we ate, Finlay occasionally making an adjustment to the sails and, once in a while, checking the progress of the other sailboat.

I could see it without binoculars now, proceeding down the coast quite far out from shore. Our trajectory took us away at an angle. We weren't going to intersect until we came about and tacked the other way.

To Patrick, we must look like a random boat out for a sail. There were a few others in the bay, I noticed, lovely triangles etched against sea and sky.

Fishing boats, trawlers, and a tour boat as well, too far away for us to hear the loudspeaker, thankfully. They came past the castle a few times a day during the season, blatting out facts and colorful tales about Ravensea and the Asquiths.

Maybe I should mount a huge banner on the tower facing the water. *Rooms for Rent*, with the website. I shook my head at the absurdity. Although it might work.

"What are you smiling about?" Finlay asked.

"Oh, a crazy idea I just had." I told him and he laughed.

"I don't think that's quite the image you want, Nora. You're a bit more upscale than that."

"True. But if we get desperate enough . . ." Ugh. I didn't want to go there, to tap the well of worry and trepidation I seemed to be carrying around.

"I've been talking the place up to my friends," Finlay said. "A number of them said they'd be interested in staying at Ravensea so I passed along the website."

I was touched. "That's so nice. Thank you." Maybe I didn't have to try to get total strangers to stay. We could mine our network for customers. "We're going to film some ads at the castle, too. People like reels."

"Great idea. The innkeeper in action, wearing your garden apron and wielding your snips."

Was he teasing me? "Oh, not me. Tamsyn. She's the actress."

Finlay pulled back to look at me. "Don't sell yourself short, Nora. You're—" Before he finished the sentence, he pivoted around on the seat and lifted his binoculars. After exclaiming, he handed me his beer. "Hold on to this, will you? We need to come about."

I knew what that meant. Duck so the boom wouldn't hit you and brace yourself as the boat tacked in a new direction.

A few deft moves and we were smoothly underway again, the beer making it through without spilling. He took the can back from me and finished it.

"What's going on?" I asked, noticing that we were headed toward the mainland.

"We're on the trail of a smuggler," he said.

CHAPTER 26

I didn't know which question to ask first. The personal won. "Did you get me out here under false premises?"

He threw me a startled glance. "What? No. I'm off duty tonight." He aimed the binoculars again. "Looks like he's heading into Sea Arch Cove."

This interesting rock formation formed one side of a small deepwater cove. Boats liked to anchor there to enjoy the beach fringing one end.

"Who?" I asked, knowing full well. I wanted to hear him say it.

"Horn. Aha. There we go. The game is afoot."

A fishing boat was approaching from the south, its bearing appearing to also be the cove.

Picking up his phone, he said, "They're here and the coastguard is ten miles south." He dialed. "DI Cole, North Yorkshire police. Your target is headed into Sea Arch Cove as we speak, with the other party approaching. Yes, that's right. Me? In my new sailboat with a friend." His eyes met mine and he made an amused, incredulous face. "Quite by accident, yes. Fortunate, isn't it?"

Reading between the lines, the picture became clear. The coastguard had been planning to intercept Patrick

Horn and the other smugglers. Was he delivering wine? Or taking it on board? I guess we would find out.

He listened. "Yes, sir. Thank you, sir."

"What did they say?" I asked when he disconnected.

"Hang back and watch." He grinned. "They decided to find me useful."

I snorted. "As they should. Otherwise they would have been waiting forever for them to show up."

Finlay gazed up at the telltales and made an adjustment to the lines. "Something must have tipped Horn off. He's a crafty old blighter. There's already been one skirmish and the contraband ended up in the Dragon's Lair."

"Oh, so that's what happened." In general, the Dragon's Lair wasn't a good place to unload smuggled goods. Boats could only approach at high tide and if unloaded, the way out was difficult. Witness the broken bottle I'd found.

We tacked past the cove, where the *Party Girl* was now anchored. Although we were far enough away that hopefully we couldn't be recognized, I put on my cap and pulled it low over my brow.

The fishing boat chugged toward us, Finlay guiding us to stay out of their wake. "Throw them a wave," he said.

Even better, I leaned toward Finlay and raised my empty beer can in a salute. Hopefully they would think we were a jolly couple out for a romantic sail. Not a detective inspector and his amateur sidekick.

The men on board waved back and when I caught one grinning, I felt a rush of satisfaction. "We fooled them."

Our heads were still close and when he turned, I had the distinct feeling he might kiss me. To further the deception, of course. Or to thank me for being such a good sport.

I quickly pulled back. Not only did I want to honor his need to keep everything aboveboard, I wasn't ready to put things to the test. What if I was getting my signals crossed? Yikes. I had enough problems without making a fool of myself.

We continued down the coastline, carefree and minding our own business, while the fishing boat also made its way into the cove.

That wasn't suspicious at all, a fishing boat loaded with nets taking a break in a secluded cove. Not in the least.

"Coming about," Finlay said.

He took us farther out on the reverse tack, so we wouldn't be too close to the cove. Even so, I could clearly tell that the two boats were moored fairly close and there was movement on both decks.

"Hope they get here soon," Finlay muttered. "We'd better not go past the cove again or they'll get suspicions."

Disappointing but smart. I stared toward the south, willing the coastguard to ride in like cavalry. Did I hear a faint buzz of engines? I thought so.

On we went, the boat heeling in the gilded waves of sunset, while closer to shore, a drama unfolded.

The high-speed Defender coastguard boat arrived first, maneuvering to block the cove entrance. Someone spoke through a bullhorn, the wind snatching the actual words. Another, larger coastguard vessel was right behind the first.

Horn's yacht and the fishing boat were trapped.

"Shall we?" Finlay asked, preparing for yet another tack. I knew the routine by now. "I'll like to check in before we head back to the harbor."

"Check in?" Was he part of the official team after all?

"I have a friend I want to say hello to." He lifted the sheet out of the cleat. "Coming about."

He trimmed the sails to lower our speed and as we approached the cove, he released them both, so we were coasting along. Coastguard officers were swarming around Patrick's yacht and the fishing boat, while several people stood on the deck of the smaller craft. I recognized two of them: Patrick Horn and Gavin Cargill, both with hands tied behind their backs. They'd been arrested.

Then I spotted a man in uniform. It took me a few seconds. "Brian is in the coastguard?" This was a new facet to the man I knew as our guest, birdwatcher, Tamsyn's date, and Celia's son. I couldn't wait to tell Tamsyn why he'd ducked out tonight. It hadn't been about her at all.

Finlay waved and Brian waved back. "He is. He's been working undercover to nab these guys."

And now he might have arrested the men who had his mother killed. I wondered if he knew that. I was also pretty sure that they had killed Hilda and Joe to cover up their crimes.

We drifted closer, our decks on about the same level.

"Thanks for your help, DI Cole," Brian called. He gave Finlay a thumbs-up. His eyes flared briefly under the hat brim when he noticed me. "Hello, Nora."

"Hello." I waved, then took a shot. "Have you arrested them for murder? If not, maybe ask them about Hilda Dibble and Joe Lumley."

Face red with anger, Gavin bucked against his restraints. "You're not pinning that on me," he spat. "I had nothing to do with either one."

Protesting too much or being honest? I couldn't decide. "How about you, Patrick? You were moored right offshore when Hilda died."

Patrick, in contrast, didn't even flinch. His eyes flashed fire at me. "Ridiculous. As if I'd do such a thing." He ducked his head. "I . . . I was very fond of Hilda."

As the robe and lipstick hinted at. Content that I'd lobbed a bomb, I didn't say anything else. Brian could sort it all out at the coastguard station.

I glanced at Finlay. "Take me home?"

"Happy to."

Once again, I felt the pull between us. Perhaps my remark did have a little innuendo in it. Quite by accident.

"Talk to you later, Officer," Finlay called. "I'm available if you need me." He switched the boat motor on and we cruised out to open water.

A smuggling case closed. Two murder cases—no, four—still open.

At the dock, Finlay and I worked together to lower and stow the sails and make the boat shipshape. The evening air was warm and still here in the harbor. People were wandering around on the wharf and the sea path and I could smell fish and chips frying.

"I really had a great time," I said, zipping up the cool box. We'd decimated every crumb. "Thanks for taking me out."

"We'll have to do it again soon," he said. "Hopefully without bumping into any smugglers."

I put on my jacket rather than carry it. "Let's hope." I glanced around, not seeing any excuse to linger. "Well, I suppose I'd better get going. Are you heading back to the castle?" I thought of a way to prolong our not-a-date. "Want to go get an ice cream?"

He shook his head ruefully. "Sorry. I just got a text demanding my presence at the coastguard station. We've been called in to coordinate."

"Maybe they're taking my brash comment seriously."

I dug around in my backpack for my car keys. "Be nice if one of them—or both—would confess to murder."

"I wish someone would," he blurted. Then he rolled his eyes. "Not to denigrate our force's excellent detective skills. Or my own."

I jingled the keys. "It's all very confusing. I've been going 'round and 'round." I took a step toward the rail. "See you later."

On the short drive back in my steaming-hot car, all the windows down, I thought about Gavin and Patrick. Gavin had been so angry. A sign of guilt, maybe?

Even if he hadn't killed Hilda or Joe, it was still possible he'd staged the accident that killed Dennis and Celia. He hadn't been there that weekend, which meant he'd probably never been questioned by the police about it.

If he'd used the back entrance, Gavin could have come and gone without anyone being the wiser.

What did his wife know about that weekend? I wondered. It was odd that she hadn't mentioned knowing Celia when we'd first discussed Celia's death. She'd talked about the sisters as if it were ancient history, a story Hilda had shared with her.

Distancing herself on purpose? It was possible she wanted to put that period of her life behind her after divorcing Gavin.

Being best buds with Hilda and lunching with Gavin's new wife kind of did the opposite, though. Plus, she'd been at Horn House with Patrick, another member of the old gang.

I put Sandra aside—mentally, that is. *Lorna*. I wondered if she knew that her husband had been arrested. She'd suspected that he was involved in smuggling. Having it confirmed was going to be a shock, I guessed.

We'd do our best to offer comfort and support. She was probably going to need it.

When I reached the castle, I continued straight through the arch to the stable yard, where I usually parked. The Land Rover was in its berth, which meant Guy and Janet had returned from their outing.

I gathered my belongings and went in through the kitchen door. "Hello? Anyone home?"

The kitchen was empty and quiet. I emptied the cool bag and put it away in the pantry. Ruffian came meowing to meet me. "Where is everyone?" I checked his dish, which contained plenty of kibble. "You're fine. I know. You want snacks." He was getting spoiled by our socials, which offered frequently dropped tidbits for his pleasure.

I fished around in the fridge for cheese and broke off a piece. "There. That should hold you." While he pounced, purring, I retrieved another beer from the pantry and went to go find the others.

Dad, Janet, Guy, and Tamsyn were sitting around a table on the terrace, enjoying adult beverages. Rolf sprawled nearby, twitching as he dreamed.

"Nora," Tamsyn cried. "How was your sail?"

I pulled out a chair. "Fantastic. I saw Brian, by the way."

She frowned. "Really? Where? Was he with another woman?"

"I'm not sure." I hadn't noticed if any coastguard officers were female. After taking my time to pop the top and take a sip, I put her out of her misery. "He's a coastguard officer working undercover to catch smugglers. Which they did, tonight, while Finlay and I watched from the sailboat."

Exclamations of surprise broke out, everyone talking at once. I put my hand up to let them know I wasn't finished. Once they finally quieted, I said, "Does anyone know where Lorna is? Gavin's been arrested." More shouts of surprise.

"I never liked him," Dad declared. "A repudious skelm if ever I saw one."

"That's very clear in hindsight, isn't it?" Guy smiled behind his beer mug.

"Gavin and Patrick were working together," I told them. "Patrick transported wine with the help of fishermen and Gavin sold the smuggled goods in his stores."

"Partners in crime," Tamsyn said. "I wonder what else they've been up to." She gave me a significant look.

"Like Celia's death, you mean?" To Dad, I said, "We have more questions about that weekend at Horn House. First, though, has anyone seen Lorna? Someone needs to tell her what's going on, if she doesn't know."

Janet put up her hand. "She's gone off for a walk along the shore. Said she's meeting a friend."

I sank into the chair. "Friend? Who?"

"She didn't say," Janet said apologetically. "I'm sorry I didn't ask."

"You had no reason to," I assured her. "Believe me, I didn't think I'd be seeing smugglers arrested this evening. Or that Gavin would be there, although Lorna had suspicions, she told me."

Tamsyn put two and two together. "The retail chain paperwork."

"Exactly," I affirmed. "She could tell the numbers didn't add up. By the way, there are a couple of cases of wine at the sacred spring. Someone ditched them there, I'm guessing. We should probably turn them in to the coastguard."

"I can go over with the wheelbarrow," Guy offered.

My phone rang, a sharp peal that startled us. "It's Finlay. I'd better take it."

Rather than annoy everyone, I picked up the phone and walked to the other end of the terrace. "Hello?"

"Nora. Have you seen Lorna Cargill? We've been trying to get ahold of her."

"She's not answering her phone?"

"No, it keeps ringing. Last time we tried it went right to voicemail."

Avoiding a call from the police? "She's not here. Janet said she went for a walk and was meeting a friend."

He made a disgruntled sound. "Maybe she couldn't hear her phone ring or is out of range. Listen, if you see her, have her call the station. Or come right down."

"I'll pass along the message for sure, soon as I see her. And I'll let you know as well. In case she's trying to dodge you." I was only half-joking. Maybe Lorna was a conspirator and concern about her husband merely a smoke screen.

Maybe she'd gone on the run. She didn't have a vehicle but it wasn't difficult to get to the train station via the bus or a ride service. Once there, she might have gone anywhere.

He gave a little laugh. "That's possible. We're not on the most popular list."

"I'll be in touch with any news." I walked back to the table. "The police are trying to reach Lorna and she's not answering. I'm going up to her room to see if she's gone."

"Running for the hills, eh?" Dad commented.

"I hope not." I started for the terrace door. "Be right back."

Tamsyn pushed back her chair. "I'm coming with you."

"Did you see Lorna before she left?" I asked as we crossed the drawing room.

"No." Tamsyn made a face. "I was up in my room pouting and patting Primrose. The stress around Ben and the new part and then Brian . . . Is he really a coastguard officer?"

I put my hand up. "Swear. In uniform and everything. Finlay said he's been on an undercover assignment here in Monkwell."

"Ooh, that's hot." Tamsyn's eyes sparkled. "He's not just a nice, boring birdwatcher, is he?"

"He's a good guy." To Tamsyn, considering a man boring was the kiss of death. She hadn't learned that boring might actually mean drama-free and kind.

After stopping at the reception desk for keys, we hurried through the Great Hall and up the stairs. As I inserted the key in the door of the King's Chamber, I felt a familiar prickle down my spine. "Tamsyn."

She spun around. "I feel him, too."

Particles of dust seemed to dance in a shaft of setting sun.

"Sir Percival," I called. "What's up? Or, as Dad would say, 'Pray tell, kind sir.'"

The particles seemed to whirl and condense, like a whirlwind. A casement window down the hall banged open. He was getting really skilled at opening and closing doors and windows.

"Is it Lorna?" I called. "He seems to be pretty attached to her," I told Tamsyn.

"Isn't she lucky?" Tamsyn murmured.

The wall sconces flickered. Another of his talents.

"That's a new trick, right?" Tamsyn wagged a finger. "Good one, Percy."

"Fairly new. And I take that as a yes." It must be so

frustrating being a ghost, not having the ability to communicate. To have to use dust and bangs and strange sounds. "Is she in trouble?"

A cannon boomed. Loudly, as if it were right there.

We screamed and ducked. "Wow," Tamsyn said. "That was amazing."

My heart still pounding, I finished unlocking the door and stepped inside the room.

Lorna's and Gavin's belongings were still there, as were their suitcases.

"She didn't leave." Tamsyn said.

"So she did go on a walk, as she told Janet. With a friend." Hands on hips, I surveyed the room. "Needle, meet haystack."

Tamsyn crossed the carpet to the tall windows. "Maybe she's down at the beach. Or watching the sunset from the bluff."

Possibly. Those ideas didn't quite sit right. "When I ran into her at the sacred spring, she was really upset about her husband being a smuggler."

"How did she get the idea to go there?" Tamsyn asked. "The spring isn't usually associated with smuggling."

"Good question." There was another place fairly close by that was. "Maybe she went to the Dragon's Lair, to check that out."

I was dressed for a ramble, Tamsyn not so much. "Change your clothes and we'll go look for her."

Sir Percival had pulled out the stops to warn us and I was going to pay attention.

CHAPTER 27

Rolf wanted to come along, so the three of us set off along the bluff toward Dragon's Cove. Before we left, I had called Finlay with an update on Lorna and our plan, not mentioning the Sir Percival factor.

At some point, if we got to know each other better, I'd have to tell him. Instead of meet the parents, we had the meet-the-ghosts gauntlet at Ravensea.

How absurd.

"What is it?" Tamsyn asked, having noticed my grunt of amusement.

"Nothing. Finlay. The ghosts. Introducing them."

Tamsyn stopped at a vantage point where we could see our beach. "Something brewing between you?" Her tone was casual, her gaze on the shore below.

Which was empty. Lorna hadn't gone down there, nor was she sitting on the bench on the bluff. We started walking again.

"Maybe. I really like him, Tamsyn. I think we had a . . . moment on the boat. But I chickened out. Plus, we can't date. Not until Hilda's and Joe's murders are solved."

It felt good to let it all gush out, the way I used to confide in her when we were teenagers. She had always given me good advice.

"For what it's worth, I think he's smitten," Tamsyn said. "I've caught him looking at you tons."

"Really?" I found myself revisiting our encounters. I hadn't noticed. Which was good. It would have made me nervous. "I'm glad to hear I'm not imagining things." I dreaded the idea of making a total fool of myself.

We tromped on, Rolf in the lead, the long grass brushing against our legs. This path didn't see much traffic. Most hikers used the main route, which traveled farther inland, skirting this headland. If someone went to Dragon's Cove, they either walked straight in or drove partway on the farm track the police had used to get closer.

A small white sedan sat at the end of the lane.

Did it belong to Lorna's friend? Or a random hiker?

"Sandra has a white car," Tamsyn said. "Remember? When we met her at Hilda's house?"

"That make and model?" I wasn't great at identifying cars, plus so many new models looked similar to each other.

Tamsyn shrugged. "I don't know." She veered in that direction. "Let's go check it out."

The car was empty and incredibly clean. We peered through the windows and spotted nothing of any use.

Then I had an idea. I went around and took a photograph of the license plate and sent it to Finlay. He could run the plate and find out who it belonged to. In this situation, where the wife of an alleged smuggler couldn't be reached, that action might be warranted.

He sent back an acknowledgment.

The long June twilight was shading toward night as we made our way down the bluff into the cove. We'd brought headlamps and now we paused to put them on. Wandering around the rocky shore in the dark was asking for an injury or worse.

In contrast, Rolf was sure-footed on the slope despite his bulk, even trotting ahead to reach level ground first. He waited for us, tongue hanging out, as if to say *What took you so long?*

"That dog is something else," Tamsyn commented as she navigated the last few footfalls.

"He really is." I scanned the beach. The tide was coming in, washing over the seaweed beds I'd so recently foraged. Which reminded me. I needed to check the drying seaweed at home.

I didn't see Lorna anywhere.

"She might not have come down here," Tamsyn said. "Maybe she went somewhere else on her walk."

"True. But where are the people from the car?" No couple sharing a blanket and a bottle of wine or strolling the shore, watching the waves.

My stomach sank. "What if she's in the cave, looking for evidence of smuggling?" Not a great place to stumble around, especially at night.

"I haven't been in there in years," Tamsyn said. "What's it like?"

"Kind of claustrophobic. The entrance tunnel is lower than I remember." When we were kids, we were a lot shorter and less bothered by this.

My phone screen glowed in my pocket, signaling that I had a message. Finlay had sent a text. "The car belongs to Sandra."

"So Sandra might be the friend Lorna mentioned?" Tamsyn was staring at the cave opening. "I think we have to go in. What if they're hurt? Or lost?"

Getting lost in a cave was the stuff of nightmares. Other tunnels branched off the main cavern. We'd scared ourselves silly a few times exploring them.

My phone rang. Finlay again? No, it was Janet. "Hey,"

I said. "We're about to go into the Dragon's Lair. If I don't call back in half an hour, send help."

A stunned silence, then, "Will do. That's not why I called, though. Guy went over to the spring to pick up the wine. He couldn't find it."

Since the cavern was tiny, that meant only one thing. "Lorna must have taken it. Thanks for letting me know."

"Are you really going into the cave?" Janet asked. "I'm not sure that's such a good idea at night."

"Neither am I. We need to make sure they're okay. You can get hurt in there, especially if you don't know your way around. And then you're stuck underground, with no cell service." I felt a retroactive shiver at how careless we'd been as children. My parents hadn't known the half of it.

"Half an hour. Then I'm calling."

"Please do. Thank you, Janet." I hung up. "We'd better get going."

We started moving as fast as we could across the stony beach without turning an ankle or slipping on seaweed. Rolf led the way, thrusting his nose into every malodorous heap he could find.

The cave opening loomed ahead like a dark mouth waiting to swallow us. What could they be doing in there?

Something was definitely off. I could sense it.

"Do you think Lorna is the killer?" I blurted.

"Lorna? Really?" Tamsyn sounded incredulous. "She's just a bystander, I thought."

"So did I. But think about it. Her whole world is falling apart. Say Gavin did have something to do with Celia's death and Hilda figured it out. Knowing her, uh, propensity for blackmail, maybe she approached Lorna."

"Why wouldn't Hilda go to Gavin?"

"Lorna would be a softer touch, I bet." Or so Hilda thought, to her demise.

"That's a good point. What about Joe? Why would Lorna kill him?"

I wasn't sure. *Unless.* "He might have seen or heard something that incriminated her. Or maybe he was going to rat Gavin out for smuggling. Joe liked tattling on people." It still rankled that he'd run to the police about Dad.

I lowered my voice, even though the waves crashing onto the shore muffled my words. "Finlay told me Joe died of a head injury, not drowning. I made an offhand remark about the stone balls in the garden and the very next morning, he was out there in the rain. It made me wonder if the head injuries were similar."

"You're really reading between the lines, Nora."

I shrugged. "I suppose. I should have asked more questions. Not that he would have told me anything."

We had reached the cliff, where a short climb was required to get into the cave. "Rolf, you wait here." I wasn't going to try to boost him. He whined and whimpered as we clambered up the rocks. "You'll be okay. We'll be right back." He huffed a huge sigh.

"That dog is comical." Tamsyn adjusted her head-lamp. "Who's going first?"

"I will. Since I was in here the other day."

She touched my arm. "Hold on a sec. Why did Lorna ask Sandra to come with her? Assuming they're together in here."

"For company? To pick her brain about Gavin?" My heart lurched. "Oh. You think Sandra is in danger?"

In the glow of her lamp, I saw her lips press together. "Maybe. She could be another loose end."

I felt the truth of that in my gut. It all made a terrible sense. The Dragon's Lair was a perfect spot to murder someone. Joe had probably been killed there, too— although I hadn't figured out how Lorna trussed him in canvas and dumped him overboard.

After my conscience wrestled with the desire to save my own skin, I reached up and adjusted my headlamp. "We'd better go in." If we could have prevented another death and didn't, well, I couldn't live with that.

Then I hesitated. "I'm going to send Janet and Finlay a text." I told them the police needed to come now, that Lorna was the killer and had lured Sandra into the cave. We were almost positive. Better safe than sorry.

We crept through the tunnel, the lamps low so as not to reflect off the condensation-slimed rock and blind us. It felt like traveling into the belly of a beast. A dragon.

As we drew closer to the cavern, I began to hear voices echoing in the vast space.

"Don't do it," a woman pleaded. "Please don't."

CHAPTER 28

Restraint went out the window. Making sure to keep my head down, I bolted. We only had minutes, seconds even, to prevent another crime.

"Stop," I yelled.

Two figures at the back of the cavern froze. The beam of my light glanced off them, so I turned it to fully view the scene.

Holding a big rock, Sandra was looming over Lorna, who was leaning back against the cavern wall, hands up.

Sandra. My thoughts skittered, trying to adjust. We'd had it backward.

Sandra was the threat. Sandra was the killer.

Tamsyn shouldered her way to stand beside me. "Police are on their way."

Well, we'd asked them to come. How soon they would get here was unclear. No need to share those details, however.

Sandra dropped the rock with a crash and ran toward the front of the cavern. Waves licked and foamed as the tide raced in. She feinted toward the far side, then turned toward us. "Get out of my way," she snarled.

We locked arms, our twin beams cutting through the

cavern's murk. "You aren't getting through us," I said. "Give it up. It's over."

Sandra glanced over her shoulder. Lorna was now holding the rock, like a softball she was getting ready to toss.

Lorna's eyes narrowed with anger. "Try it. I dare you."

Sandra took a step back, hands up. "Help. Help me, Nora. Tamsyn. She's the killer. I was only trying to defend myself."

Had we gotten it all wrong? An elbow in my side interrupted my spiral of doubt. "We'll let the police sort it out," I said, rather than argue. "So, no more rock throwing. And stay at least twenty feet apart, you two."

Hands over her face, Sandra bent over and began to sob. "I didn't mean to kill her. I swear. She . . . she—"

"She who?" Tamsyn asked tartly.

"Hilda?" I guessed. "What did she do to you?"

I was being sarcastic but Sandra took the question at face value. "She was dredging up the past. Trying to put the blame on me. Telling me I'd go to jail for being an accessory. She made me so angry."

The pieces came together in my mind, which was so satisfying. "You helped Gavin kill Celia. Not directly. You gave him an alibi, right?"

"He was my husband. Of course I did."

In the silence as we digested this, the waves frothed into the cavern, edging closer to where Sandra was standing. At high tide, they'd reach Lorna's position.

I thought about Sandra's meeting with Patrick at Horn House. Setting the long-ago murder aside, she was up to her neck in his present-day crimes as well. I would bet on it.

"What about Joe?" I asked. "What did he do?"

Anger flashed over her face. "He was going to go to the police and report the smuggling unless we cut him in." She sneered. "He was too nosy for his own good, always creeping around and listening."

I thought it was more likely that he'd been ignored while working, as so many tradesmen are. Unfortunately for him, he tried to use the information he overheard to his own benefit.

"So you hit him on the head and Gavin wrapped him in canvas and dumped him overboard."

"We did. And he deserved it." Sandra sent Lorna a triumphant look. "You might be Gavin's wife but I'm his real partner. He was going to ditch you and take me off to the Canary Islands. 'I always loved you best,' he told me the other day. 'Lorna is a bore. She wouldn't know fun if it bit her behind.'"

Lorna gave a cry of rage and launched herself forward, onto Sandra. So much for staying in her corner.

The women grappled and rolled, screaming, pulling at each other's hair. What now? Get down there and pull them apart?

Something struck the back of our legs and we broke apart with a scream. Rolf pushed through and leaped down onto the cavern floor. With pants and woofs, he went over to the wrestling women and began to nudge them with his huge face, giving licks in between.

They rolled apart, screaming, this time in disgust, and rose to their feet. Rolf went back and forth, still butting them, as if pushing them apart.

"He really is an amazing dog," Tamsyn marveled. "Now that we have Rolf guarding them, want to go back out and call the police? Make sure they're on their way?"

"If you're okay alone for a few." She was, so I hurried back through the tunnel.

As I emerged, I saw blue and white lights strobing in the field. Other lights were snaking their way down the cliff. The cavalry had arrived, right on time.

CHAPTER 29

"What a beautiful day." I stepped out of the cool, candle-scented interior of St. Elmo's onto the front steps, pausing to take in the sweeping view of the water from here.

Finlay was with me, and we planned to retrieve the dogs from his flat and then meet Tamsyn and Brian for a fish-and-chips picnic on the waterfront. They were behind us somewhere, in the throng of parishioners.

"How are you, Nora?" Father Patrick asked, clasping my hand between his. "Everything going all right?"

The two murders, now thankfully solved, and the arrest of the smuggling ring had set the village abuzz. My first foray into church after the excitement had been met with curious glances and whispers, which was entirely natural. Father Patrick's eyes, though, held only compassion and genuine interest.

"It is, thank you. We have an amazing opportunity coming up." I lowered my voice to a whisper. "The team from *Britain's Got Ghosts* will be filming at Ravensea." They were paying us handsomely for the privilege of investigating our dearly departed. I was already thinking about how to incorporate their findings into our marketing. Lean into your strengths, right?

His brows rose. "Fascinating. I'd love to watch them work, if they don't mind."

"I'll certainly ask. I'm fascinated as well to see what they do." I moved aside to allow Finlay to shake the priest's hand and then we continued down the steps to the sidewalk.

Finlay's flat, above the Lazy Mermaid, was a couple of blocks from here. We strolled along, smiling hello at passersby. Town was busy, the summer season in full swing.

Sandra had confessed to killing Hilda and Joe and trying to kill Lorna. She'd had a mix of motives. Not only had she covered up Gavin's role in Dennis's and Celia's deaths, she had been jealous of Hilda. She wanted the primary role as Patrick's henchperson, on the ground scheming to push owners out of their properties.

She was a nasty piece of work, Janet said, and I agreed with her.

As for poor Joe, he'd overheard an argument between Sandra and Hilda after they'd left the castle social that first evening. He'd been retrieving a tool from the van so they hadn't seen him.

He'd tried to take a page out of Hilda's book and get money out of Sandra. Her first plan had been to push slates off the roof onto Joe when he came back from lunch. A quick escape in Gavin's van and it would have been ruled an accident. Instead she almost hit me and Tamsyn. Plan B had been killing him with a rock from her own garden. She then called Gavin, who rowed Joe's body offshore and dropped him into the drink. She'd also ransacked Hilda's home to throw suspicion elsewhere.

The extra wine in the cave had been left there by one of the smugglers. During the melee when they'd almost been caught by the coastguard and scattered, a couple cases had gone missing. Accidentally . . . or on purpose. Lorna had found it by accident, when exploring the castle grounds.

The Lazy Mermaid was doing a brisk trade, but a glance inside revealed that Liv wasn't there. She tried to take Sundays off with her family. We had plans for lunch with Darby next week to catch up.

Finlay unlocked his door and we went up, greeted by ballistic barking and excitement from Rolf and Lady, who had become good buddies. The odd couple, I dubbed them. One huge with black fur, the other tiny with a white coat.

I slowly spun in a circle. "I love what you've done with the place."

We were in the main room, which had tall windows on three walls, a beamed ceiling, plaster walls, and polished wood floors. Books filled built-in shelves and the furnishings were comfortably overstuffed.

Finlay had promised to cook me dinner one night. That event would mark a new phase, I was pretty sure. Right now we were hovering on the line between the friend zone and something more.

"Thanks. I finally unpacked the last box." Finlay clipped a leash on Lady's collar and I did the same for Rolf, since we were in town.

"Look at him. He hates leashes." Rolf wore a mournful air of resigned patience.

"Don't blame him a bit." Finlay moved toward the door. "Ready?"

Tamsyn and Brian had been waiting for us up on the bluff, close to the spot where we'd spotted Brian in his maroon-and-orange jacket. Seated on a blanket, they were deep in conversation.

We joined them on the blanket and dug into the containers of fish and chips they'd picked up on the way. The dogs gnawed on the doggie bones we'd brought for them, with only occasional longing glances toward our food.

"Any news?" Finlay asked Brian.

Brian shook his head. "Still all in the lawyer's hands. It's very complicated."

Patrick's arrest for the murder of his brother had set off an unexpected chain of events. In a twist of fate, it turned out that Dennis had been Brian's father.

Brian Taylor, birdwatcher, coastguard officer, and all-around nice guy, was the true heir to Horn House. Things hadn't shaken out quite yet, but it was possible he would be taking over the hotel empire. He was Patrick's only living relative.

"Until things are settled," Brian went on, "I'm trying to keep my head on straight." He put an arm around Tamsyn. "Thanks to this one, I might succeed."

She tilted her head, regarding him with a smile. "I'm not sure . . . it looks a bit crooked." She yelped with laughter as they playfully tussled.

Finlay and I looked on fondly. I'd never seen my sister so carefree. She'd decided to take the new role even though Ben was going to be in the show. She was *so over* him, she told me. She was going to do what was right for her career. The production company had already booked the castle for a shoot.

I closed my container lid. "Ready for an after-lunch walk?" The dogs leaped to their feet. They were ready.

Tamsyn and Brian stayed behind to enjoy the sunshine and each other. Finlay and I strolled along the cliffside path, taking our time and allowing the dogs to dawdle and sniff whenever they wanted. Which was a lot.

At another favorite viewpoint, we stopped and Finlay

reached for my hand. Standing side by side, dogs sprawled at our feet, we took in the scene. Waves crashed, seagulls cried, lovers kissed, and children ran and screamed with joy.

Ravensea Castle kept watch over it all.

ACKNOWLEDGMENTS

A special thank you to my literary agent, Jill Marsal, and my editor, Kelly Stone, for believing in this series! Your help, encouragement, and insights are appreciated more than you know. Thank you as well to the St. Martin's team: Olya Kirilyuk and Sam Hadley for a gorgeous cover, Katherine Minerva and Steven Roman for precise copyediting, and Sara LaCotti and Sara Eslami for their dedicated publicity and marketing efforts. It's a pleasure working with you.